Terraweaver

TERRAWEAVER

CHROMA: Book Two

MAYA GOULIARD

Second edition

ISBN: 978-1-967608-05-8 (paperback)
ISBN: 978-1-967608-04-1 (ebook)

Book Cover Design by Maya Gouliard.

First Printing 2024.
www.mayagouliard.com
Mayagouliard@gmail.com

Calmillusion PRESS
INDEPENDENTLY PUBLISHED

For Katie:

who everyday proves that hard work and love are the best recipe for life; who taught me how to be a mother; who loves her siblings with all her being; who doesn't just stop with knowing the how, but pushes to understand the why; who answers when I text; and who loves me when I am at my best and just a little bit more when I am at my worst.

Acknowledgments

Writing book two was a whole different experience than Waterweaver.

When I published Waterweaver, I wasn't even sure anyone would want to read it, let alone love it. My goal had been just to complete the project.

Immediately after publishing Waterweaver, I drafted book this book (Terraweaver.) Then I let it sit, unsure if it was worth the time and effort to finish.

I want to thank all of the amazing readers who reached out and gave me the belief in myself that this journey of Lara and mine is worth the effort. People I didn't know read my book and told me they loved it.

Above all, this book was, and is, about gaining confidence. And often that takes community, so thank you all.

An extra big THANK YOU!!! Goes out to Kim and Sarah, who went above and beyond, and helped me see that I am not just a person who published a book —

I am an author.

-Maya

Contents

REALMS OF CHROMA

RED - PIRON
ORANGE - LARAN
YELLOW - AMARA
GREEN - GREVENDALE
BLUE - AZURAL
PURPLE - MORCHAST
PINK - VAALEAN

CHROMA

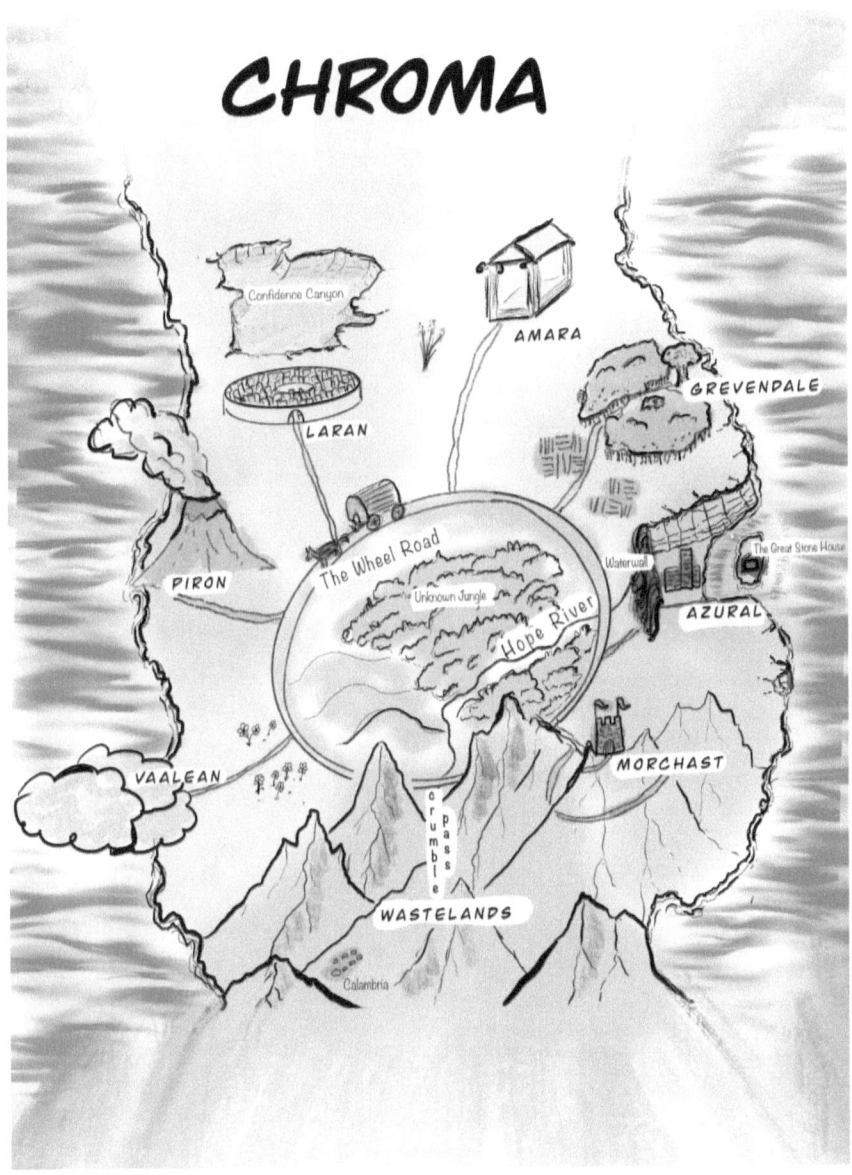

Preface

The sun beat down on layers of packed earth, highlighting a multitude of shades in lines from burnt sienna to a bright dusty orange. The old man stood sturdy and strong against the wind, appearing as one with the ground and canyon walls. But the dragon towering beside him, although looking comfortable and at home in the setting, stood out against all the color around him: as if he were more than all this grand wonder of nature. His white fur flowed in the wind, as if it were trying to pull him up into the skies.

They both looked out at the expanse of the canyon before them, each of them deep in his own contemplation. A comfortable silence sat between the two, a comfort that came from years of deep connection.

Without a word, they both started walking into the burnt orange hues of the sunset toward their home. It had been a long time since anything had changed for them, their mornings, evenings, and nights held the same disquiet, that nothing would ever change, when they both felt deeply that it must.

Home

Lara pushed open the back door, carrying the basket with their laundry. It was only a few items. She had gotten into the routine of every morning gathering the few pieces from the day before, right after breakfast. She enjoyed the peace of the early morning yard. Sheila the goat was always a bit happier to see her first thing. Lara reached down to pat her bony head and then slid her hand down one of the goat's long soft ears. The velvet smoothness always made her just feel a bit more at peace.

Sheila pushed her head into Lara's knee forcefully. "Oh, something I should know?" Lara asked with a glimmer of laughter. She looked over and sure enough the water bowl was empty.

Lara walked over to the laundry line she and James had strung up between the house and the trunk of their dead tree. Branches had been cut down for firewood years ago, but the thick trunk of the once sturdy ash tree still stood. Considering that most trees in the Wastes had long since started keeling over, this one's roots must have been deep and strong.

Once she had set the basket down, she turned to Sheila. "Shall we play a bit?" she asked. Ever since returning from Azural, she had tried very hard to be responsible and in control with her waterweaving powers. The magic was always there, she could feel the water rush by in the river no matter where she was in town. She knew how full the well in the town square was at all times. She found that she could even tell if any of her neighbors were dehydrated. The water practically sang to her. She felt a tickle of it from the clouds high in the sky, it pulsed through the blood in her veins.

But she didn't want to be too different. She knew that all of her fellow townspeople loved her still, but now they looked at her askance and with hooded eyes more often than not. Her power had been on full display that first day back in Calambria. Pulling waters from the skies to make it rain, filling the almost dry Hope River again, these were not acts of just anyone. The sparkling blue magic had surrounded her that day on the Wish Dragon fountain in town, and she found that the image had stuck in their minds.

She was no longer simply their neighbor Lara, the girl they had played with as children in the dirt field behind the schoolhouse. The woman they had trusted to teach their children after the teacher had left town. The friend they had worked with when they were repairing the fence to keep the wolves out. No, she could no longer just be that old Lara to them now. She was something more. She was something bigger. It was a bit disconcerting from her end.

But in her back yard, it was different. Sheila didn't care. The goat just wanted her water dish —and her belly- full. Lara closed her eyes for a moment and let the glimmer of fun seep into her responsibility to this nanny goat. For years Sheila had supplied them with milk that many in the town had desperately needed. This goat had supplied the milk that created the cheese that Lara kept as her special treat each day. As much as the goat needed them, they needed her. Lara opened her eyes and marveled at the magic accumulating around her upper right shoulder. She had been a waterweaver for months now, but it was still amazing. The light emanated around in ribbons of thin blue from the stone grafted to her arm. The magical light caught the morning sun, and the sparkle reminded Lara of the ocean in Azural, the sun hitting the peaks of the waves, and then just as quickly disappearing only to have a glitter hit from another place. Lara's sparkle jumped along as the ribbons slowly moved.

She smiled at Sheila and playfully whirled as she shot the ribbon of light toward the river. She couldn't see the river from their yard, but she knew it was there. She had walked the path a thousand times, but she also could just feel the water. She sent the magic in a high arc so that it would land directly into the center of the river. The magical light dissipated as it floated away, but a ghost-like effect lingered for a few moments as the magic moved away from her.

She turned to Sheila again, looking at the water bowl next to her. She tried to gauge how much she was scooping up from the river. Could she control it enough to fill the bowl? She pulled what she thought she needed and leaped again, although it was unnecessary, and pulled the magic back toward the bowl. She used her right arm to create an arc in the air as if she were painting the water across the sky and pointed at the bowl at Sheila's feet. The arc of water followed the path she laid out and landed in the bowl, filling it.

Lara stopped it before it overflowed and sent the rest of the water back in a stream across the sky. Lara looked contentedly at the blue magic arches in the air. She stood silently as she watched the glittering magic slowly filter back down to the ground, settling in.

Sheila was not watching the blue, she was lapping up the water. By the time that Lara watched the last of the magic disappear into the ground, she saw that Sheila's bowl was empty and the baleful eyes looked up at Lara entreating her for more.

"All right, but no more games, I have to get this laundry hung." This time Lara just pulled the water she felt in the air around her, gathering it up and wringing it out above the bowl. A hint of blue hovered along her shoulder, but barely enough to notice unless one was looking. The goat didn't care if it was a big fanfare or not; she just loved to drink her fresh water.

Lara knew that her powers gave her the ability to dry these clothes by simply sucking the water from them, but she loved the way the clothes smelled after drying in the sun. It had been so long since they had the option to sun dry clothes. For most of her years as a mother, the sun had been hidden behind thick dark clouds. Now, the blue skies boasted a bright sun.

Strangely, the sun didn't help to warm the town of Calambria. Lara wondered at the elements and their connection to the magic stones. Was it yellow that pulled the sun's warmth down to them? The water stone's magic was abundant here in Calambria now that she had returned it. What would happen if they brought all of the stones home?

Lara threw yesterday's blouse over the rope and pulled at the corners. Then she ran a hand down the center of the wet fabric. The fabric, cool and rough, had been mended more times than she could count. That was the last of it.

She turned to head back inside with her empty basket loosely held by the handle in her left hand. She was almost at the door when her entire vision was flashed with a bright splash of pink.

Oh no. *What did you do now?* She didn't have to reach out to contact Fleck, because the flash of pink had linked them tightly. Her answer came two-fold: first, she saw a quick image of the living room, all the books on the floor; second, she heard James's shout, "Lara! He has done it again!"

Rushing in, she saw the sight of the books with her own eyes. She turned her back to it to see James. He stood in the center of the single room they used for both kitchen and living room, his hair disheveled.

"I was over here washing the dishes when all of a sudden there was a blast of air. I'm not sure what he was trying to get at, but the books all flew off the shelf." He looked like he was still a bit in shock. Then suddenly he laughed. Lara noted that his eyes were looking past her, so she turned around.

There atop a fairy tale book sat Fleck looking pleased as punch. He stared in wide eyed adoration of the full-size dragon in the image. "Of course!" James said. "He remembered the story from the other day. Aren't you just the smartest little baby dragon that ever existed?" James cooed.

Lara rolled her eyes. Of course, James would forgive anything. He loved animals so much. Lara, on the other hand, was getting just a little tired of the flashes of chaotic light that were hitting her and was starting to give her a nagging headache.

"Fleck. You could have just asked me. You know, sent a picture of the book or something. You didn't have to just blast it down."

James sat down next to Fleck on the floor as Lara began picking up the books. "Once upon a time, the Great Dragon Selephor ruled over the skies of Chroma. His flight path took him across the land." James voice always relaxed Lara. He had a way of keeping things succinct and clear in his tone. She rarely misunderstood what he was saying. He had a way with his own words, but even reading someone else's he was melodious.

Since returning to Calambria, Lara had gathered all of the storybooks she could find on the Pelanor. Hoping for hints about what to expect for this little one. They read them over and over again. Curled up on James' lap, Fleck didn't look much like the dragon in the drawing of this children's tale. He looked more like Granny Winslow's cat, but with much longer of a soft nose and a bit longer of a body, like a fox.

The only book she had that had confirmed Fleck was a Pelanor, or Wish Dragon, or Guardian Dragon, was the leather-bound book of Siegel's Journals. He had written it ages ago, and she had been lucky to find it in the Library of Azural. And been lucky it was in her pack the day she had been arrested.

The journals were all over the place in their lack of organization, so reading them for information was a bit of a hunt. She still hadn't learned anything about these flashes of color she was getting every single time that Fleck used any magic. Actually, she hadn't found anything about the psychic link connecting to a human. He had referenced the link they have with other Pelanor a few times though. He had conjectured that it was how they all communicated, through telepathic images.

As she finished placing the last book on the shelf, James stopped short of the end of the tale. Lara looked over and Fleck was fast asleep in his lap. She scooped him up and set him on the cushion by the fire. He was still so young, and although he was no human, she was constantly reminded of her own children. The bursts of energy, the enthusiasm, and the need for a good old nap.

James smiled as he slowly stood up. "Well, back to the dishes."

"I can do them if you like. I finished the laundry." Lara said.

"No need. Weren't you going to go into town to check on Jada, Farmer Oswald, and then go by Sally and Fiero's?"

"You wanna come?" Lara asked.

"No. I am almost done reading my book. And besides, someone better stay with this troublemaker. Tell Sally and Fiero hello for me. I'll see them tomorrow for dinner. Remind them I am making chowder. It's Sally's favorite." He said, heading back to the sink.

Regrets

Lara pulled her chair in close to the table and buried her face in her folded arms. Jada sat across from her waiting. The table was small. Jada had never had children, and her kitchen was not the center of her life, unlike the large carpet that covered most of the room holding musical instruments of all kinds. Although Lara had spent many evenings in this room with large groups of neighbors singing, she had spent even more with her best friend simply chatting with each other.

"I just left." Lara stated. Then fell silent, her mind a jumble of emotions and words. How to explain? "I was about to be arrested and instead I ran. I didn't just run, I broke through their beautiful glass window and then consumed by all of the emotions of wanting to save Calambria, I pushed their waterwall down."

She paused. "When I arrived at Azural, they had been closed off from the rest of the realms and The Wastes for over 40 years. The wall had completely closed off their only connection with everyone outside. Do you see?" She realized her voice was muffled in her sleeve.

Looking up into Jada's eyes, she repeated, "Do you see? They didn't even believe that the Wastes existed. I made some powerful enemies there, and left the realm unprotected, taking away their stupid wall."

"Sounds to me like you did them and the rest of the Land of Chroma a favor. Sometimes you just have to rip the baindaid off," Jada stated.

Lara gave a half laugh, "Oh Jada, you always agree with me. Even when I am wrong. I know I could have done better. And I left all of my friends there, I didn't get to say goodbye to anyone. It was all so sudden." Lara pictured her last glimpse of Van, Delly, and Iris as the guards had led her away. They had been nervous for her. She was sure they knew what had happened. She imagined all of Azural had heard some version of the story. She wondered what most folks thought. Many of them would likely make her out to be a terrorist as Shauna had proclaimed. There to take their resources and then she removed the wall that was their only protection from a scary world that was out to take from them.

"So many people in Azural had no inkling of what life might be like beyond the wall. It was so strange, Jada. It was so different. And it was so, so blue."

"Well, we have our blue skies now too, thanks to you. I don't think I would worry too much about folks who have never had to worry about dying of thirst. And I also imagine that the wall being down will be good for them. It is about time they realized that the world has changed." Jada paused, thinking and then added, "and their part in it."

"So true."

"What do you think happened to your young friends?" Jada asked.

"Iris will be fine. She was smart and friendly and had strong support from her family. Van, I think was happy in blue. I think he might just find his place there. The only one I really have worried about is Delly. She had gone to Blue because she was looking for something different. She certainly found it, but she never did seem to fit into the system of it all. She made great friends with Van and Iris though. I think she is good at that, probably from all those years her mother took her traveling around the realms." Lara pictured the three as they chatted in the gardens in Azural and felt keenly her regret at having to leave them with no explanation. "I just left so suddenly."

"I'm surprised you got out at all by the sound of it." Jada stood up and walked over to her cabinet, pulling out a loaf of bread. "And you got that book on Pelanor, that's a blessing." She placed the loaf in front of Lara and tore off a hunk. The yeasty smell of it hit Lara's nose, and she was compelled by her stomach to grab a piece too.

They both sat there in silence eating the bread. Lara let each bite melt a bit in her mouth. She thought about her time in Azural. She had learned so much, but the thing that she had learned most of all was how different the realms were. "I wonder what the other realms are like?" She said as she broke off another hunk. "If they are based on the emotions of their stone like blue was, there is no telling what they might be."

Jada studied her bread, "I think yellow is full of wheat fields, and green must be a garden, red is full of bullies and orange is full of," she said the last word in staccato emphasizing the two syllables, "pump-kin's." Then she stood and started prancing toward her piano, the folds in her three-quarter length black skirt swirling around her. "Pumpkins, pumpkins, pretty pretty pumpkins."

Lara sat happily listening as her friend composed a quick children's ditty about the pumpkin patches of Laran. Maybe she could send a letter with some of the brown traders to her friends at Azural now that the waterwall was down. Someday, she would get a chance to find out how they were doing. She also spent some time envisioning her son Pete in yellow fields of wheat, he was holding a loaf of bread and dancing to the funny tune Jada played. Brie she couldn't imagine. Try as she might she really didn't know where she might have ended up, but she had a feeling she hadn't stayed in Laran for long. She could see her fitting in for awhile in all of the realms. Brie was quick to make friends, but then Lara never saw her settling down.

Fallow Fields

Lara walked the worn path toward the Oswald farm. She had only been back from her journey a few weeks and in the short time since her large show of magic in the town square she had brought the rains and river back— immense changes.

Lara could clearly tell which homes had been left deserted by the families who had fled over the last few decades. Their buildings still sat with the dirt and grime carried by the wind, stuccoing the sides of homes, building up along fences and sticking to windows.

All of the homes used to look like this, but now the inhabited cottages stood out in stark contrast. No longer was water such a scarce resource that people chose to leave the dirt. All of the windows had been washed clean. Sides of houses had been splashed with buckets of water, rinsing the years of build up down to the ground.

The yards were still empty, the gardens that used to grow, no longer an option. As a child before things had gotten so bad, many of the homes used to have stone paths with wildflower gardens along the sides leading to their front door. Vegetable gardens in the back yard. A few of the houses Lara passed, like Jada's, for example, had cleared their stone path. But Lara thought it was a losing battle. The dirt continued to shift back over the edges of the stones without the vegetation to keep the dirt in place.

She thought of the neighborhood gardens from her childhood. Her favorite place to visit had been Granny Sanders, who back then had been around Lara's current age. Her front yard had been full of pretty wildflowers that she encouraged Lara and Jada to cut and bring home to their mothers.

Granny's vegetable garden in the back had been in a raised bed built with solid brick walls to hold the dirt in. Granny had even let them walk along, chasing each other along the outer rim of the garden beds.

After running around the two little girls had loved to lean on the wall, they could simply reach over at chest height, to play in the dirt. The ground had been so full of life. The rich black soil, which Granny Sanders had tilled in early spring, had been soft and heavy to pick up, and Lara had loved the feel of the earth as it clumped together when she squeezed her hands into fists around it.

Jada would hunt for worms and squeal out in delight as she found them. She would bring them over to a corner of the garden beds where Lara would build a home in the dirt. Tiny clumps of dirt set up as houses and streets in a uniform pattern. The worms would disappear into the earth, and the girls would move on to whatever next piqued their interests.

But Granny Sanders gardens were gone now. Lara and her children had helped dismantle the garden beds years ago, the town using all the bricks they could find to support fencing around the exterior of town. Griff and Ben had become experts at leaning the posts just so against the stacked bricks.

At the end of the path of village homes was the entrance to the Oswald Family Farm. There was a Turnstile gate, but the gate was always open now, and Lara continued down the lane. The path ended in a circular roundabout. The farmhouse was larger than many of the village homes, but the Oswald family had always been large, and all of the generations stayed in it together.

Lara could hear the chatter of folks talking in the kitchen as she walked by,

"I'm just going as far as the Wheel Road, Granny. I'll be back before the end of the day."

Granny Oswald's voice was scratchy but loud enough for Lara to hear through the window, "It's dangerous Jane. It's best to let someone else do it."

Jane huffed so loudly, that Lara was reminded of the girls when they were teens. Lara closed her eyes and smiled, remembering the good old days where she had always been surrounded with the energy and excitement that teenagers brought.

But Jane, and her own children too, were not teens anymore. "Granny," Jane's voice had softened, "Lara proved to us all that we can accomplish things. We need to connect with these traders like the color realms do. It might be our only chance to survive. We have water now but look at how many hours dad is out in the fields still. It is better, but we still have so many needs. Water alone will not fix our issues."

Lara considered joining them in their discussion, Jane was right. Calambria needed so much more than the water. All of the magic stones brought different resources; water was just the one they had needed the most. Jane was doing what she could, and Lara needed to continue doing what she could to help. For now, she was here to talk with Farmer Oswald.

She continued past the house and followed a narrower path, but still large enough for a cart. The path led through what used to be fields full of vegetables. Now they lay fallow, unplanted from lack of seeds, but also from the inability to grow anything.

Only one plot was left to produce the foods for the whole of their community. It was right up against the back end of the fields, at the foot of the great mountains to the south of town. The dirt here was richer from erosion on the mountain and still held enough nutrients. A large plot of wheat shifted in the wind, and she saw the meager fronds of small carrots and the leaves of the turnip plants and potato vines. Lara was here to help water the plants. She also wanted to see if she could help the farm cultivate more food for the community.

Farmer Oswald was on his knees, bent over a plant in the center of the field. She called out "Hey Dillon!" And he pushed up with his arms sitting on his heels.

"Lara! Just the magician I wanted to see." He stood up with a slow motion Lara recognized. She was sure that it was from the same stiff joints she had now, and imagined how difficult it must be for him in these fields. She hoped that Jane and Jeff understood too. Of course they did.

His children were around the same age as Lara's, and Lara had taught them to read after the schoolteacher had left town. She remembered those days as some of the happiest in her lifetime, but children grow up. And sometimes adults have to remember that they change too.

Farmer Oswald joined her in the main row between the potato crops and the carrots. She always thought of him as "Farmer Oswald" because that's what her kids had called him. Even now, those wispy memories from the life she had lived reminded her of all she had accomplished. "I don't really think I like the word Magician," Lara said as he came close enough that they didn't have to shout.

"Hmm, how are we supposed to refer to you? Waterweaver? Stone Grafted?"

"Honestly, Dillon. I prefer Lara."

Farmer Oswald looked up at her with his bright light hazel eyes. The sudden softness around his eyes was accented by the harsh wind-worn skin of his gaunt face. It was obvious to Lara that he completely understood the layers of what she was saying here. "Lara." he said simply. No need to get into details between old friends, he understood that she wasn't comfortable with people treating her like the powerful mage she had become. She was still the girl that had played tag in the field behind the schoolhouse, the mother who had sat for hours each afternoon reading with the village children, the friend who came with James to dinner on special occasions.

He got that quickly. It occurred to Lara that because of her lifelong relationship with all of her neighbors in this tiny village, they would likely behave the same. She needed to trust them, not fear their reaction to her.

"Well, I thought I could see if this magic stone might be able to help out with the food situation." She looked over the neatly spaced field. The Oswalds had worked hard to feed Calambria. She saw the network of irrigation channels that had been dug from the river. The largest snaked next to the mountain, and Lara felt the natural pull of the water. This main stream was a natural occurrence. The channels dug from it started thick and slowly thinned out as it cut off to each smaller field.

Dillon saw her studying it, "You've already helped a ton. That stream over there had been completely dry for about five years. We had been having to take a cart over to the main riverbed and fill urns there and then cart them back and water the fields." He walked toward the initial cut off from the stream. "This water is already making a difference." He pulled up a carrot from the ground. "Look at this."

Lara could see the change. "Why, that is almost twice the size of the ones you brought to market before I left for Azural!"

"But still so much smaller than what Grandad used to grow. The problem is water is only one piece of a healthy garden. Here, watch this." He led her over to a row of three wooden boxes that came up to his shoulders. "These are our compost bins. I collect leaves and any of the natural waste I can find around town, and we put it in that first one. Then after a month or two, we transfer it over to the next, adding dirt from near the bottom of the mountain. This gives the leaves time to break down and mix with the dirt, enriching it with any nutrients I can find."

He opened the middle bin by swinging the front open like a gate. Then he motioned for her to look more closely. Lara got down on her knees and reached out to touch the almost black dirt. "Go ahead," Dillon laughed, "get your hands into it. I think it will help you understand." Lara reached out and grabbed a handful, and her memories of childhood days in Granny Sander's garden came back full force. She pulled a handful up, clumped tight in her hand and smelled it. The smell reminded her of autumn as a child. Lara also remembered that the death of things often fed future life.

"You have real dirt here," she said in awe.

His eyes turned sad. "Lara, these bins are all we have. The family and I collect every piece of food waste and loose leaf we can find and put them in here. These bins are the only nutrient rich dirt in all of Calambria."

Lara set her handful down reverently. Then dusted off the remains precious, healthy black dirt on her hands over the pile.

"Go ahead, let's see a bit of that waterweaving, Lara. If you don't mind," he pulled his hands through the dirt in the bin creating a small channel, "can you fill this with a touch of water?"

Lara reached to her center, listened to her heartbeat and focused on Calm. When she had a tie into the regular beat, she turned that emotion to her magic. The stone embedded in her shoulder glittered a small flare of blue sparkling light. It flashed down her arm, and water arrived at her call. The channel filled, and they watched as it quickly sank into the banks and dirt below. The top layer on both sides of the channel held the moisture leaving them darker from the damp. "Lara, do you see how the dirt holds the water here?"

Lara nodded, and he motioned for her to follow to the far side of the planted fields. Lara was struck by how much of the farmland wasn't even planted at all. These fields were lying empty because they wouldn't grow food. Dillon crouched down again, scratching out a similar hole in the ground as he had with the compost. "Here, add some water to this channel."

As Lara repeated her process, the magic filled the ditch with water. The result was completely different. This time rather than the water soaking into the dirt, it sat on top of the hard packed ground. Slowly, the water turned muddy, but the ground did not absorb the water at all.

"This is the state of things," Farmer Oswald said. "Our land needs more than water magic to thrive. I have been considering following in your footsteps and heading to Green. Jane and Jeff are not excited about the idea of going themselves. I had thought I was too old to do something like that. I thought I had missed my chance." He looked at her and smiled. "But a magician friend of mine reminded me I still am fully capable of learning new things and going on adventures."

Sorrowful Farmer

Lara followed Farmer Oswald back toward the place she had originally found him. There was a small bin half full of turnips. "Want some help?" She asked.

"Sure. I was just finishing up this section here." She watched him pull a few and got to work herself.

It didn't take long before her lower back ached, her arms felt warm from the motion of pulling, and her fingers were tight from gripping. This was hard work, and the Oswalds were always so kind about sharing their bounty. She felt the satisfaction of knowing that each tuber she pulled was going to nourish someone in town, and it amazed her how simple it was to push the pain out of her immediate thoughts.

The sun shone so brightly overhead that she had to squint her eyes. Yet, there was no heat from it. It was as if the sun's rays were choosing to warm a different village. Lara pictured the sun beating down on the yellow kingdom, orange and green getting a touch of it too. So much still was missing from their home. She had worked so hard and caused so much trouble back in Azural, leaving chaos behind, and what did she have to show for it? Of course, essential water to drink, but really, only two more inches on a carrot?

"Let's take a break and have a snack," Dillon called from the end of the row. "I generally just pull something from the ground and eat right here, but if you'd like we can head back to the house?"

Lara shook her head, "No, I am fine with a few carrots out here. I appreciate the peace."

Dillon pulled a carrot from the ground and, dusting it off, brought it over to her, "Sorry, it's a bit dirty."

"No problem there." She quickly let out a blast of sparkling blue water and rinsed the carrot. "Although, I have always been of the 'a bit of dirt won't hurt' family."

As she crunched into her carrot, a shot of green and a matching headache, blasted into her mind and there stood Fleck. His eyes bright green with the aftereffects of his magic.

"What the...?" Dillon shouted.

All of the townsfolk had met Fleck at this point, but many still hadn't experienced his magic.

Fleck sent her a pleading image of him happily eating a carrot. "Oh, my goodness. He just is jealous of us eating carrots without him. I think they are his favorite." She handed over her carrot and pulled another from the ground, cleaning it off quickly so she could feed herself before Fleck wanted this one too.

Wide eyed, Dillon watched Fleck for a few minutes. He was quite a sight propped up on his hind legs clutching the carrot. Fleck looked adorable until his sharp teeth came out. Dillon shuddered a bit and looked over at Lara. "Reminds me of the Rabbits and the Sorrowful Farmer tale, remember that one?"

"Oh yes. I don't think Fleck has heard it yet though if you want to tell him."

Dillon looked over at Fleck and seemed to consider the animal. Fleck had turned his curious eyes on the farmer and was clearly waiting to hear the story. "He looks so intelligent. It is a bit disconcerting."

Lara understood what Farmer Oswald meant, but she also had a much closer relationship and more time to have processed things. "He's a Wish Dragon, Dillon. I know it is the stuff of fairy tales, but it is real. He's going to be wise and powerful. We just got to meet him when he was a baby. Go on, tell him the tale."

Maya Gouliard

The Tale of The Rabbits & the Sorrowful Farmer

Once upon a time, there was a tidy little farm in a remote village. The farmer who lived there took immense pride in his trade and followed a strict routine each and every morning.

Early, before the sun even woke up, the farmer left his house, quiet as a mouse. He tracked across the worn path outside to the barn and fed his animals. Always in the same order.

First, he fed the ducks because they were the loudest.

Second, he fed the pigs because they were the hungriest.

Third, he fed the goats because they were next to the pigs.

Finally, he fed the horse.

The farmer had one grand horse. He was not a farm horse; he had come from far away and was retired here from his adventures. The old horse was more friend than farm-worker, so the farmer always saved him for last. He stayed and talked with the horse while milking the goats until the sun had risen. The horse munching his oats as the farmer shared his woes.

The farmer always had woes. He worried day and night. Today he was worried about the mice, yesterday he had been worried about the rain. There was always something out of his control, and as he talked with his horse, he felt better.

Having shared his thoughts, he felt lighter and went about his hard work in the fields.

His days went on like this for many a year, and he was content.

But no one can avoid change, even one who wants to the most. The horse passed away, and the farmer had to say goodbye to his beloved friend. And so, in the mornings he could no longer feed and talk with his friend the horse. The farmer had to learn to live without his company.

Each morning, he continued to follow his routine, quietly feeding the ducks. Then feeding the pigs, then feeding the goats.

He milked the goats, but he didn't share his thoughts. Instead, they shifted around in his head. They grew and grew. And with them was the added sorrow at the loss of his friend, and each morning the newest worries added, the farmer grew more on edge.

The fears and sorrow the farmer carried in his mind came with him to his fields and as he counted his rows of carrots, he worried about harvest coming soon. He worried about the lack of rain the last few days. He worried about the seeds he had to order in town.

Terraweaver

Walking along a row of carrots, the fronds of thin fluffy green leaves reaching up past his ankles, he took comfort in the regular pattern of the vegetables growing at his feet. Step, there is another plant, step, another plant, step another plant. The beat of it helped him. Step, another plant, step. he stopped short.

There was no green frond of carrot here. Instead, he saw an empty hole from where the carrot had been just yesterday.

What happened? He looked left. He looked right. He listened for a clue and heard a crunch crunch crunch coming from the row behind him. He slowly turned and found a large family of rabbits all happily munching on his prized carrots.

"Shoo you!" He screamed. His pent-up emotion let out in the one outburst.

A few of the rabbits ran, but most stayed. They looked at him with their big eyes. And all of the hurt inside him hated them for it.

"I said shoo!" He shouted.

A few more of the rabbits darted away, but still many stayed. Their eyes big and brown. His pain became more apparent to him, his hurt obvious in their large soft eyes.

"Shoo you terrible creatures, these are my carrots!" He stomped his foot hard on the ground as he shouted. The pain raw and palpable to him. A few more of the rabbits ran, but still three stayed. They sat there eating the carrots and looking at him. Their eyes kind and understanding.

"Don't you see?" He said, his blustering spent. "You aren't supposed to be here. These fields are mine, and the carrots you are eating are meant to be harvested in three weeks' time." They listened. He continued. "I am supposed to pick up the wagon from town in two weeks time, and the neighbors are coming to help with the harvest. I've already seen there is a chance of early frost this year, and I don't want to risk losing the crops."

They sat there listening as they chomped.

The farmer felt better.

The next few days the farmer continued his routine, but when he was out in the fields, he searched out the rabbits who listened as he shared his thoughts on the days to come. He had found some new friends.

After harvesting his mornings with the barn animals continued, but he realized that the rabbits would not have his carrots to munch. So, he gathered up a small supply and headed back to the barren field. He set a pile of carrots down and the rabbits came.

And to this day, the sorrowful farmer lays out a pile of carrots, and he always has at least a rabbit friend or two to share his day with.

ʔʔʔ

Fleck had sat back on his haunches and looked a bit more like the squirrel Stella had described him as that first day in Azural. His tail fluffed up high behind him. Lara had felt his emotions flow as Farmer Oswald had shared the story. Although they hadn't figured out how to speak with each other, they were definitely getting the hang of understanding one another. And he obviously understood the story, as his emotions had run the gamut from sorrow to humor.

Lara noticed that the story had even pulled Fleck's attention from the carrot he had been so intently eating earlier.

"Did you like the story?" Farmer Oswald asked Fleck, and Fleck chittered back as if sharing his thoughts.

Lara felt the intention behind the words, "He most certainly did. His favorite part was the carrots though."

Dillon reached his hand up in a wave, and Lara turned to see Jane heading toward them.

"Hi Jane!" Lara called out.

The young woman was the same age as her oldest daughter Anna, and they were fast friends similar to how Lara was with Jada. The community in Calambria had become tighter as fewer and fewer residents stayed.

"I am so glad to see you, Lara," Jane said loudly as she walked up. "I was talking with Dad about maybe traveling to the Wheel Road to try to connect with some of those Brown Travelers you interacted with. Granny is not so keen on the idea."

Dillon smiled, "Oh, Lara knows Granny well enough. Remember how we all got in trouble for trying to climb Mount Grist when we were teenagers?"

Lara laughed, "Oh Jane, you thought you kids got in trouble. Mrs. Oswald said she couldn't care less what Jada and my mother thought, she was not going to let us all go and," turning to Dillon she asked, "how had she phrased it?"

Dillon could barely get the words out with his laughing, "Oh Jane, it was one of her best. She wasn't going to let us all go and likely get our feet stuck in a tree root, trip and fall into a pond and drown with no one to ever know, and our bodies would freeze with winter blizzards and we would be left only for the birds to ever know where we had died."

Lara shook her head back and forth. "We argued with her for at least half the day saying there was absolutely no way that all three of us would trip, and if one of us did, the other two would pull them out of the water before anything happened. She did not agree."

"Well, she hasn't changed much. Dad, I need you to talk with her. I am going to head to the Wheel Road; she just seems to have a problem accepting it."

"Speaking of a bit of a problem, I have to get going. I am meeting the family at the tavern to chat about Fleck."

Jane looked from Fleck to Lara and back again. "What's the problem? Is there something I can do to help?"

Lara wrapped her arm around Jane's shoulder, "Oh thank you. I am happy to have as many minds as possible. I am planning to explain it all to them, so why don't you come along."

Family Meeting

"Maybe we just should take official turns." Sally said. She was huffy because she had asked Anna four times to pass the book to her, and when Anna had finally finished looking at it, Fiero had pulled it over to look. "Should I make a sign-up list?"

James was always Sally's pair when it came to shenanigans, so he immediately piped in. "I agree. Let's do it in order of age: Me next, then Jada, then Mom, then I think it would be Anna, then Jane, then Fiero, then…" He looked at the table next to him, there was no one else there. "Maybe that kid, and then of course Sally." He smiled at her, and Fiero looked up at his wife a bit surprised.

"Oh, here Sally." He scooted his chair out and encouraged her to sit down on his knee. They leaned in together, heads side by side over the images on the page.

Lara had left Azural in a blur, and she was lucky she had her pack with her at all, but the luckiest piece had been this book she had checked out from the library. It was a compilation of old journals written ages ago by a man named Siegel. In Azural it had been categorized in their extremely ordered shelves under fairy tales.

Anna stood up, but she had no reason as the tavern was empty. They had all come in on her off day, so there was no need to bus a table or cook. But she couldn't stay still. She started pacing back and forth, and Lara had a flash of memory of a ten-year-old Anna pacing this exact same way in front of the fireplace during family meetings. "I mean, it is clear as pen on paper. Fleck must be one of these Pelanor. I mean just look at the first image of the baby stage, that could be him, aside from maybe the ears being a bit shorter."

"Yes," Lara continued, "and the book says that Pelanor are Wish Dragons. At first that was the hardest part for me to grasp, but I am telling you so many strange things are happening."

Everyone looked up at her except Sally, who continued carefully turning the pages while still perched on Fiero's lap.

"The first is the psychic connection we have. I know what he is feeling, I can see images from him. But that goes further, so, connected to that, the second is that he is intelligent. He responds to my thoughts and often will send me images and feelings that feel like questions or responses. They are not just 'here is the random tree I am about to climb.'" She paused here. So far, she had only told James about this part. "And third, he can use magic."

"What? Like he is a waterweaver too?" Fiero asked.

"What kind of magic?" Jada said on top of him.

As the others were responding with so much interest Sally looked up from the book, "Wait, what did I miss? What's going on?"

Anna looked at Sally with the dismissive look only an older sister could perfect and said to Lara. "Explain, Mom. What kind of magic."

Lara started from the beginning for Sally's benefit. "I started noticing small things surrounding me from the beginning of having Fleck around. The ground would shake, for example. But then, it got stronger. The first big instance was when he returned to me by teleporting from outside the waterwall at Azural. I could feel him faintly far, far away, and then there was a flash of orange, and he was right in front of me."

Lara paused, but no one seemed like they wanted to interrupt so she continued, "That was just a few days before I connected with the water stone and got its magic. After I stonegrafted, things were moving so quickly, there wasn't much time to think much about any of it. Now, things have gotten... a, well, difficult over the few weeks since we returned."

She started listing occurrences, ticking them off on her fingers, "He started a fire in the backyard, we caught him flying in the living room to reach a book on the top shelf, he grew a vine that was reaching all of 6 feet by the time we saw what he was doing." She looked at James.

"It was inside the house." James stated very matter of fact to mimic Lara's professional presentation, then he grinned. "It was hilarious, if we hadn't stopped him, we might as well have been living in the green realm."

Lara commented, "And it was beautiful too. Jada, remember how your aunt used to have all the plants inside by her kitchen windows?"

Jada laughed, "Yes and we used to pretend that we were hunting in the jungles in the center of Chroma."

Sally stood up. "Wait, so let me catch up. Fleck is using magic? Like all of the Color Realms magic?"

"Yes." Lara stated.

They all thought quietly for a moment.

James was the first to break into everyone's thoughts, "But your mom hasn't even told you the worrying part." He looked at Lara, and she motioned for him to go on. "Every time Fleck uses his powers; she is getting affected. First, a bright flash of color in her mind. And then she gets a splitting headache."

Anna looked most alarmed. She was everyone's protector, but especially her mama. "Are you okay?"

"So far. It only happens one or two times a day, and the headaches dissipate within a few minutes. It seems to be happening when there is a reason for him to use it. Like I explained, I often am connected enough to him and his thoughts that I know kind of what he is planning to do next. But most of the time, when he uses the magic, it is instantaneous, as if it is instinct rather than plan. He wants to be warmer; he starts a fire. He wants the book on the shelf; he flies up there."

She reached for the book that lay open in front of Fiero and Sally, "I really am hoping this book has some answers."

Jane had been quiet the whole time. She had been friends with Lara's children their whole lives, and had often been present for family meetings, but she generally stayed as an observer. But she piped up now, "It sounds like we should stop looking at the pictures and start reading all of those little words."

James nodded in agreement. "Yes, the journal entries are probably the key here. And, as Jane just said, they are little words. I was going to read it but got a headache myself after the first page. My glasses are helpful, but they are old. We need some young eyes willing to take this on."

There was a chorus of ascent from the younger generation around the table.

Jada said, "I think it is a good idea if you start recording these instances too. Maybe we can start piecing together things a bit."

"Good idea." Lara said. She felt a world better. This is what she had missed most being away in Azural. Her friends and family working together as a team on the problems that came up. "Oh, thank you all."

Tiny Chaos

A few weeks later Lara joined Jada at their usual seats at the far end of the bar. The tavern was always busy, but these seats were generally the last to be filled. Either because they were right next to the kitchen, or because everyone just knew they were Lara and Jada's spots.

"I can't believe that I made it in time for lunch." Before Lara sat down in her seat, she fished out her journal and placed it on the bar in front of Jada. "Take a look."

Lara and Jada had been meeting regularly for lunch to discuss what they lightheartedly called "The Fleck Mystery." As if they were kids again playing sleuths. Although the name harkened to the happy-go-lucky play time, this had become a rather serious endeavor.

Fleck was using his powers more and more, and every time, Lara was getting a blinding flash of bright color and now, more often than not, a blinding headache too.

After her first few weeks back home when it had only been happening occasionally, Lara had simply talked about it openly with her friend and her family. She had thought to keep Fleck a bit of a secret, or at least not a center of attention in town, until she had figured out a bit more about him.

Unfortunately, that was impossible. Fleck had begun using his powers regularly and publicly. Lara opened the journal to the most recent page. She had begun taking notes of the incidents.

Tuesday -

WHEN - COLOR - WHAT - WHY
7am- green - no idea what - no idea?

7:30 - red - charred marks on the side of house - no idea?

9:45am - pink - books pulled off shelf with wind - wanted a story read?

"It seems that all of them have to do with his desire for something in the moment." Jada said slowly closing the journal.

"When we first connected, I was getting a lot of images and feelings from him, but we didn't get these flashes of color. And he wasn't popping off with all of this magic either."

"Well, all you have to do is look at the fountain in the square to know that Fleck has a lot of growing up to do."

"Yes. He hasn't grown physically very much yet. I'd say he is about twice the size he was when I found him. But I will be honest, these magic flashes I am getting are very difficult. I can't seem to close them off."

"What would happen if you try to reach out to him right now, when the magic isn't 'popping off?'" Jada asked.

"I'm a little bit nervous to. When I left Fleck with James, he had still been asleep on the cushion in front of the fireplace. Curled up like a kitten, his fluffy tail wrapped all the way around himself, and his face tucked underneath it with just the tip of his nose showing. I love that floofy tail."

"Love that floofy tail," Jada concurred.

Lara closed her eyes and reached out to Fleck. She had gotten better at it. Rather than reaching out with a question looking for an answer, she had begun sending him a feeling and an image. She had been extra careful lately to send calm thoughts his way. Yesterday when she was at Sally's house, she had sent him an excited look at a pack Sally and Fiero had made just for him. He had instantly popped over, landing on top of the pack in Fiero's arms unexpectedly. Lara had been again blinded by orange, and Fiero and Sally had heart palpitations.

She sent him a feeling of calm and a mental image of the river turn where it pooled into a calm flat spill off. Although she felt the connection it felt muffled.

"I think he's still asleep."

"Poor little guy. He's at it one hundred percent when he is awake." Jada laughed.

"Yeah, but sometimes I think that is the best way to live. Days lived to the fullest and then nights, and naps, in a deep sleep. I find falling asleep difficult sometimes."

"I think that happens when you have a lot on your mind. I have this mystery in my mind at night too," Jada answered her.

"Where is Anna?" Lara asked suddenly as she realized she hadn't seen her yet.

"She's in the storeroom. There was a delivery from Farmer Oswald's daughter. She just got back from the Wheel Road."

"That's fantastic. It's a pretty rough path, but I knew if we started trying, we might connect with some brown traders." Lara thought back to her friends she had made on her trip. "Did Jane have any luck?"

"Oh yes. She had brought that collection of older jewelry none of us around town used, to see if it was worth something. Apparently, the brown traders felt like it was more than enough, saying there were plenty of folks in the realms interested in unique jewelry pieces and insisted on only taking a few pieces in exchange for a box of vegetables. Jane could have gotten more, but she had to carry it back."

Lara thought of the path she had traveled between the two mountains to reach the Wheel Road. Now the river ran down the center again. The original path the townsfolk had used before the river went dry, ran along the edge of the water, but it was crumbling adding the danger of falling into the water below.

"I need to practice more with my magic. I can probably use it to make something like the canals in Azural. They run on their own, pulling and pushing boats along. That could make it easier to reach The Wheel Road that way?"

"That's a great idea. I don't get to watch you water weave as much as I'd like," Jada said.

"I'm nervous, Jada. I didn't get very much training before I left Azural so suddenly. And the raw power of it when I tore down the waterwall was scary. I sometimes wake up with nightmares of it engulfing me. Or worse, of the waters of the Hope River swelling beyond my control and drowning all of our homes."

Jada reached her hand out, placing it gently on Lara's right shoulder. She moved it over where the stone lay beneath Lara's top. "You have been doing great. This is a life changing power. Many would be using it to make the world what they want of it. I am super proud of how you are processing this. The town is better. There is no rush to you figuring this all out."

A clatter behind them turned them both on their spinning stools. Stan had dropped a full tray as he was delivering it to the larger table in the back. Soup was on the tray, on the floor and all over Stan. He stood there looking embarrassed and a bit unsure of what to do next. With Anna off the floor, he was the only one out here.

Lara jumped up. She had worked a few shifts here over the years. "No need to worry Stan," she said. "I don't know a single employee of this place that hasn't spilled a tray. When Sally worked here, she dropped a tray full of drinks all over the table and the guests her first day." She gently took the tray from his hands and set it on the ground. Carefully picking up the broken pieces of the clay bowls.

Lara stood up with the tray of spilled and broken bowls, the soup sloshing around to the lip of the tray. "Why don't you go get yourself cleaned up. I got this."

"At least let me take the tray. I can clean all of this up too." Lara handed him the tray holding on until she saw he had full control of it. He headed into the kitchen.

She was about to tell the table that she'd get them replacements in a jiffy, when she saw Jada walk out of the kitchen with a new tray, four bowls ready to go.

With Jada serving the table, and the bowls cleaned up, the only part left was the spilled soup. In that moment Lara had a small crisis in her mind.

She could easily go to the back and grab a towel and a mop.

Or...

She envisioned how Fallon would handle this. Magic sparkling through the room, as he danced around the spill, pushing water and pulling water until the floor was dry and clean.

She envisioned how Shauna would handle this. Succinct, a thin stream of magic, pushing the mess into a pile and then using the water to move it to the bin, pulling the water away and the food pieces dropping into the garbage.

It would be simple enough, but then she envisioned how her friends and townsfolk might look at her after doing either of these. The stark reminder of their faces the day she returned, the shock and awe they had shown. The otherness she had felt.

She headed to the kitchen and returned with a few dry towels and a wet mop. Why change what worked? Once the mess had been cleaned up, she placed another dry towel over to dry it as best she could.

Anna and Jane came up from the cellar just as she was standing with her pile of dirty towels in hand. Anna's dark eyes didn't miss a thing, and she joined Lara and Jada walking toward the kitchen.

"How many bowls broke?" She asked with a flat, defeated voice.

"Only three. I know they are hard to come by, I'm sorry." Lara walked toward the kitchen, and the two followed. "Jane, how was the trading attempt? I heard you got some vegetables?"

Jane grinned from ear to ear. "It was such an adventure. The path next to the river was difficult though. I could have traded for so much more; they were really interested in our jewelry. Something about the black stones sure to be a hit in the other realms. But I could only bring back what I felt sure I could carry along the path. I think we could bring more people next time to transport and get even more. Or maybe we can find some solutions to getting the path more stable so a cart could travel it."

"Or" Lara said slowly, thinking about logistics, "I might be able to figure out a way to move a boat or raft along upriver. My water weaving can't do much about the dirt and rocks around the river, but I think I can figure something out in the water."

"That would be great," Jane said. "I've never been on a boat."

Anna piped in, "Is there even a boat left in town?"

"I think we might need to solve a couple problems, but there is definitely enough wood from these half fallen dead trees that we can fix up a nice raft," Jada said. Then laughed out, "I love how I say we when I have never worked with wood a day in my life."

"It's the teamwork mentality though. We can all pitch in," Anna said.

"Well, I guess I have some thinking to do," Lara said. "I'm gonna go sketch."

She opened the journal and started a loose drawing of the path of the Hope River from The Wheel Road to town. She thought about the best place to drop items off in town. *Where would the best place be for a dock?* Sometimes when a problem didn't have a clear solution, she repeated the words in her head.

Where should the dock go?

After her third or fourth time repeating it, she realized she had made a mistake. Her mind had been a bit too focused, and she felt a stirring response from the little firecracker back at home. He was awake, and with her deep thinking the connection between them had become an open pathway.

Before she could send calming thoughts his way, he popped right over to her. The bright explosion of purple before her eyes blinded her for a moment. She scrunched up her face to abate a bit of the pain, but as usual, the color could not be blocked. It was inside her mind.

After a few moments, the sharp pain subsided. She slowly opened her eyes, letting the stiffness in her forehead and cheeks relax. There on the bar in front of her, adorably cute little paws were already holding a carrot. She sat and watched as his soft muzzle opened just enough to show shining sharp triangular teeth. She continued to watch as he brought the carrot up and started devouring it. Tiny shavings of carrot escaped, and the poor vegetable was gone in no time. When he finished with the orange root, he moved on and ate the green fronds too. Then he slowly started preening and licking his paws. As he did, she saw the talons pop out. These were as sharp as his teeth and curved. The teeth were hard as rock, and pin prick sharp, and, unlike the claws of a cat, the edge was like that of a knife. Dangerous.

She was at once reminded of one of the images in Siegel's journal of a full grown Pelanor Dragon. The massive body hunched forward ready to attack, its sharp-toothed mouth in a wide roar, one forearm up and talons out ready to slash. It was a scary image; she felt a chill thinking about her little Fleck becoming that.

He had finished his grooming and sauntered over to her, jumping into her lap and turning a few times before reaching his front legs to her chest and rubbing his slender long cheeks along her chin. His feathery soft ears tickled her ear at the same time as the force of his head pushed hard against her.

Did you have a nice nap?

His response was a contented reply, filled with warmth from the fire, and she thought the sound of James reading aloud in the background.

Oh, you lucky ducky. Did you get more stories?

Fleck finally had gotten enough cuddles and decided to go wander around.

At this point everyone in town had met Fleck, and he was a bit of a hit. Few of them saw his dangerous side. He was adorable and young, and the townsfolk were all happy to watch him bound around and chitter with them. He was so expressive that many of them practically held full conversations.

Lara went back to her journal and turned back a page.

1pm - purple - teleported from home to tavern - no idea? To join me?

She went back to her sketch of the river and chose a spot for unloading. As she tried to imagine what kind of magic to use to adjust the current but not mess with the overall flow of the river, she couldn't help but have her mind pulled to the mystery of Fleck. His antics were adorable to most in the town right now, but what about when he grew? How would her friends and neighbors react to a full-grown Fleck? Would she still have this connection? Would he be out of control and a monster? Would he even fit through the tavern door?

She thought of how smart the little guy was. She knew he had emotions and often was encouraging her and supporting her. She might never have succeeded in Azural if he hadn't been there for her. She owed him so much. She would repay him. She would support him too.

But to do that, she needed answers.

Mayor Kelton

Lara sat in her favorite perch on the edge of the stone water fountain in the center of the square. She could still picture it as she had as a tiny tot. It had been surrounded by a neat square of short cut green grass. The shop windows had been bright and full of amazing fun.

As a child her favorite locations had been the candy shop and the fabric store. The candy shop had been run by Mr. Smiles, at least that is what the kids had called him; she realized now that was likely not his real name. Granny Winslow had run the fabric store. She was still in town, but too old to run a shop, and the possibility of bringing in fabric had disappeared ages ago. For a while, the shop had turned into a mending area, but nowadays most everyone knew how to mend up a tear, or to reinforce a weak area in the fabric.

With the many shops closed, the ones still here were extra important. They were, of course, useful, but also a key part of human connection in the town. The tavern and inn that Anna ran was there to the east.

Directly in front of Lara to the south of the fountain was the town hall. This massive building harkened to the glory days of Calambria. It seemed very out of place now with all of the smaller dilapidated buildings surrounding it. Lara climbed the wide steps leading up to the entrance and walked through the heavy double doors that brought her into the meeting hall.

Lara recalled her first thoughts walking into the Great Stone House in Azural. This room would fit three times over in their Great Hall. But here in Calambria, instead of feeling like a small room, it was grand. There were small offices in the building, meant for leaders in the community, but now only one office was occupied. That was Mayor Kelton's. Lara geared herself up and walked through the room to talk with her.

Her steps echoed through the hallway. Mayor Kelton's office was in the back of the building, the entry door behind the speaker's podium. Lara skirted around the back row of chairs and knocked on the office door.

Mayor Kelton was a small woman about Lara's age. They had grown up together but never become close. Lara and Jada had been fast close friends, and their antics and rough, silly play had been too childish for Diane. She had always been serious, and when she had been elected Mayor, there was no question from anyone in town that she was the one for the job. Lara and Jada had jokingly started calling her Mayor Kelton instead of Diane, and now Lara found herself unintentionally doing so.

Diane was behind the large desk that had been built at the same time as the building. The desk was imposing, built at a time when the mayor had been expected to be imposing. Now, it was as out of place as the candy store would have been. A reminder of past days.

The mayor looked up from a large ledger full of pristinely printed numbers and pierced Lara with intelligent, dark eyes. When she saw it was Lara, the eyes softened a bit. "To what do I owe the pleasure?" She said as she stood and walked around the desk to greet Lara. "I haven't seen much of you since you got back from saving the town." It was a loaded statement, and Lara reflected that it was for that very reason that she had kept her distance.

"I know," Lara replied choosing her words carefully. "I am still trying to come to terms with these powers myself. I don't feel too much changed, and then I realize that everything has changed. It isn't a simple switch to flip."

Mayor Kelton nodded her head sagely, her adorable, bouncing, tight black curls softening her look now more comforting than belittling. "I agree with your choice to keep the waterweaving to a minimum, but we should talk about what changes this has created for our community."

"Yes, I actually came to chat with you today because I was thinking of something more I could do but wanted you on board." Lara said.

Mayor Kelton gestured to the comfortable seating area to the side of the room. "Why don't we have a seat together? Then you can tell me about it."

Lara shared her thoughts about connecting with traders on The Wheel Road. She shared about the canals in Azural and how the magic was left behind in the water to continue the pull of the boats without the continuous intervention of the weavers.

"This is fantastic!" Mayor Kelton exclaimed, with more excitement than Lara expected. "I think our biggest need right now as a community is getting better connected with the rest of the Land of Chroma. I don't want to dismiss your work bringing us water, it has been lifesaving, and our community would have had to leave. But we are still short on all of the other resources. The crops won't grow, the air is cold, the dirt itself is crumbling. I have been thinking that our next biggest step is strengthening our food supply and trading abilities. I have even considered meeting with Farmer Oswald and asking if he would consider traveling to Green. I know you have inspired him quite a bit."

Lara's initial response in her head was to downplay her part in it, but she had already talked with Farmer Oswald and knew Mayor Kelton was right.

The mayor stood as she continued. "Well, I don't like to sit around talking about something when we know the answer. Let's discuss the logistics of this magic water way and how we go about making it happen. I'll get some paper to take notes. The sooner we move the better."

Trade

Lara stood beside the river looking across the water at where the dock was going to be built. She had specifically talked with Mayor Kelton about limiting the number of people present, and the mayor had done a wonderful job. The only people with her were James and Mayor Kelton. James for moral support and the mayor in case they had to make any changes mid-project.

The plan had been simple. Lara would create an undertow in the water that would pull along the river's edge. When they had refined the plan, they agreed that it needed to be on the far side of the river from town to allow families access to the natural river flow. There had been discussion of pulling the magical water across the river to a dock, but Lara was not confident enough in her abilities, and worried about messing with the flow of the river towards the farmland south of town. They decided to build a bridge across the river instead.

The river continued through the mountains after passing by Calambria and emptied into the sea on the far side, and although the journey was treacherous for anyone who lived in Calambria, Lara could feel the water as it followed this path. Never in her life had she even considered what happened on the other side of those mountain peaks to the south. She was amazed at how many questions lay unanswered simply by not asking them. That was a much safer place for the passing river water to travel, than to risk closing off the waters and causing flooding in town.

And so, the plans had been drafted: construction of the bridge would start next week. They would need wood to build the bridge, and a raft.

Ben and Griff, who knew the situation with available wood best after their years of fence building, were already out dealing with old tree trunks that had lost their footing. In the meantime, Sally and Fiero were getting together strips of leather and rope for binding the wood for the raft.

Mayor Kelton was very clear that she wanted something in place right away. Later they could improve upon the bridge and maybe even build a nice boat, but the town needed to get something in place immediately. Lara appreciated her leadership.

"Well, are you two interested in a little magic?"

"Can't wait," James said, while Mayor Kelton just bobbed her head in brisk answer.

Lara closed her eyes and thought about her town. She had refined her use of the blue magic and used emotion tied to responsibility the most often. She felt the need to help her community, and that emotion tied in so nicely with her communities need. This waterway was going to help feed her family.

Opening her eyes, she saw that the blue ribbons of magic had begun to encapsulate her arm. They swirled slowly getting brighter as they waited for some direction to go. Lara pushed at the water in front of her. The riverbed slowly opened in front of them. Lara held the rushing water to her right against a tight imaginary wall. The ground in front of them showed the rocky bed. Before they started walking, she split off a touch of the magic to pull the water from the path before them, so it was dry and less precarious. "We better hurry and get across so that I don't end up flooding the town." The water she held back was slowly rising as the river continued to push along. When they passed through the center of the riverbed, the wall reached over their heads and loomed dark, the push of the current hitting her wall of magic.

"Look, a fish." James laughed as a catfish swam near his feet.

Lara giggled and the wall bubbled inward. "Stop making me laugh, I have to concentrate." She pushed back on the water to get better control of it.

When they climbed up the far side of the riverbed, Lara let go carefully. She started in the center feeding the water through, slowly releasing the magic so as not to flood the banks with a deluge of water.

"Well, that was interesting," Mayor Kelton said, "Can't say I've done that before."

James laughed, "To be honest, I am not too excited about doing it again, even doing it to get back home. Maybe we should just swim back."

Lara laughed. "It worked though. I am open to suggestions for the return trip. Now as we discussed, for this next part, I will have to create a layer of magic that loops around under the water. There will be a flow that continually pulls itself with the magic powering it. Should the trip toward the road be by the river's edge or the trip back?" She asked.

Mayor Kelton bent over and drew in the dirt in front of her. "I made a detailed sketch back in the office. I should have brought it along, but this should do." She drew out the rough lines of the edges of the Hope River, then added the bridge across it at the far end. "This is the bridge at The Wheel Road. The plan is that we will add a dock in place here," she drew a small rectangle next to the ground. Mayor Kelton looked at Lara to check she followed the drawing. Lara remembered her difficult climb up the side of the riverbed on her journey to Azural. The river would now be full, so the dock would easily be at an accessible level to the road.

Lara nodded and Mayor Kelton continued, "Here is where we stand now. She added a box of similar size over the edge of the water at this end of her river image. "Here is the bridge we so desperately look forward to," she grinned at James, then drew two arched lines across the river on the far side of the dock.

"My thinking is your magical water way will create a loop drawing the raft up this edge of the riverbank, then it will turn right at the far dock and pull back around toward town. It will travel back more closely to the center of the river." She drew a looping line with small arrows along it.

Lara agreed, "This looks good to me. Now, let's see if I can make it happen. I think I am going to have to take a little trip, but you better stay here. Here goes nothing."

She stood on the riverbank and envisioned the path of the future raft. She didn't want to take any major risks, so she decided to begin with a nice slow leisurely trip. The water magic flowed from the stone in her upper arm, and she could feel it tingle along the waves of her tattoo. She created a force of water from the river and used it to pick herself up into the air. She opened her eyes and saw she was indeed hovering above the water where she intended for the circular path to begin. She left a touch of the magic below in the water and pushed herself forward over the water, working upriver while constantly leaving a magical path below.

For now, the magic just stayed there like a rope she was holding onto, lengthening as she traveled toward the Wheel Road. She passed the area she had initially met Fleck; it was underwater now. *How much the world has changed* she thought, sending him an image of the water below. He responded with a chitter, but was interested enough in Sally's workroom happenings that he didn't pop over to her. She realized she probably shouldn't have risked encouraging the interaction.

As she saw the bridge of the Wheel Road coming up ahead, she carefully controlled her pace. She calculated roughly the space needed for the dock and the raft to pull up to it. Not wanting to push the water too far under the bridge she decided to turn a bit earlier. Slowly she laid her magic tether into the water below turning a tight corner where she imagined the raft would stop to tie up and then turning another corner headed back in the direction she had come.

The return trip needed to be far enough from her first trip that the current wouldn't work against the raft on the way back. She pictured Jane sitting happily on a stack of crates loaded on a raft. The crates full of food and other necessities Calambria had done without for so long. Continuing to lay the magic down, she found the energy easy to create. This was a prime example of how the emotion used to power the blue stone matched up with real life needs. Here she was responsible for helping her community and she used that responsibility to power the stone.

She could see the sparkle of the initial water magic rope she had set in the water as she moved along. Coming back to James and Mayor Kelton on the bank, she looked for the start of her magic. When she found the tip of it, she lashed her magic rope to it, imagining a tight knot like what she would use to tie the laundry line up. Then she slowly settled herself onto the ground next to them.

"Whew," she said. Her body was shaking. It had taken a bit of strength in her muscles to keep the water pushing her along the path.

Now that she had stopped, the muscles suddenly felt tingly and weak, she wasn't really in the physical shape to take on this type of task easily.

"Did it work?" Mayor Kelton asked walking over to the river and looking closely at the water. "It doesn't seem to be moving."

Lara walked up next to her, "Look there. Do you see that sparkle there?" Lara pointed at the water.

James came up on her other side. They both searched below in the murky blue waters. "I guess it is easier for me since I can feel it there. I know exactly where to look."

James looked back at Lara, "I don't see it, but I didn't bring my reading glasses. I wish I could see that fish again. Hey, he isn't going to get hurt by this is he?"

Lara rolled her eyes. Her husband loved every animal under the sun. "I am planning to keep the forced current very slow. Any fish should be strong enough to swim out of it if they get pulled into it. It will be a nice leisurely trip for the raft too. Here, I am going to grab ahold of the magic I just laid and try to power it up to run on its own."

Lara reached down and pulled it back slowly with her magic. Then, like pushing a child in a swing she gave it a good solid shove. The water below started to ripple slightly, and the ripple pushed one side as it pulled the other.

James and Mayor Kelton both cried out together, "It's working!"

Lara let go with her magic and they all watched as the water continued to slowly pass by her, heading upstream. James turned from the water and picked up a small stick. "Let's test it out with a small tester raft," he said.

He twined three small sticks together and dropped them into the river. They bobbed a bit beneath the surface then buoyed up and began to flow upstream.

"Well, maybe we should be timing this trip so we know how long a trip takes?" Lara asked.

"I don't think we need to worry much about how much time it takes. It will be much faster than a walk down that precarious path. And we can transport so much more! This is so exciting." Mayor Kelton sounded uncharacteristically childlike in her glee. "There is so much we need to do. I need to get this bridge and raft built asap. And we should come up with a clear plan about what in town we have to trade. And there is the discussion of how to distribute what comes in. I am very happy with Anna getting most of it for now. So many in town would rather have her cook for them anyway. We can work up from there. This is really going to change things for the better. I just know it."

They grew quiet as they all stood on the riverbank, shoulder to shoulder, imagining the changes that might come. "Whoever sees it first wins," James said.

"You are so competitive," Lara said.

"I am also the one without his glasses," he laughed. They looked at each other grinning.

"I win!" Mayor Kelton called out. "There it is!" The tiny little raft came slowly along down the center of the river bobbing along. As it came in front of them, it slowly turned the corners that Lara had laid in the water and made its way to head back toward the Wheel Road. It had worked.

Carrots Again

Lara followed close behind James around the carts set up in the town square. As far as she could see, everyone was out today. There might only be a fraction of who they had started with as the population, but when everyone was in the tiny space around the Dragon Fountain it certainly felt like a crowd.

Everyone had brought items to share and trade. Suzette had a small cart piled high with clothing that she had mended. Some items were original items that she had pieced together to create amazing, quilted jackets and skirts. Others were just favorite clothing that people had given her to mend and last just one more year.

Lara generally did all of the mending for her family, but when she walked past today, a skirt caught her eye. She always loved the look of the patchwork skirts. They brought fun layers and volume to the skirts, and when she saw others in town wearing them, she often thought they just made life a bit happier. The materials were all worn and threadbare, but Suzette had found a way to layer them on top of each other so that the finished skirt was more substantial. Lara walked over to Suzette's cart and picked up the skirt that had pulled her over.

"Oh, Suzette!" She exclaimed. "This is lovely. Wait, I recognize that pattern there." She pointed to a larger square patch near the center. "This was an old shirt that Pete used to wear almost every day." She turned to James, who had trekked back through the crowd to return to her. "Do you recognize this?"

"Oh ho! We couldn't get him to wear anything else," James said. "Wait, I think he used to say, 'It's comfortable and warm and why would I wear anything else?' I had a hard time arguing with that."

Suzette smiled, "Well, it was meant for you then, Lara."

Lara opened up her leather pack Sally had made her, flipping the lovely etched map of Chroma over as she set the pack up on the table. She looked inside at what they had brought for trade. "Is there anything you are specifically looking for right now?" Lara asked. "We brought a few books, and I have — "A flash of yellow hit Lara's mind breaking her off mid-sentence. The headaches were getting worse. She pushed her hands to either side of her forehead, trying to hold the pulsing in her mind tight to control the pain. Although the light subsided within an instant, the pain lingered for a few minutes.

When she found she could breathe evenly without sending daggers through her brain, she slowly relaxed her arms to her side and opened her eyes. James was right there next to her. Suzette was looking at her with deep concern. She then noticed that it was quiet around her. The market had paused, most people in the area were turned and looking at her also.

"I'm fine," She called out to no one in particular. Then turning to Suzette, "Really, it's nothing. Where were we?"

James behind her turned to the others in the area, confirming that everything was fine, and the folks continued back on their paths between carts.

Suzette reached her hands out and set them on Lara's, stopping her from reaching into her pack. "Lara, I don't want anything from you in trade. You have done enough already for us. Think of this as payment for the water you brought, a small down payment actually."

Without thinking Lara blurted out, "Oh no, I..." but she saw in Suzette's eyes the truth of it. Lara had brought water. Before she had returned, water had often been one of the items traded here at the market. She remembered clearly spending a few hours slowly filling bottles at the river and carrying them up to markets to trade for needles and other items needed back home.

She switched her attitude. "Suzette, I can't tell you how much I love this skirt. I will think of you every time I wear it. You and my Petey. Thank you."

She was still feeling uneasy about the trade as they made their way through the crowd toward the book cart. She wasn't comfortable with the idea of using people. She wasn't comfortable with the idea that they owed her something. She had done it to help, not to get things for it. The skirt was in her pack, and she realized she had a lot to unpack here. She had been avoiding using magic in front of her friends because it might change how they saw her, but she realized in that moment that it was too late. They all were there that day she had made it rain. They all knew her, and they all knew what she had become. She needed to come to terms with that.

They came up on an opening in the crowd and James slowed to walk beside her. "What color was it?"

"Yellow. I still don't know what these other powers are. The only obvious ones are green for plants and the red for fire. That one scares me, for obvious reasons, but these other colors scare me because I have no idea what he is doing."

James looked around searching, "Where is he?"

Lara created an image of where they stood next to the old schoolhouse and sent out in a wide circle around her. She felt him connect to her from over in front of the inn. Rather than walk the short distance between them, or wait for them to join him, he flashed over. The instant flame of purple seared Lara's brain, and she doubled over with her hands to her temples.

After the pain had subsided, she drew in a deep breath and righted herself, standing up. Again, people around them had stopped. She gently waved her hands at folks. "No need to worry, I'm fine." She said. But she turned to see James looking like there was indeed something to worry about.

"You screamed out this time, Lara. Is the pain getting worse?"

"I don't think so, and I feel fine now." She paused, thinking about the pain. "To be honest, it's completely gone."

Fleck scurried up her arm and circled around her neck like a scarf, his long soft tail wrapping around her neck a second time and tickling her ears. "What I don't understand is how he always reacts to my emotions as if he is feeling them himself. But there is no way he is feeling this pain. He wouldn't constantly be doing this. And somehow it isn't registering to him that I feel it either?" She shrugged her shoulders and his poofy tail moved up tickling the tops of her ears.

"What's up?" Jada waved with a concerned look on her face, calling to them from Farmer Oswald's stand. James and Lara made their way over to say hello.

The farm stand was piled with the vegetables for trade. Lara and James pulled the pack out and traded Jane the shawl that Lara had finished crocheting for a portion of carrots, potatoes, and turnips. James took one of the carrots and started snacking on it right away. As he bit into it, the crunch pulled Fleck's attention.

Lara almost lost her balance as Fleck scurried and perched on her right shoulder leaning forward with both paws toward James' carrot. James laughed and broke off a piece handing it to him. Fleck took it with exuberance and scuttled back into a comfortable circle around Lara's neck but with his front claws holding the carrot.

"These are definitely his favorite," James laughed. "It's a good thing you are so cute Fleck, because these outbursts of yours are causing Lara a lot of trouble."

Fleck finished his carrot so quickly that Jada laughed. "I swear he must just be inhaling them. Can you imagine how many carrots it is going to take when he is full grown?" She put her hands to her cheeks. "Oh my. I hadn't even thought about that."

Lara's eyes got large also. "Oh no. What will it look like him walking around the crowded little square?"

"You two are worrying about tomorrow's problems when we have a today problem."

"What do you mean?" Jada asked. But right at that moment it happened again. A flash of green took over Lara's mind. Nothing but sparkly green and sharp pounding pain. When she felt that her mind was her own again and the pain had passed, she righted herself from the crouched position she found herself on the ground.

Fleck was no longer perched on her shoulder, instead he was sitting on the booth in front of them. And it was completely changed. One of the carrots had grown. A lot. It was so heavy it had broken the table. Fleck happily sat chomping away at the carrot that would probably feed this village for weeks.

Lara looked around her in shock. And found that everyone else was also looking in shock at the scene. There was no simple waving of the hands to folks and get back along your regular day.

The whole town watched as the tiny dragon sat atop his prize. He devoured the carrot, eating his fill. When he finally felt content, he looked up and jumped into Lara's arms, leaving more than enough carrot for everyone else.

James apologized for leaving so quickly and pulled Jada and Lara into the path between Anna's Inn and the empty candy shop.

"It's getting worse," James said, the fear in his voice surprising Lara. "I'm sorry Lara. That last one scared me. You may feel fine now, but in the moment it happened, and you screamed out in such anguish, I thought we might lose you."

"But I feel fine now."

"But what about the next time he wants to just pop over somewhere, or needs a drink of water when he isn't by the river, or wants a storybook off of the top shelf?" James set a hand on Lara's arm and then pet Flecks long sleek snout. Lara heard Flecks purr in her ear and felt his happiness radiate through her.

She focused a bit on that feeling. The connection between them was so tight that she knew how he was feeling, she could even feel his satisfaction with a full belly. She could gauge his emotions, and he could react to hers. The connection was obviously what was causing this. "I wish we understood this connection better. But Van and Delly told us about other people who had connected. I can't believe that they all deal with this pain constantly. Or maybe they do? How would we know?"

Find Mentor

Jada perked up. "That's it. You are going to go and talk to them. Those journals by Siegel were written ages ago by someone who didn't even have this connection like you do. You need to talk with someone who has firsthand experience. And Fleck should be able to meet some other Guardian Dragons too."

Lara stood in shock for just a beat, and then it all clicked into place in her mind. "Of course Jada, you're amazing."

"Didn't the kid from Green… what was his name again?"

"Van," Lara said.

"Right, didn't you say that Van had seen two dragons in Green?"

"Yes, two of the weavers there connected with young dragons. Van had said they were much larger than Fleck, so maybe they are adolescents?" She thought about how lovely and calming going to Green felt, until Lara immediately felt her stomach drop. "But I don't think I can go to Green. I would have to go right past Azural. I'm not ready to confront them there again. I left them so suddenly." She stalled, a bit overwhelmed remembering the flash and crash of her magic breaking the windows in the court room, the well of emotion she built up to pull the waterwall, the city's 'protection,' down as she left.

She reached her left hand up to burrow her fingers into Fleck's fur at his belly. As she pet him, his purr rumbled through her body, and she felt it calm her enough to keep going. "Granted, I realize that the powers-that-be in Azural were already at odds and there was a lot going on, but I am the one who destroyed the wall and ran from a guilty sentence. I just think it might be best to wait a little bit longer before I walk back in that corner of the Land."

James and Jada shared a look and then James nodded. "We understand, Lara. You went through a lot to get water for the town. Don't forget about how much has changed here too— for the better — because of what you did."

Jada nodded in agreement, "I get your emotions, from all you shared, you made some great friends there. I don't think you need to completely write it off, but I don't see the need to go there yet. Wasn't there another dragon they mentioned seeing?"

"Of course! There is a fully grown Pelanor in Laran. I could travel around the Wheel Road to Orange from the other direction. Not only would I not have to go anywhere near Azural, but I would get to meet someone who had been attached to his dragon for decades." Lara spun to look intensely in James' eyes. She whispered because she was almost scared to say, "And maybe I can find out about Brie?"

"Yes, although we all have discussed that she may not have stayed in Laran, it is where she was planning to head first. It would be wonderful to hear how she is. And" James added, "one thing in the fairy tales is that the fully grown dragons could," he looked up and motioned to Fleck "well actually, I should rephrase. We know they are real now. The fully grown Guardian Dragons can communicate with words. He would have real answers for you and Fleck."

"Can you imagine?" Jada said, "I wonder what little Fleck might tell us if he could use words?"

Lara laughed. "Carrot. Carrot. Story. Carrot."

James laughed for a minute along with them. Then he sobered up. "I can't believe I am encouraging you to leave again. I missed you so much last time. And this time it will seem even more quiet without Fleck, too."

Lara thought about it for a second, "Maybe I should stay? We can figure this out."

James shook his head, "No. You need to do this. We need the answers."

"And besides, James needs your stories when you come back to add to his journals. Your adventures make his town history much more interesting than Mayor Kelton's accounting of the town census."

"Hey," Lara said, pushing her friend, "what James does is important. It is how we remember and learn and teach future generations."

"I know. But I also know that the chapters with you and Fleck in them will make the book much more entertaining."

James

The covers on Lara's bed were heavy. She loved the feel of the weight of them when she fell asleep, but come morning, she always felt differently. She pushed legs out and arms out to cool them and try to balance the heat that had built up as she slept.

James never liked having a lot of blankets, so they had come to a happy place where they each had their own blankets on their own side of the bed. She looked over at him through her half-awake eyes. He was an early riser and sat with his back against the headboard, his reading glasses perched low on his nose. The book he was reading was one he had read many times before, so she didn't feel bad interrupting.

"Morning," it came out more as a mumble than a chipper greeting.

He looked over at her, her face half buried in the pillow and her right arm flung up between them. "Good morning," he said happily.

"Um- humm," she agreed, then stretched out her arms, while still keeping her body buried in her blankets. She closed her eyes and squeezed them preparing to open them fully for the day. This was a routine she had. Usually after opening them, she was much more awake.

When she opened her eyes, she saw James staring at her arm. The bright blue stone sat perched there between them. When the stone had magically grafted into her upper arm right below her shoulder, it had hurt for only a searing moment, and then the magic had overtaken her. The blue tattoos that looked like waves on the sea reached out down her arm toward her elbow, slowly dissipating until they were gone. The tattoos reached across her collarbone and her back, but right now James and Lara both just stared at the waves on her arm.

James reached out and touched her elbow just where the tattoo ended and traced up her arm. "Does it hurt?" His eyes found hers and she shook her head.

"No," she said. "That actually feels pretty good."

Hope River

And so, about a month after she returned home, Lara packed up again to leave for the Color Realms.

This time felt so different. First, she was leaving town a different way. Last time she had walked along the Crumble Pass, which had been the empty riverbed left behind when the Hope River had run dry. This time she was going to be riding the fledgling trip on the new trading raft.

Many of the people in town joined them at the edge of the river, but only her family and Mayor Kelton crossing the plank with her to the far side.

Mayor Kelton had decided to put all of the energy in building a really good raft first, so rather than a bridge there was only a narrow walkway of a large log across the river. The bark had been removed, and the log had been leveled, but it was narrow, and everyone walked with careful steps.

Lara followed last after a final fierce hug with Jada. Her friend had some final advice: "Get this mystery solved, but don't forget to have fun this time. We aren't all about to die, so that takes some of the pressure off."

Fleck pranced across in front of her, looking all innocent and adorable. He was wearing the pack Sally and Fiero had made him that matched Lara's own pack. He was so proud of it, and his steps seemed lighter as he held his shoulders erect to show off the pack to those around. She had to remind herself that he had no intent of hurting her when these flashes happened. He was just a baby. An adorable little floofy tailed baby. With enormous unexplained powerful magical abilities. Maybe not the best combination.

Sally wrapped her arms around Lara as soon as she was across the log. "I'm going to miss you, but don't worry about us. We will keep busy while you are gone and will not worry nearly as much now that you have made it back once."

Anna was close and rather than waiting her turn, grabbed both Sally and Lara, creating a pile of love around her. Lara loved these two. She was so proud of them. So proud of all of her children. Anna whispered, her voice muffled by the tight embrace, "Keep an eye out for Brie. I'm worried about her."

Lara pulled back to look Anna in the eye. "I don't see her having ended up in Laran, but I will obviously keep an eye out. I don't think you should worry though. She is strong, and she will find her way."

Anna rolled her eyes just a touch, "I know, I just wish she would be a little more predictable."

"That isn't who she is," Lara said softly.

James came up and put his arm around Lara, they faced the kids, creating a small circle. From this vantage Lara couldn't see the townspeople lined up behind them. Instead, she was surrounded by the folks who knew her best. "I'm a little scared that I am leaving for the wrong reason. Last time it felt right, I was leaving to help all of you. This time feels more selfish."

Although they all spoke denials at once, James was the firmest. "Lara. You are important to us. This trip is important, because you are important." He nodded to the kids across from them. "We all want you to figure out what is going wrong with Fleck and your connection. Also," he finished, "there is nothing wrong with you going on a trip to see the world. Calambria learned so much about the color Realms from your last trip. The information you bring back is valuable."

"Spoken like the historian you are," Lara stated.

Sally smirked and said, "Also, it's okay for you to just go have fun. If Orange is all about excitement, then it will be a great story."

Mayor Kelton interrupted here, "I know that goodbyes are difficult, but..." she was attempting to be tactful, "the whole town is waiting to send you off."

And so, with a final round of quick hugs, Lara and Fleck were loaded onto the newly built raft and as they released the rope tie, the current carried her along the river.

She could hear Mayor Kelton attempting to give her planned speech about connections with the outside world, but all of the folks yelling goodbyes drowned her out. As the mountain range came up, Lara yelled out "goodbye, love you" to her girls and James and then they were out of sight. Fleck stood on his hind legs standing tall like a ground squirrel trying to see them for a few more minutes. But when it was evident they would not pop back into view, he instead started darting around the edge of the raft looking for fish in the water.

The pace of the raft was intentionally slow to keep crates from falling into the water, but it was a bit of a torturous pace when she was so ready to be on her way. It felt hard to be so close to her family still and know that she wouldn't see them for such a long time. But she also remembered that her last trip had flown by once she had been truly on the road.

She considered the road to Laran. Her last trip had taken her East past the Purple Realm of Morchast and straight to Azural. This trip she would be turning West. The path should pass the Pink and Red Realms before reaching the orange one.

Her doubts took over. She didn't know how long the trip she was about to take would last. She didn't know where in Laran to find the Weaver Soren and his dragon. She didn't know if it was safe to walk the roads by Red. She sat looking down into the dark water depths and worried about all that could go wrong.

Fleck broke her out of it. He always knew when she was going down a dark thought path. He came over to her and jumped into her lap. Patting her face with his tiny paws. *Thanks Fleck.* Not only were there still so many unknowns, but also, she had done it before with less information than she had now. When she had arrived at Azural's wall, she had not known about the Realm beyond their basic tenets. She had been on a pressed timeline because of the water shortage back here in Calambria.

Her young friend Delly had been from Laran, and Lara had learned a lot about the Realm from her. She knew they had very few rules, and that the weavers often did shows of magic for fun at their regular festivals. That alone was a huge change from Azural where rules and order had taken the lead in all decisions.

Another difference was that for this trip she was not on any schedule aside from she would miss her family and friends. Lara stood as she saw the bridge of the Wheel Road coming into sight, grabbing the rope to tie off. James was right, she needed to figure out the headaches. They were getting worse.

Pink

The path down the road to the left started out by looking exactly the same as the one she had traveled to Azural in the opposite direction, just the mountains were on the left side of the path. She and Fleck were getting good at traveling together. He was super fast at gathering kindling for a fire, so while she set up and cleared the space for them to camp at night, he ran around getting all of the small sticks and tree bark to feed a fire. She generally found a few larger pieces. Then as the fire started roaring, they sat and thought with each other.

We have come such a long way Fleck, she thought.

He sent her an image from his memory of the Wastes empty riverbed and an agreement of amazement.

The next morning, after cleaning up their camp area, they were back on the road . The mountain peaks loomed tall to the South. On the North side of the road there were thick trees. *I wonder what is in the center of Chroma?*

Fleck looked toward the trees and chittered excitedly. The feeling she got was a mix of excitement and comfort. She wasn't really sure what he meant by it. *Sometimes I wish you could use words* she sent to him playfully.

It was on the third day of travel that they noticed a change. Tiny soft pink buds were popping up in the dirt by the side of the road. The mountains were changing to foothills now, with rolling tops rather than the harsh points. It was around dinner time when they crested a hilltop and Lara had to just stop short. Fleck on the other hand raced ahead gleefully.

In front of them to the left of the path was a field of pink. Lara couldn't see anything else for miles. It looked like a puffy cloud that would just welcome you in and cheer you up. She left the path and followed Fleck out into the field. The flowers reached up to her ankles at first, but as she walked deeper into the field they came to her knees. Lara recognized the tulips, but the rest she could not name. They were in every shade of pink, from the lightest almost white to a shocking bright solid in your face pink, that almost hurt her eyes.

Fleck bounded along following the path but staying in the field of flowers. She could see him at the top of his bounce, and then he would disappear again into the sea of pink flowers. She just loved him so much. His adorable fluffy fur looked extra poofy, and he had his pointy ears folded back on his head, and as he dove into the flowers. He pounced on a nearby flower bud and made a happy tiny roar of pleasure that Lara had never heard before. It was high pitched and cracked in the most endearing way.

The field continued as far as Lara could see, and as they walked throughout the day Lara wondered just how large this field was. She really had heard nothing about Pink, she wasn't even sure what the official name of it was. It was not until the next morning as they walked along the path that they saw the Spoke Road toward the Pink Realm. They had a lovely sign made of wood with Pink and white large, beautiful script letters as tall as Lara that read "Welcome weary traveler to the Realm of Vaalean. A realm of safety, healing, fun and relaxation."

Lara had no idea how to pronounce a word with two a's in a row. She looked down the spoke road but saw nothing that gave a clue to the Realm. She couldn't see anything but more pink fields on either side of the Pink Spoke. *Well, that is a trip for another day maybe.* She sent to Fleck, and they continued on their way.

Sitting at the fire that night Lara studied the map on her pack. She was getting just a touch nervous. The next Realm to pass was Red. Everyone knew that those in Red were all about power and force. She had heard fears of passing red soldiers on the road. When folks talked about the dangers it was wolves and Red. After she had seen the way wolves reacted to Fleck that fear had been removed from her list, but she still had not come across any red soldiers. It is amazing how the unknown is often even scarier than the known.

Her mind began racing a bit with scenarios where she came across soldiers. At first, they just passed her by, and she kept her head down avoiding eye contact. Then as she continued to worry over it the images changed. They stopped her and questioned why she was on the road traveling. They questioned her about Fleck, they tried to detain him and take him. As the scenario played out in her head she got a mental push from Fleck.

She looked up at him and his eyes glowed from the fire in front of them. Was he bigger than the last time she saw him? Had he suddenly grown? No, she just realized she had been seeing him every day and it just hit her how much he had grown since she had first found him. He was still small, cute and cuddly, but he was less the size of a squirrel and more the size of a small fox.

Once he had her full attention, he pushed an image on her of when she had pulled the waterwall down. The magic of blue pulsing around her in ribbons of power. Ha. It hadn't even occurred to her that she could likely hold her own now. She had always just considered the blue power to be a lifesaving force, but it could be harnessed in other ways. Indeed, Shauna had held Lara captive in water, keeping her from moving.

She didn't have as much to fear from Red as the average everyday traveler. It was a bit of a wake-up call that she was not an average everyday traveler herself. She was a waterweaver. A color weaver. She was one of the Stonegrafted.

It took her a bit longer to fall asleep that night as she worked over the realization that indeed the red soldiers might have something in her to fear.

Red

Lara looked down as the skirt she had bought from Suzette swished around her knees. The patches each had memories, of friends and of family, but definitely of home. The morning had started off cool and so she still wore her cloak. She had brought the blue cape she had received as a student at the Great Stone House in Azural. The memories of her mornings walking with the other students in the chilly air, their matching capes adding to the feeling of being in it together. She loved that her clothes could bring all of these memories to mind.

This morning there had been quite a few brown carts passing her by, headed toward Pink. She realized that the path had deeper grooves from the heavier traffic.

This reminded her that Calambra was off the beaten path. Not only being left in the Wastes, but also between the two smallest Realms. There was a lot less need for the Brown traders to travel to purple. The Northern half of the Country definitely had become the most populated, due to them being home to the most useful resources: heat, water, food.

The traders' carts reminded her of her friend Nessa from her first journey, both in build and artistry. They all had intricate carvings of lovely wooden landscapes. They also all had the same friendly nature, waving jovially, laughs and pleasant 'good days.'

She got the impression any of them would have stopped for a chat had she invited a conversation. There was such an air of acceptance from them that she had never felt in Azural.

Although the cart path had changed a lot, the real change was in the land around them. To the left of the path where the lovely pink fields had flowed, now there was harsh red dirt. Dirt like Lara had never seen before, hardened and course. When she kicked at it, a light dusting came up, but she couldn't imagine planting any seeds in this. Indeed, there were very few plants on the side of the road.

Off in the distance she could see a single large mountain, but instead of the dark misty peaks near her home, this mountain had a flat top, a flow of bright lava falling down the sides of the mountain in rivers of glowing red. Lara wondered at how anyone might live so close to such a fearsome dangerous landmark. But Red was about danger, about bravery, about power. As she was thinking about this, she heard a call from ahead of her, "Hold!"

Lara snapped her head toward the voice and saw three soldiers standing across the path ahead of her. She was surprised at how closely they matched what she in her fears had imagined. The fierce looks on their faces, the broad stance and angry red uniforms were one thing, but the long blades they all had scabbarded on their hips were beyond what she had imagined.

She had never seen a sword before. She had seen drawings in the fairy tales she read to the kids, but never in a real-world setting.

These three swords were safely in their scabbards, but the soldiers' stance gave the clear impression that they were trained and ready to pull them out at a moments notice.

Lara wondered in this moment if she had been wise to wear her blue cape. Had blue made enemies of all of the Realms by being so closed off. Would that hurt her in this encounter? She also didn't know what Red thought about the Wastes. She had thought of how to handle this though and slowly breathed in her calming breaths. She had enough control to call on the water magic if the need arose, but her plan was to try to simply pass as just another traveler.

They blocked the path and looked at her with commanding looks. "What ya doin' on this side of the world Bluey?" The older gentleman in the center sneered. Both of the younger two on either side of him snickered as if it was the funniest joke they had heard.

Great. More bullies. I had hoped we might be wrong about what to expect from the Reds. Lara thought. Although Fleck didn't send words, she felt she could almost hear a wry chuckle from him.

"Hi there," Lara started cheerfully, "I wouldn't call myself Blue exactly, I am actually from the small village Calambria to the south of here between Pink and Purple."

"Interesting choice of cloak then." The youngest man on the right stated his hand resting lightly on the helm of his sword.

"Well, the clothes we have in the Wastes are fairly thin nowadays, I appreciate the warmth this cloak gives me." Lara watched their reaction with keen eyes. How they reacted to her mention of the Wastes was something she was desperate to know. Did the other realms ignore the state of the world around them? They gave no similar reaction to that of the senators in her first meeting in Azural, so she assumed that the Wastes were not a strange unknown to these soldiers.

"Makes sense," the older gentleman said, "Can't say we have seen many from Blue around here though. Didn't really think they were open to travelers. What is your business on the road today? Traveling to Azural again, the long way round?"

"Oh no, I am headed to Laran. Thought it would be fun to see the fairs I heard about that happen there." She had planned this as her way to explain herself. She wasn't prepared to explain Fleck to every stranger they came across. Too many questioned the reality of Pelanor, from her experience.

The youngest of the three perked up at this, but he wouldn't speak to Lara. Instead, he turned to the man in the middle. "Sir, I've been to a few, they are amazing. I saw a rock weaver right up close. They let you stand right by them when they weave. The orange light actually spun all the way around me."

"I am so excited to see it for myself." Lara shared.

The young man turned his attention back to Lara, "Oh, yeah. It was super amazing, there was music too, and," He cut off suddenly as Fleck moved up next to her to sit down.

"Is that?" The other young man stuttered, "That, is that?" He drew in a sharp breath at the same time as drawing his sword, and finally got out, "Is that one of the Dragons?" He had his sword out in front of him pointing at Fleck, and the other two followed suit.

"Wait!" Lara was confused by the fear in their eyes. "It's fine, he's just a baby." As she tried to get between Fleck and the others, there was chaos. Fleck did not like the swords in his face at all, and reacted quickly with an unexpected flash of fire, with a matching flash of red in Lara's mind. She staggered to her knees from the pain splitting her head. When she finally regained control enough to look around her, she saw red flames emanating from Fleck's feet, and he slowly glowed red as red sparks began to build up along his body. The fire didn't actually hit the three soldiers but instead set the ground, between the two of them and the soldiers, ablaze.

The red soldiers immediately jumped through the flames, they didn't seem too worried about fire, must have been a familiar environment training in Red. The sword of the oldest soldier already in an arch to flash down to cut Fleck. Lara immediately responded, her need to protect Fleck, he was her responsibility, engaging instantly with the stone in her shoulder. The blue magic flashed from her shoulder, down her arm and pushed a rope of water out, she blasted it into the man's chest, sending him to the ground. He spluttered as the water splashed into his face, and Lara pulled back on the stream of water, pushing it to put out the flames around them. The other two stopped up short.

Lara had seen the look on their faces, and she had experienced it before, but never toward herself. It was fear. These three commanding soldiers were scared. Of her. She moved to pull Fleck into her left arm, making sure to keep her right free.

"We really don't want any trouble. He's just a baby."

The young man was the first to pull himself together enough to respond. "Yeah, we don't want any trouble either. I think you should be on your way, Waterweaver."

The youngest echoed his words, gruffly, "Yes, move along, and take that dragon with you." He squared his shoulders but left the sword next to him on the ground.

The other young man was bending over to help the older man up and Lara realized he was sopping wet. Her stomach tightened up in regret, but she could still feel Fleck's heart racing. She had protected him, and no one had gotten hurt.

She hurried down the path trying to get a comfortable distance away from them before she set Fleck down. When she finally reached a turn in the road, so they were out of sight, she crumbled down on the side of the road and cried. Tears of stress and fear fell free from her as she let all of the emotion out. Fleck curled up on her lap, she felt confusion from him. *We really don't know our way around these different Realms. It seems that Red is very scared of you. Another question to add to the list for Soren.*

Off in the distance she studied the red mountain top. Fleck could use the Fire magic. It had been powerful here so close to the heart of the red stones magic. Maybe the soldiers had been right to fear him. She wondered what a fully grown Dragon might be able to do once they could control these powers. She wondered at her own powers and what she might be able to do if she was pushed.

Orange

The main Spoke Road into Laran was wide and open. Lara noticed the differences from Azural at every turn. The people of the Orange Realm welcomed outsiders with open arms. Lara and Fleck walked down the path that was plenty wide enough for carts to pass by them and also have carts pass from the other direction leaving the realm.

When Lara had turned onto the Orange Spoke from the Wheel Road she was joined by other travelers on foot. Most were in yellows and greens. It appeared that the three realms had a lot of interaction, unlike small and far-removed Pink and Purple, and Mistrusting Blue and Red. These folks were happy and comfortable with the others on the road.

Lara joined in the throng of people happily. Most of them started walking faster as they got closer, and Lara began to feel the pull of excitement herself. She heard the drums first, a steady beat that as they got closer, turned into a more layered sound. The deep base rhythm encouraging her feet to move step by step closer, while the other lighter drums brought her shoulders moving in a slight dance as she walked with the wind whipping around, making her cloak dance along with her.

The land around them was open with large boulders cropping up at odd angles and moments. Lara saw layers of orange in all shades in the rocks and thought about the ages it must have taken to wear away at the rock to leave it set there for all to see. She pictured the rivers that must have cut away at the rock over eons. Now, it was dry. The blue stone at her shoulder felt that more than her own eyes.

The wide-open space let her see far into the distance, but the city of Laran was wide and low, there were no tall buildings like in Azural, so it wasn't until she was right up close that she began to see details. There was a wall surrounding Laran, but by the looks of it, it was more aesthetic than there to keep people out. It was a work of art; obviously work of the orange weavers. It was rock pulled right from the ground. It reached about the height of ten feet. Lara realized, as soon as she walked through, the purpose of the stone wall. Her cloak stilled and settled. The high winds of the plains were held back.

When the throng of people she walked with hit the edge of town, they were joined by more people from the town proper. The sea of people she was surrounded with changed from a mix of yellows and greens to almost all oranges.

Fleck, why don't you jump up? I don't want you getting trampled underfoot. He agreed and jumped to perch on her shoulder. He was too large anymore to hide under her cloak as he had in Azural.

She didn't need to ask the way to downtown, the crowd took her there. She saw children running ahead of parents who chatted amiably with neighbors as they walked toward the ever-loudening beat. As they neared, Lara could make out the sound of wood flutes adding a borderline frenetic feel to the music. Lara was pulled in, but also felt herself on edge, as if she might need to escape.

The crowds didn't push, but they were close, the cities buildings began to close in on her immediately next to the path, with small openings she could look and see narrow alleyways that led to more buildings and paths. She worried she might feel completely crushed by the crowds, so she considered turning down one of the alleys for a quick reprieve. But she was in the center of the path and realized there was no way she would make her way pushing against the crowds' flow. Her only choice was to continue forward.

She slowly maneuvered her way to the side so that she was positioned on the edge of the crowd so her right shoulder with Fleck was next to the buildings. That gave her a bit of a feeling of space, but as the people walking next to her began to touch her left shoulder, her stress peaked.

Just as she began to again consider turning down the next alley to come along, the buildings suddenly gave way and opened into a vast town square. Only it wasn't a square, like back home in Calambria. This was an enormous circle that looked as if a giant boulder had been plucked up to leave a divot in the ground.

Lara quickly stepped to the side to allow the others walking down her path to pass her by. Resting her back on the warm stucco of the store behind her. From her vantage she could take it all in. The bowl of the downtown area was surrounded with stucco and adobe covered buildings in oranges both bright and muted. None of them stood taller than two stories, and they all had large signs cut into stone next to their doors. Lara could read the signs on the far side of the circle even though they must be almost a mile from her.

In front of the storefronts was a wide level pathway that had room enough for hand-pulled carts and at least ten people to walk side by side. The people passing her by, waved or nodded, but she was aware that many gave her blue cloak a second look.

Beyond the outer path, the ground sloped at a comfortable angle toward the center of the bowl. The outer area was full of what Lara thought were vendor booths and then in the very center of the basin a tight crowd of people stood. There Lara saw amongst the crowd, sparkles shoot into the sky. From this distance she couldn't see the weavers, or what their magic was doing, but from the sparks flying, it looked like there were easily twenty of them down there.

I think our questions about Soren might best be answered by an orange weaver. I wonder what they call it? Groundweavers?

Fleck did not like that name at all, but his curiosity was pushing Lara to head back into the crowd, and she found that hers was piqued too.

"Alright, here we go." Lara said aloud. She had gotten better about thinking to Fleck, but it was not always her first inclination. Words would occasionally come out even when she hadn't intended it.

She didn't have to push her way through the crowd, she found that she was simply pulled back into the throng. The mass of people was all heading to the center of the bowl. Although she felt a bit claustrophobic, she never felt suffocated. The people here were friendly, and they were used to moving around close to each other. They weren't bothered by a brush from the sleeve of the person next to them, but also, none of them pushed to get past each other. Lara began to feel there was a bit of a dance to the experience. The people moving to the sounds of the drums.

As they came closer to the center, Lara found the space opening up. At first, she was confused, until she saw that there were many patches of open space. These were walled off with a low rock wall, similar to the outer wall of the city, but only knee high. When an opening came up, a few people would pour through and the folks on the path would lessen.

She paused at the entrance to the next one as it came up to study it, and then quickly realized that she needed to step inside to avoid being in the way of those still headed to the center. The sheer volume of people amazed her. Once she had stepped past the short wall, she looked around. The walled off area blended into the sea of people if you didn't look down. It was no wonder she hadn't seen them at first.

There were tables set up in the center with bright woven blankets laid out on top. As Lara walked closer, she saw that the beautiful blankets were simply a backdrop for pottery. An old woman sat on a stool next to one of the tables, calmly watching shoppers. When she saw Lara though, her eyes popped, and she stood up. She looked to be the age of Granny Winslow, but she walked with a pep in her step that came from a healthy life.

"Hello there. I see a lot of new faces here on market day, from a lot of different places, but I don't think I have ever seen a stranger here in a cloak that color."

She let the statement sit for a moment, and Lara realized again that it might have been better to wear her old black cloak. She was way too conspicuous in this blue.

"Hi," Lara began, but was immediately interrupted.

"I mean, we have all been hearing rumors, of course," she leaned in as if she was keeping a secret, but she continued to speak in her full, strong voice. "Rumors, about that wall of theirs in Azural coming down. About them having to start facing the world. About folks seeing the blue towers of their city for the first time."

Lara didn't know how to respond and was a bit overwhelmed too. She had caused that. She had stood against the powers that be in Azural, and now, it seemed there were rumors abounding throughout the realms.

"Even heard," the old woman scratched out, "that a woman was accused of stealing a blue stone..." Lara's eyes snapped up to the woman's grizzled face, aged from years of wind here in Laran. She held her gaze for a heartbeat, but before she could respond in any way, the woman continued, "But how do you steal a stone? The stones choose who they connect to. Can't steal that."

Lara paused, waiting to see if she was still going to speak, and after a long enough pause decided it might be safe to respond. "My name's Lara. I'm from Calambria, in the Wastes, but I did visit Azural…"

"I'll bet you did." the woman cackled. "I'm Ida Mae. Now, what brings you here? Looking for a cup, or maybe a bowl?"

Lara's eyes started perusing the table and noticed now that the pottery, although all the same orange-ish brown shade, was covered in unique geometric designs. She did see a few items she really loved; those bowls would be perfect for Anna. But she had no money and wasn't here for the shopping.

"Actually, I am here in Laran to find Soren and Exu. Only, I am not sure where to start? Might Soren be one of the Weavers at the festival?" Lara asked.

Ida's face fell, and Lara saw the woman age before her eyes. The sorrow on her face was such a shift that Lara worried something truly terrible had happened.

Ida took a slow breath, then another one, finally responding. "Soren has left us for the canyons up North. I don't think you will get to speak with him. But maybe one of the others can help you? I'm not sure what you needed with Soren, but there are plenty of terraweavers around here who would be happy to chat, especially with a…" Ida looked markedly at Lara's right shoulder, "someone with a story to tell."

How in the world did this woman seem to know so much about her? Lara couldn't figure it out. But she had enough questions that needed answers, and at the top of the list was Fleck. Everything else could wait.

"Thank you, Ida Mae. I think you are probably right. I think I had best follow those orange sparkles and find out if my questions can be answered. One question that you might be able to help with though, do you have any suggestions for lodging for tonight? I am overwhelmed."

Ida smiled, "Most homes here are community housing. There is usually a room or two available in any house you come across, but I'm going to share the address of the house we live at. You'll want to be staying with us." Ida Mae stated it like it was a done deal. She motioned to a second rickety folding stool that Lara hadn't even noticed before. A man about Ida's age sat snoozing in the sun, luckily the stool had a slim back that seemed to be doing a surprisingly good job of keeping him upright. "The Kindred House is what we call our home, and there will be a room waiting for you." She paused to confirm that Lara was paying attention, then nodded and continued. "If you head up to the main circle path up above, look for Tamarind Road on the West side of the city. Follow that down until you reach The Rock Grinder (that's a restaurant) and take a left there. The Kindred House is just on the right, past the second building."

Lara tried to commit that to memory. New places were always so overwhelming. West, Tamarind, Rock Grinder, left, Kindred House after second building. You going to help me remember that?

Lara thanked the woman and then headed back into the flow headed to the center.

Terraweavers

Ahead of her, Lara could already see the magic. Sprays of orange sparkling light flowed in circles with tiny pebbles arching to create patterns in the air. People around her ooh-ed and aah-ed at the spectacle. She could tell a lot of the people on the outer edge had seen it many times before and could also tell who was new like her. As she got nearer, she began to bump into folks for the first time since arriving in Laran. She, and many others were craning their necks upward to see the magic, and at the same time still trying to push forward to get a front row seat.

Fleck had woken up from his most recent nap in the sack and had crawled out onto her shoulders. She could feel his excitement too. However, his was tinged with a bit of something else. She tried to understand it and the closest she could get was he felt a bit like she did walking into her home. Like an edge was taken off, and he was just a little more comfortable.

She had expected to see a stage, but as they reached the center of the basin, she saw that the terraweavers were just standing around milling about with the people. She counted about seven of them and made her way over to the nearest one. He was a gruff older man, who was dressed unlike anyone she had ever seen before. The terraweaver was pulling the ground below him upwards and downwards, creating a ride for those nearby, up and down, reminding Lara of waves she had watched on the ocean. The magic poured not from a stone on his shoulder as the blue stone Lara had, but instead from his left thigh. And Lara could see it clearly, because his pants were cut off at the knee.

Although Lara was very interested in his clothing, cut off at the arms similarly to the knee, her attention was pulled to the stone. Now that she had so much familiarity with her own stone, she found herself comparing what she saw to her own. The stone was a similar size, and also had the variegated coloring, but the oranges ranged from a light yellow orange to a deep almost purple-brown, orange. It looked like the side of a mountain cut out and pulled into a tiny shining rock. There was also a tattoo into the skin like hers, but instead of looking like waves of water, the tattoo started with a jagged edge that looked like the edge of a cliff, then reached out in lines made up of imperfect circles, that Lara took to represent rocks and as it dissipated outward shrunk tiny pebbles.

The magic sparkled just as her blue did but with a bright orange light that filled Lara, and she could tell Fleck, and all those around her, with emotions much different than Blue. She felt excitement, community and confidence. Like she could do anything.

Axel had taught her to be hyper aware of her emotions. She had been learning to keep tabs on them and found this new confidence a bit foreign to her. She realized it must be the proximity to the orange stones. She looked around for any sign that they had a plan or organization. Maybe there would be some banners like they had at The Great Stone House in Azural to show what emotions the orange stones worked with. She could see nothing. The terraweaver in front of her was still focused on moving the ground beneath him, and she didn't see any way of getting closer.

Why don't we look at a few of these other terraweavers Fleck?

He sent his agreement, and she could feel the excitement pouring out of him. His youth mixed with the raw emotionally charged energy in the basin was definitely combining.

They swiveled through the crowds toward the person sending an artistic display of pebbles into the air that they had seen from further out. The woman there was gorgeous. She spun and danced, and the magic swirled around her and upwards as if it was a continuation of her own movements. The terraweavers dress was sleek and made of a multitude of silken orange ribbons in every shade of orange, that flowed outward when she spun and then stuck with her body when she moved a slower motion. Her long sleek hair was a deep dark burnt orange color that swung outward and around her with the motions. She was oblivious to any of the people around her, with her eyes closed, she gave all of her emotion and energy to the dance.

Lara was hoping to talk with one of these terraweavers, but even though she was able to get right up next to them to see the magic up close, she was not able to get any of their attention.

The next terraweaver they came up to, was a young girl. Juggling rocks the size of her head, she couldn't have been more than ten, her light skin was covered in adorable freckles and her hair was tiny corkscrew curls that caught the light of the setting sun highlighting their copper color. Lara was so taken aback that she stood slack jawed for a moment. When she finally had a moment to get her wits about her, she saw that the girl was staring right back slack jawed at her!

But wait, no. She was staring at Fleck.

The girl's magic sparkle disappeared immediately and the rocks she had been juggling dropped with loud thuds to the ground.

"Oh, Wowwy Wow Wow!" She squealed as she ran toward them arms outstretched. "A baby Pelanor! Aren't you the cutest thing in the whole world?"

Fleck radiated pride, and Lara couldn't help but giggle a bit at how his stature straightened up on her shoulder. His fur smoothed back along his neck but puffed out a bit around his ears.

When she was right in front of them, she reached out to try to pet him, but she was too short. Fleck immediately jumped down and sat at her feet. The tips of his ears came up to the hem of her ruffled skirt right above her knees. Lara saw the stone there, and Fleck did too.

As the young girl reached out to pet Fleck's fluffy space between his perked-up ears, Fleck reached out to touch her stone. Neither seemed to have any qualms about personal space, and Lara felt that Fleck had made a fast friend here.

"Hi there. This is Fleck, and I am Lara."

"Oh, hi! Is he yours? He is just beautiful. I've only ever seen one Pelanor before in real life, and he was all grown up."

"You must be talking about Exu? I was hoping to introduce Fleck to him and meet Soren myself. Do you know if they are around here?" Lara knew that Ida had said they weren't, but hoped she might get more information from an actual terraweaver, no matter how young this girl might be. She might know more than the potter had.

"Oh no. Soren left for the canyon almost a year ago. That was right before I connected with my stone, so I don't know much about what happened. You probably should talk with one of them." She casually put her thumb out and shook it over her shoulder in the general direction of the other magic displays.

"Can I pick him up?" She asked.

"Fleck is the one in charge; he's super smart. You can ask him directly." Lara responded.

The girl looked at Fleck formally, preparing to ask him, but he leapt up before the words were out of her mouth and she again squealed her delight. Lara felt the joy in her soul, it was so fun to be around that kind of enthusiasm. Fleck also was filling up on the happiness radiating from the young girl.

"Who's a cutie? Wooja wooja," she said as she scratched him under the chin. After a few fully invested moments, the young girl actually looked at Lara. Her eyes were clear and bright, a lovely light brown color that caught the light of the setting sun in a similar way to her curls, glistening golden orange sparking as she looked at Lara with laughing eyes. "My name's Kit. That's short for Katherine, but no one calls me that. Except for my grandfather, who says I was named after my grandmother, and he wasn't going to forget it by shortening it that way. He says I have the same spitfire personality she did, and it would be a shame not to let my name show it." Her words tumbled out, and Lara was reminded happily of the days her children would run on so fast that the words barely caught up with their quick thoughts as they came out.

"Pleased to meet you. Might you be able to introduce us to someone who could help us locate Soren?" Lara asked.

Kit giggled and tucked Fleck under her arm, bracing him on her hip. He didn't look to mind at all and snuggled his nose into her neck and wrapped his long fluffy tail around her waist. "Come on," She said turning and beginning to weave through the crowd, "it's almost time for the trials anyways."

As they moved through the crowd Lara noticed a change happening. The wide sky above the city's walls had turned darker and the atmosphere although jubilant had subdued a bit and had a tinge of seriousness. People were starting to file away from the center of the basin and were lining the edges. She saw lots of them sitting on the short stone walls that cut off the vendor spaces like Ida Mae's. There was definitely some kind of larger show about to occur.

As the center cleared out, there were still many who stayed behind. The group was as diverse as before, just less of them. Young and old, she saw a mother who lined her two children up seated on a wall next to her husband and then kiss her cherub baby's cheeks and then her husband's and turn resolutely toward the group in the center.

Kit pushed past a few of them and as they looked down, they parted way for her, and Lara behind her. Now that there were less shows of magic, Lara suddenly noticed she was becoming a bit of an interest to those gathering. Her out of place, blue cloak pulling the eyes toward her. She began hearing "water," "blue," and "Azural" murmurs.

"Dale!" Kit shouted as they neared a group of three terraweavers standing next to a thin pole with a long triangle of orange fabric snapping in the wind at the top of it. They were standing directly in the center of the basin. The three weavers were all as different as you could paint three people. One was the beautiful young woman who Lara had seen dancing earlier, one was a stocky short man who looked to be in his seventies, and the third was a tall wiry man with short cut hair and a wild beard.

Dale must have been the taller man because he turned and Lara could see his quick eyes taking in Kit, Fleck under her arm, and Lara in her blue cloak. She wondered again at how much the people in Laran had heard about from Azural. The earlier conversation with Ida Mae put her ill at ease now.

Dale reached out a hand, offering a shake to Lara immediately. "Hello, I'm Dale. I am in charge of the trials this week, so I don't have much time to chat. Are you here to try for a stone? I don't think I have ever met someone from Azural before." He seemed genuine, and Lara wondered how a simple woman selling pottery would know more about her than one of the leaders of the Realm.

"I'm Lara. I'm actually not here for the trials; I am hoping to chat with Soren. You see…" Lara gestured toward Fleck, who was now curled on the dusty ground around Kit's feet as she rubbed his tummy. "We are needing more information about Pelanors, and hoped he could help us."

Dale's eyes darted to the older man beside him, and Lara saw the old man give Fleck a distinct long look as if deciding something and then give Dale a slight nod. "Well Lara, we have been told that Soren is not to be disturbed until he decides to come back on his own. But Gage here seems to agree with me that you bring a unique reason to disobey his request."

"Oh, thank you!" Lara responded, relieved that she found help so quickly.

"Only problem is," Dale answered, and Lara could feel her heart tighten, "the only way you are going to get to him is if you can connect with an orange stone. You best jump in the group over there and join in tonight's trials."

Orange Trials

Lara's confusion spilled out of her mouth, "But you don't understand. I just got here. I don't plan to stonegraft orange. I don't know what's going on, is there no training school?" Then in hushed tones, she leaned in to whisper to Dale, "And I already have a stone, I am a waterweaver."

His eyes widened a bit at that, but he simply said. "We don't have any rules about it. The stone decides. That is," here his eyes twinkled a bit, "if you can get to it." He looked at her blue cloak again and then he nodded to himself. "I've never heard of someone connecting with two stones, be exciting to see if it can happen." A loud deep bell rang out and Lara's eyes followed the sound up to the outer ring of the path around the basin. There was a large round metal disk that had been hit, and the sound rang over the whole of Laran. "Well, times up for chatting right now, I have to get this show on!"

He turned away from her and she had no choice but to turn toward Kit with confusion, hoping for answers from the young lady. But all she got from her was, "Don't worry, I'll hang out with Fleck while you are attempting the trials. You better give me that cloak of yours, you won't get far with it on."

Lara unhooked her clasp, and Kit grabbed the blue fabric and flicked it over her shoulder. Then she scooped Fleck up in front of her, his back paws and tail dragging in the dust until she repositioned him like a baby doll and skipped off toward the other terraweavers sitting behind the pole.

Lara turned toward the folks milling in the center and wondered what the heck to expect. She walked to the group and turned slowly as the last of the large ringing of the gong died out.

Around her she felt the group of a hundred or so stretching and moving, so she began to also, she reached down to touch her toes and stretched her arms in front of her and to the sides. The muscles in her arms and thighs felt tight from having walked all day and now stood still without so much as a moment to rest.

Dale stood in front of the group and began speaking. As he did, the magic flew around him until he looked like an orange ball of light, his words ringing out loud enough for the whole of those in the basin to hear.

"As dictated by our founding Terraweaver Carlie.

Each night at sunset the orange stone trials shall begin.

The tradition has been kept for these last decades.

Come forward risk takers.

Come forward adventurer lovers.

Come forward if your heart is full of exuberance, enthusiasm and confidence.

Come forward and maybe tonight you will be added to the stone casting family!

All you need to do is make it through the course to the stones, and then it is up to the stones if one will choose you.

Good luck!

Determination!"

The crowd around her shouted back, "Determination!" Lara took in the randomness of the crowd, so unlike Azural. There, those attempting to stonegraft were all so similar. Here, she saw all ages, all sizes, and multiple colors. She felt uplifted.

"Courage!" Dale shouted over the crowd.

Lara joined in with those around her this time, responding, "Courage!" And she felt just a bit more courageous.

"Let the trials begin!" And he threw his arms into the air and jumped. As he landed the force of the magic inside him pulsed through his leg into the ground and toward the pole, he had been standing next to. Lara could see the sparks of orange as they spread across the basin starting at the pole and expanding toward the edges of the central area. The ground began to rumble so much that Lara and a few others who hadn't been prepared, fell to the earth below them.

Lara watched, still sitting in the dirt from her fall, as a familiar sight rose slowly from the ground. The large circular building looked identical to the oculus room in Azural. From the arched roof to the wide closed door, Lara felt she could have been in the center of the Stone House gardens just next to the pedestal of blue magic stones. The center of this room must hold the orange stones. It rose but didn't stop, with a crack and rumble through the earth, the oculus room pulled away from the ground, dust and pebbles raining down around it, the air grew hazy as the Oculus continued up into the air.

Around this central Oculus room, from the earth below, rocks the size of boulders rose into the air. Lara watched with awe as wave after wave of boulders in all shapes and sizes rose from the ground she had just been standing on. As they raised into the air, some stopped, and Lara began to see layers of a path laid out into the sky. Some of the boulders higher up settled into place, just sitting there in open air, while others began a slow-motion side to side.

As she squinted to see the furthest ones, she saw the shadow of the oculus room stop high above. It was now the tiniest island just hovering up there. That was the home of the Orange Stones. The crowd around her started moving to the left and she followed along.

After standing and shaking off the dust, she had ended up near the back of the line of people since she hadn't really known where she was headed. As she stood, the dust began to settle around her and as the sky cleared, she had some time to study what was happening.

This thing was massive. The boulders in the sky were a kind of obstacle course built to get to the island in the sky. The first row of boulders were smaller flat stones, reminding Lara of steppingstones leading through a garden, but they rose into the air instead of through a garden. Also, they weren't really all that close together. Already Lara was seeing people miss a stone and fall to the ground or slip and catch with grasping arms at the stone in front of them. The fall was only a few feet at first, and those who fell simply stood up and dusted themselves off and went to the back of the line.

Before too long Lara was at the front of the line. The first stone was simple enough, she gave a quick hop and was standing easily with both feet on the stone. Her mind knew she had seen multiple others climb this path successfully but also questioned how sturdy these flying rocks were. After all, she was in the air. She gave a little forceful jump in place to confirm that the rock would hold firm. She realized that she would feel a lot more confident if she could see her feet and so she pulled up her patchwork skirt in both arms and leapt to the next steppingstone.

The next few were fairly simple and before she knew it, she was seven stones up. The eighth stone was a bit further away and she felt a moment of nerves. The feeling slowed her, and she took a beat to look up from the stone in front of her, then immediately regretting it. She was higher in the air than she had realized. The ground would definitely be jarring if she hit it from this height.

Slowly she hiked up her skirts and skipped to the next steppingstone. But her boots were not made for the smooth surface, and the added distance had made her right foot slide along the top of the stone. With her arms clasped around her skirts she lost her balance and fell backwards scraping the back of her leg on the edge and banging her right hip as she flailed to turn and catch herself. Awkwardly, she fell to the ground with her arms reaching out to grab at the step but finding nothing but air instead. She landed quickly with a not-so-gentle thud on the sandy ground below.

Well, that was embarrassing. But Fleck only responded with pride and so she stood up and dusted herself off and got back in line.

As the line slowly moved forward, she watched those on the course a bit more carefully and realized that most of them were not wearing shoes, and of course none of them had skirts on. She sat down and untied her boots, chucking them to the side of the line. Then she thought about her skirts. She didn't have much choice there; she couldn't very well change in front of all of these people. She reached down between her legs and pulled the back of her skirt forward and up, tucking it into her front waistband. That worked fairly well, and now she could look down and see her toes curl in the dusty ground.

The next time on the stones she found the sensation strange on her feet. The stone was cool compared to the ground she had just been standing on. Again, the first few stones were a simple hop, skip and jump and then as they began to spread out, she was happy to not have the boots on anymore. This time she easily made the jump that had tripped her up before. Before she knew it, she had reached the last steppingstone. And realized she had not even considered what was after the steppingstone path.

Here in front of her was a large boulder about three feet across, which would be simple to connect with. But it was moving. The boulder followed a simple path right to left, without much speed. She looked beyond it and saw that there were large boulders all ahead, moving up and down and around at different speeds. She was not prepared for any of this, but she jumped anyway.

Exhaustion

Lara had lost track of time; she had felt a compulsion in herself to just keep trying. The need to make the next boulder each time she fell, pulled her back into the ever-shorter line. A few had made it much further up the path than her, and from the ground she could see athletic feats on the boulder's high overhead. Closer to the ground, a few had walked away, giving up for the day. Not Lara. Even though she was exhausted, there was a thrill she was unfamiliar with feeling. With each trip, she made it just a bit further and that kept her optimistic about what she could achieve next attempt.

Even with all of her work and time, she had only made it to the second larger boulder. The falls to the ground were enough now to knock a bit of the air out of her too. This time she was convinced she would make it just a bit further. She was standing on the last of the steppingstones readying herself for the timing when the boulder pulled right in front of her when all of a sudden there was another loud ringing of the gong and the stone she was on started descending. She bent her knees to keep from losing her balance. All of the boulders and stones were returning to the basin. As they reached the ground her comrades jumped off and moved to the side, so she followed suit. Eventually, the larger boulders reached the basin, and all of the people were back.

Everyone stood silently as the oculus descended. Lara noted that Terraweaver Dale was standing staring with intensity at the Oculus as it came to settle into the earth. Just as Lara felt the rumble of the ground opening for the large stone structure, she saw that a young man summersaulted off of the edge, landing not far from Dale's feet. He stood up and Lara saw he was about the same height as the older man, he had the same look about him too. This was definitely Dale's son. Next to them, the earth consumed the Oculus and covered it until it was smooth and even. Lara could not even see that the ground had been disrupted.

Dale walked to the pole that stood again in the center of the basin, his back to his son and addressed the crowd before him. "Well attempted!"

Everyone echoed from the large crowd in unison, "Well attempted!" and Lara felt a thrill of accomplishment, even though she had not reached the top.

Immediately, the crowd began to disperse and as Lara made her way to Fleck and the terraweavers grouped in the center, her body began to tell her how unhappy it was. With the goal gone and the next immediate jump out of her mind, the muscles in her legs began to stiffen and her arms tingled.

Fleck ran to meet her and jumped into her arms. She cringed as his body impacted her already sore one. What she wanted more than anything right now was a place to lay down. She thought of the Kindred House and began to wonder if she should just head over there right now or ask these terraweavers more questions.

Dale was busy talking with the tall wiry young man who had reached the oculus. Instead, the woman in silk came toward her.

"Hello Lara," her voice practically sang, "Kit tells me Fleck is yours."

"I'd say we are each-others, more than he is mine."

She laughed, "Soren used to say the same type of thing. My name's Liv. I'm Kit's aunt."

"Nice to meet you. I have so many questions, but I don't think I can make it much longer without a good night's rest. We started this morning in the fields outside of Pink. I'm a little surprised at myself for making it this long without falling asleep. Would you be able to meet with me tomorrow?"

Kit came running up and around her with Lara's blue cloak in her arms. It had been folded carefully, and Lara was fairly sure she had gotten help. She accepted the cloak with thanks and shook it out spinning it around to place it on her shoulders and regretted the motion when her arms yelled at her. But once it settled around her, she remembered how cold it was, and her toes suddenly felt the chill more obviously. When she looked at her feet, Kit jumped into action rushing off with a call of, "I'll get your shoes Lara!" Fleck jumped down and joined her in a rush.

"Of course!" Liv looked down at the blue cloak and pointedly said, "To be honest, we all have a lot of questions for you too. Where are you planning to stay?"

"I was invited to stay at The Kindred House. Are you familiar with it?"

Liv nodded and they agreed that they would meet at The Rock Grinder Cafe on the corner for lunch. "My treat." Liv had said as she danced away.

Lara turned to say a friendly goodbye to Kit but was instead almost bowled over by the ferocious hug the young girl gave her. "I told Fleck that I would see him tomorrow. Don't make me a liar!" She laughed over her shoulder as she skipped after her aunt.

And suddenly, Lara was almost all alone in the darkness in the center of the basin that had been filled with people just moments before. She saw the crowds up above moving down the outer streets from the upper ring, and realized she needed to get her bearings. Remembering where the sun had set, she turned West and started to look for Tamarind Street.

Although the city was large, she found that it was very easy to follow Ida Mae's basic instructions. The West end of town had about twelve main streets spoke out of the basin and all of them were labeled with large stone signs that she could even read from the path up to the outer ring. This street was about the same width as the one she had entered town on, but now with most of the people gone, she noticed a lot more details about the buildings around her. None were very tall, one to two stories, and they were made of the same orange clay and rock that was beneath her feet. There were tons of open windows, that bright light shown through, bringing flickering light to the streets and alleyways. Although it was night in a foreign town, the lights created a warm, almost homey feel to the strange streets.

Lara's feet ached, she had decided not to put her boots back on and was carrying them along with her pack. The chilly night was helping numb the pain in her feet, but she was feeling it everywhere else. When Lara saw a few round tables and chairs set out to the side, she looked up and saw a cozy little shop. The sign read 'The Stone Grinder,' and Lara wondered why that name had been chosen. She turned left, and there was Kindred House. It was a building like all the others, but this one had a lovely stone sign with a cut out of the sun setting behind the stone walls of the city.

Lara went to the door and knocked, and although you could likely knock her over with a feather from weariness, the shock of who opened the door was enough to have her forget her pains and rush forward into a tight hug.

Friends

Delly's infectious smile and Lara's exhaustion had Lara laughing hysterically. She couldn't believe it. Tears of happiness ran down her face, as Delly pulled her inside toward a lovely warm family room filled with soft cushions, couches, and blankets. The softness was a perfect balance to all of the hard stone underfoot and in the walls.

The room had six people all sitting around and three of them stood up from the couch when they walked in. They were all obviously siblings of Delly's, they all had the same high cheekbones covered in freckles, bright eyes and curly red hair. They all looked very excited to have Lara and Fleck there. Fleck ran around greeting each of them, while Lara sank onto the couch that Delly led her towards. The fireplace was right in front of her and Lara felt it's warmth immediately seep into her sore, tense muscles.

Delly sat beside her and Lara just looked at her. Her young friend looked just as she had back in Azural, but the surroundings made her look different. Lara looked at the family around her and smiled.

"You came home." Lara said with a contented sigh.

"Well, lots happened after you left. But we will have time to chat about it in the morning. You can barely keep your head up. Do you need to eat first, or sleep first?" Delly asked.

Fleck jumped up onto the couch with Lara and pushed her chest slightly. She had no energy left to fight it, and she laid down into the soft pillows. Fleck curled up and Lara didn't even have time to feel guilty for not answering. She was fast asleep.

When Lara awoke the next morning, everything hurt. Her muscles felt each small motion, and she slowly furled and unfurled her hands into fists. At first the motion was stinted as her fingers almost clicked into place, rather than her having control of the movement. After a few minutes of slow moving, they were back under her control, and she stretched out her arms and legs. The couch felt luxurious compared to the ground she had slept on the nights before.

Everything was quiet around her, and she also didn't see Fleck. She reached out to him. *Good morning*

And got a quick happy push from him, moments before he raced into the room. Behind him came Delly, and Lara's mind reeled with all of the questions she had for her.

"Hi!" Delly greeted her warmly. "We wanted to let you rest. I remember my first attempt at the Orange Trials, and I was super sore for the next week. And I was young! Oh, sorry, not to…"

"No worries, Delly. I know I am not young anymore." Lara laughed. "You are so right; I am super sore. But I am also so very happy to see you. We have so much to discuss. I want to know everything that happened after I left."

"And I want to know everything that happened with you when you got home!" Delly exclaimed, "and I want to know why you are here in Laran?"

"Of course, but can you go first? I have been so unsure of how I left things back in Azural."

"It was amazing! Iris, Van and I were waiting outside the building since we couldn't get in to see your tribunal. So, we were just sitting out there worrying over you. Iris' mom, Hyacinth, came out during the deliberation time and told us that it wasn't looking good for you. We were so worried. Then we heard a crash and Lara, I can't tell you how amazing you looked. You were glowing blue and the magic looked like it was crackling. It was a little crazy to us, because we had just learned that morning that you had stonegrafted, and there we were watching you use more power and water magic than we had seen from any of the instructors."

Delly had been talking a mile a minute, and had just reached the couch with the glass of water she had been bringing to Lara.

She took a deep breath and continued, "And then you took down the waterwall! It was epic. I still can't believe it and I saw it with my own eyes. The whole realm watched as the water streamed back into the riverbed toward the rest of Chroma."

Lara's face fell. She knew that her choice would have long lasting repercussions, and she hadn't spent any time in that fateful moment thinking them through.

"Don't worry," Delly said after seeing her reaction. She sat beside Lara, pulling her leg up and hugging her knee, she leaned forward and pierced Lara with an intense look, before continuing. "Nothing much has changed. The ground at the base of the waterwall is still wide with water, it is a bit like a moat, so the only way into Azural is that same bridge, it just is so much more open. Oh, and the sunsets there are so much more enjoyable." Delly laughed and reached down to scratch Fleck between the ears. He was staring at her listening as intently as Lara. "You know most of the senators agreed with Shauna. The majority definitely do not want outsiders, so they have set up more guards at the bridge, and they always have two waterweavers on duty also. It's turned a bit more serious."

"Oh no." Lara put her head in her hands for a moment. "What have I done?"

"Oh wait, I'll be right back with some breakfast, you must be starving." Delly jumped up and ran back into the kitchen.

Fleck didn't follow this time, instead he leapt onto Lara's lap and snuggled under her chin. She never should have acted so rashly. Was she responsible for the armoring of one of the realms? Was she responsible for creating chaos?

Fleck pushed his forehead into hers hard to get her full attention, then looked at her with his clear, light grey eyes. He only sent one image. It was the town square with all of her loved one's dancing and rejoicing when she had brought the rains and blue skies.

You're right of course. The mess started long before I got involved. Sometimes drastic measures need to be taken. Sometimes there is no simple solution.

Fleck purred his agreement, and Lara took a long deep breath, trying to relax the tension that came into her neck and shoulders every time she remembered the day she left Azural.

Delly returned and was talking the moment she entered the room, "I, of course, had already decided to leave Azural. Do you remember? I had realized it wasn't where I wanted to stay, and when the waterwall came down and you left, I realized it was time to just do it instead of talk about it. It was hard leaving Iris. I love her so dearly. I don't think I have ever had a kinder friend. But because she is so wonderful, she supported me in heading back home. I packed up my stuff and walked over the bridge, and left Azural the day after you did.

"Let me tell you though, the guards were already at the bridge, but they didn't seem to mind one bit my leaving. You know, a lot of the people in Azural never accepted me, treated me the same as you were treated. To a lesser extent, of course. It really is better here in Laran. Everyone is welcome here!" Lara marveled for a moment at how Delly could speak for so long without even taking a breath. "But what about you? Why are you here? Granny Mae told me she just found you wandering into the Basin! We are super lucky she realized who you were. I am glad you wore your blue cloak!" Delly pointed over to her cloak hanging on a coat rack near the door. There was not an empty hook, cloaks hung on it in all lengths and different fabrics, but they all had one thing in common. They were all orange, at least a majority were orange. Lara's blue cloak, a deep contrast to the bright, warm colors, hung next to Delly's matching school blue. Lara's eyes moved across the room and saw again, the tapestries and woven rugs, all in multitude of shades of orange.

It took her a moment to realize that Delly was done speaking and waiting for Lara, her arm outstretched with a small plate with a baked bun and bright orange slices. As Lara took it, the smell of the citrus almost had an invigorating essence on its own. But when she bit into it, she definitely felt her energy perk up.

"I am so glad I found you. Laran is amazing, but I am a bit lost. I didn't intend to do the trials. I came here looking for Soren."

"Granny Mae told us. That is definitely going to be an issue. Is it to find out more about Pelanor? I don't know if you might be better off heading to Green. Soren has been AWOL, and I don't think he is coming back anytime soon."

"Well, I came here first for a few reasons. I am hoping to see if I can find any news about Brie, and to be honest, Green is too close to Azural. I am not sure I should be going anywhere near there."

"Oh my, good point!" Delly exclaimed.

"I don't know about Brie. Laran is a bit chaotic, as you have probably already seen. We don't track people who do the trials here. I don't know, I mean we could ask around. Do you still have that family portrait you brought with you to Azural? It might help if we showed it around to some of my friends?"

"Oh, that would be wonderful, yes. I brought it with me, it's in my pack. I mean she was still at teenager when my husband drew it, but I think the resemblance is good."

"Ok." But now tell me all about what happened with you!"

Lara told Delly all about her first few months back at Calambria. About the rain, about the renewed hope. Then she started on the problems with Fleck. "And so, I am concerned that if we don't understand soon, it might get even worse. Each attack is harder on me."

"And maybe Soren will know how to help, or Exu will." Delly stated. She understood immediately. "Well, I think that the terraweavers were right. You will need to stonegraft with orange. Traveling into Confidence Canyon is not possible unless you have the ability to move mountains, literally." Delly stated.

Lara tried to stand and felt every angry twinge. "Honey, I am not sure I can walk to the restroom, let alone get back out on that course."

"Oh, sorry! It's right this way. Here, use my shoulder." And Delly led her down the narrow hall, walking carefully as Lara's muscles slowly warmed up and became a bit more able on their own.

"I got it from here," she said, "thanks."

When Lara got back into the living room she asked, "There were so many people in here last night, where is everyone?"

"Oh. The whole family sells stuff in the basin. Business starts picking up mid-mornings."

"Wait, what time is it? I was supposed to meet that Terraweaver Liv at 11."

"It's 10 now, where are you meeting her?"

"Right at the place on the corner there, Stone Grinder."

"Ok. We still have plenty of time. Let's discuss a plan. You will of course be staying here. We had a room for you, but I didn't realize you were going to be doing the trials. Wow! I don't know anyone who has two stones! That would be amazing. If anyone can do it, you can."

Lara's heart warmed at how much her young friend believed in her. It amazed her how hearing it from someone else helped her believe it herself. If Delly thinks so, why shouldn't she think so?

"It is not going to be easy." Lara said. "I think the first thing I need is better clothes."

"Oh, that's easy. And we need to get you into a group that does the training and stretching beforehand. But I was saying about the room. Since it is upstairs, I think we should find a place for you downstairs. Trust me, you aren't going to want to be going up and down those the first few weeks."

It suddenly dawned on Lara the amount of time she was signing up for. Was this really what she wanted? She had hoped for a quick journey and meeting to get her answers. This was not going as she had expected. She looked at Fleck and contemplated her options. Maybe they would be fine. Maybe he would outgrow it, and they didn't need to meet up with Soren and Exu.

"My brother Sammy's room is down here; I will talk with him. I am sure he will move upstairs for a bit so you can use his until you are in shape to get upstairs."

This added to Lara's doubts. She didn't want to be putting people she had never met out of their rooms. She really needed to think this through, but her lunch with Liv was soon. Maybe after that she could find a quiet place to be alone and think.

Lunch with Liv

Delly walked at a clipped pace next to Lara toward the Grinder. Lara pushed through the stiffness in her calves as she kept up. "Will you be joining us?"

Delly's forward motion stuttered just a bit, as she gave Lara an askance look. "I don't think so." She pulled the words out slowly, and Lara read a lot of missing information in the statement. "I really need to get over to the market. I usually am there hours ago."

"I really appreciate you hanging back so I didn't wake up all alone. And these clothes are amazing." Lara laughed. She looked down at the soft orange pants she had borrowed from Delly. They were loose enough to move comfortably, but tight enough that they wouldn't catch on the rocks and also closed tight at the ankle. Lara was able to move very freely. Her top was unlike anything she had ever worn before. The material stretched and held her tightly. Delly had explained that they were what everyone wore on the course but happily gave Lara a flowy top to wear over it, in a lovely pale peachy shade of orange.

"I really am so excited you are here Lara. I am just so happy to be able to help you."

The pain in her calves finally broke through and Lara stopped walking for a moment. Delly realized a few steps further ahead. She turned back and walked the few steps to meet back up with her.

"I just can't even put into words how much you, Iris, and Van meant to me back in Azural. And even now. It is like you are my guardians."

"Oh Lara," Delly laughed. "We are your friends, and that is what friends do. Come on," and Delly wrapped her hand under Lara's shoulder and pulled her along.

Lara was amazed at the vitality that being around her young friend gave her. It helped her see the world with enthusiasm too.

When they reached the Stone Grinder, Liv was already seated at one of the outdoor tables. Today she was wearing another sleek silk dress that came past her knees. It was such a vibrant shade of orange that it made all of the other oranges surrounding her look dull and boring.

Liv was definitely a center of attention. All the people walking either whispered excitedly to each other or even waved hellos to her. She was seated with her back to the crowded streets and missed most of the acknowledgments. Lara gave Delly'shoulder a quick squeeze. "I'll meet you in the basin this afternoon?"

"Of course! Do you remember where you found Ida Mae yesterday?"

"Not specifically, but I will find you." Lara laughed.

As Delly started walking away, Fleck ran after her and then realized that Lara had not continued. He stopped and sent her back a quizzical push. "Do you want to go with Delly?" After affirmation from him and agreement from Delly, Lara watched the two of them filter into the crowds headed to the basin.

As she turned to weave her way through the last few feet in the crowded streets, it was the first chance she had to feel the emotions of meeting with this terraweaver. She was excited, but she was also nervous. Her experience with the waterweavers in Blue had been so closed off. They had kept their secrets close and were not the quickest to befriend. Lara had a feeling after last night that this would be different. She would know soon; Liv turned and saw her walking up and jumped to meet her halfway.

What Lara noticed more than anything was how graceful she was. The movements as she stood weren't just a person standing, there was a dance to it. Liv was magical in her movement.

"Lara, come sit down." Liv gestured to the seat across from her, and Lara was very glad to sit in the seat. It had its back to the side of the building, and she was able to watch everyone around her. Lara always felt ill at ease sitting with her back to people, especially here where she was a bit on edge already.

As she sat, the server immediately came up to the table. It was obvious that the establishment thought that Liv was a VIP and there were a few of the staff on the ready. "Get whatever you'd like, it's my treat."

Lara smiled at the server; it was a young man with scraggly brown hair. His shirt and apron were crisp and clean. Lara thought of Anna back home. She would love to work in a place with so many people, but Lara could not imagine her willing to wear a uniform at all. "Do you have coffee here?"

"Cold Brew, cappuccino, drip, latte?" He asked.

Lara sputtered out an awkward laugh. "Sorry, I have no idea. I have only ever had a single cup back in Azural." Lara paused when she saw his eyebrows raise at her mention of the Blue Realm so continued quickly. "It had some cream and sugar in it." She shrugged. "How about I trust you. Anything sweet and creamy with that lovely kick that coffee gives us."

"Certainly. I will make you a cafe latte with cinnamon and honey added. That will give it a nice sweetness." And he was gone before Lara could thank him.

When the man had walked away, she gave her full attention to Liv. "Good morning."

"Good morning. We have so much to discuss. Is Fleck with you?"

Lara smiled, "Oh, not right now. He was so excited to see Delly, that he got up super early with her. He hasn't wanted to leave her side all morning. He went down to the market with her, but if he needs me, he will find me." Lara was a little concerned about that part, because he had taken to just popping to wherever she was, and that might go poorly.

"Oh, well I am as happy to see you as him. I have never met a waterweaver before."

Lara's mind raced through how Liv would know she a waterweaver instantly, going over conversations she had had, until she remembered her quiet moment with Dale before last nights trials. So, the information was likely out amongst all the orange stonegrafted then.

Lara felt a bit on edge. How would this leader in Laran feel about her story? For a brief moment she wondered if she should keep the story to herself. But she brushed that away quickly. She had always thought it was best to stick to the truth and work things out. Sometimes it was difficult at first, but not facing reality would be harder in the long run. She needed to be open with Liv, so that Liv trusted her enough to be honest back.

Lara had always been quick to talk about herself at a personal level. James had always been a bit frustrated with her willingness to share almost everything with everybody. He liked to keep things more private. Lara had trained herself early in their marriage to be more aware of what and how she shared information, but her default was always to chat about everything. She loved hearing people's thoughts on matters.

"Have you met stonegrafted from other realms?" Lara asked.

"Oh yes. I have met so many. Most of us travel a little bit. The only one I have left now that I met you is Purple. I don't think they leave often, and they are so far off the Wheel Road that it is a big deal to travel there. But I know people who have been there. Blue on the other hand… That waterwall did the job of keeping people out. What was it like there? You are from the Wastes originally, right?"

Lara immediately started into her tale. She shared about her home well running dry, about the town meeting deciding someone should go to Azural to try to get help returning some of the water magic. She shared about her experience there as an unwelcome student. Then she paused. How would Liv react to Lara not completing the trials?

Liv took her pause to mean that she needed a break, "I can't believe how brave you were to head out into the world like that after so many years at home. You know, bravery is something we value very highly here in Laran." While Lara had been sharing her story, the table had been filled with plates full of snacks. Lara laughed to herself at how orange all of the food was: the baked muffins to fresh fruit. She grabbed a muffin and let eating it give her a chance to reset her mind. And plan a bit how much she should share.

"I thought bravery was more of a red thing?" Lara asked.

Liv laughed, it was a light-hearted tinkling of a laugh, that sounded like tiny bells but seemed to lack the sincerity of a good hearty laugh. "Oh, sure. But Orange is a bit of red, a bit of yellow. We claim courage as one of our most important values here, but what is courage without bravery?"

"Can you tell me a bit about how you became a terraweaver? My experience on the trial course last night was telling. It is no joke. And how did Kit ever do it?"

This time Liv's laughter was hearty, and Lara got a real feeling of Liv's love for her niece. "Kit has more determination than anyone I have ever met. She started on the course as soon as I did. We actually completed it together. I was in the chamber with her when she stonegrafted. I have never in my life seen a smile so huge as hers that day."

Lara wondered at this. "You were together? In blue it is a very intimate, solitary experience. The rules of blues trials are quite particular." But then Lara remembered that she actually didn't know how they did it usually. Her experience was so secretive and against the laws of Azural. It might be different for others? No, they still wouldn't have had two people stonegraft at the same time.

"Oh, we don't have any rules here. If you make it through the course, you are worthy of trying. The stones decide the rest."

"Axel told me a bit about the founders deciding that each realm would have trials to earn the right for a stone. I guess I really just didn't think about how very differently each realm would interpret that."

"You met a founder?!" Liv almost screamed this, and Lara was a bit taken aback by her reaction. Was it so very strange?

"Yes. Axel was a great help to me." Lara sighed and took a sturdying breath to gird herself. "You see, the rules in Azural were against me from the start. They do not let their weavers leave the realm. And they were not happy with my story about how my land was wasting away. They didn't believe that things could be that dire."

"That's what happens when people hide away behind their walls. They can't see the truth beyond their own needs. Everyone knows the wastelands are real." Liv shook her head.

"Well, not everyone. The laws and leaders in Azural were set against me taking a stone back to Calambria. But Axel helped me. He had been worried, he said, about the repercussions of him and his friends' rash decisions in their youth. He helped me connect with a stone without completing the trials, and he helped me escape when the senators wanted to lock me up for 'stealing' a stone."

Liv gasped. "No way! The stones choose. People don't get to control that. That stone connected to you." Liv pointed at Lara's arm, and then she raised her eyebrows in question. "Can I see it?"

"Of course!" Lara pulled her arm out of the loose sleeve of her over shirt and was even more appreciative of the flexibility of the tight sleeveless undershirt.

Liv gasped at the sight of the blue waves and stone on Lara's arm. Even Lara was a bit surprised at how vibrant the blues were here surrounded by all of this orange. Lara thought about how honest the story she shared was, and the blue sparkle spread from the stone and pulled the water out of her drinking cup. Lara sent it into an arc in the air, pulling it around to create a bubble that caught the sunshine, glinting in the light. Liv stared, and then Lara realized that it was quiet. The whole street was staring. She smiled awkwardly and pulled the water back into her glass. Giving everyone a half wave once her arm was free of the magic.

A round of applause broke out and Lara could feel her cheeks warm in embarrassment at the unexpected attention.

"Oh, you must join us tonight before the trials. Everyone will be talking about the Waterweaver now." Liv said.

Lara sputtered, "I haven't really performed the way you all do. I am not sure."

"Oh, pish posh," Liv laughed, "you could just do that bubble thing the whole time and you'd be the biggest attraction there. Folks around here really look forward to our shows." Here Lara noted that Liv's eyes were taking on a dreamy far-off look, "They absolutely love us," she sighed.

Lara considered that look, and thought it sounded like Liv enjoyed being the center of attention more than Lara might. She bit into a lighter colored baked good and was surprised by the flavor and texture. Her mouth dried out even as it enjoyed the tasty morsels of dried fruit. As her eyes popped Liv laughed, "That is an apricot scone. I know the flavor is amazing, but you might want a sip of that latte." Lara looked down and realized she had let her drink sit as she had shared her story. The steam was no longer rising from it. A sip of it was the perfect pairing to her scone.

Lara took a few moments to enjoy the flavors in front of her as she built up the courage to ask Liv to reciprocate.

"I would love to see your stone up close too." Lara finally ventured.

"Of course!" Liv slid her leg over to the side of the table. The orange stone sat just above her left knee on the outer side of her thigh. A soft orange glow started in the rocky outline of the tattoos. Lara marveled at the sparkling orange flecks of of light that lifted from the tattooed lines, and felt the thrum of excitement as she watched the ground begin to shift. Liv used the magic to pull a pedestal of rock from the ground to prop her foot on so Lara could see the orange stone more clearly.

It entranced her fully, and then she felt a stirring from Fleck. His excitement at the possibility of seeing the stone was too much, he jumped to her at once, and Lara only felt a searing pain through the flash of orange in her mind and then everything went black.

She awoke to a bit of turmoil. She had fallen onto the ground and as she opened her eyes all she could see were worried eyes staring at her: Fleck's large round light grey, Liv's light brown and the deep brown of the server. They all let out a collective sigh of relief as she opened her eyes.

"Are you alright?" Liv asked.

"Here, have some water," said the server.

A quizzical push from Fleck that was then mirrored in his whole body pushing into her to confirm that she was alright.

"I'm okay," she cracked out, taking the water from the server with a nod of thanks. The cool water refreshing her throat, and she realized it also refreshed a bit of her energy too. Laran was a very dry climate, and she hadn't really done much waterweaving since she arrived. She wondered if the lack of water in the area was making her weaker now that she was a weaver.

She took a moment while laying there to look up at the sky. It was a vast open space with not a cloud in sight. She closed her eyes to recenter herself and tried to feel for water but could feel nothing below her and extraordinarily little around her. She could sense the glasses of water and a few skins that passers by had, but there was no lake, no reservoir below them. How were these folks getting water?

As she made her way back into her seat, she was about to ask Liv just that, when she noticed that the scene around them was more chaotic than just reacting to her. Everyone on the sidewalk had stopped and were staring - oohing and ahhing over Fleck. He was creating quite a scene. They all seemed to know what he was, and no one wanted to move on. There were cries from the backed-up people out of eyesight. "What's the hold up?"

Yet, everyone just seemed to be glued in place.

Liv stood fluidly and spun to face the crowd. She looked as if she were center stage in the Basin. She lifted her left leg, and Lara caught the flash of sparkle near her knee, before bringing it down in a light stump, that rumbled the whole street. All eyes turned from Fleck to look at Liv.

She raised her arms, and the thin, silken sleeves of her dress billowed a bit in the breeze, she created a striking image, and the crowd stilled and quieted. "Can you believe it?" Her voice rang out almost sultry, and Lara was a bit shook by the difference. The Liv before her did not feel like the same one she had been sitting with a moment ago. "We have another Pelanor visiting us in Laran. Come to the Basin this evening if you want a chance to see him. For now, we need you to keep moving, or else things could get fairly complicated in this tiny space." She spoke with authority. Lara was amazed at how quickly everyone listened to her. There was obvious respect for her. Was that because of who she was, or because she was a terraweaver? There didn't seem to be any rules around this place. It was almost like a polar opposite of Azural. And yet, the people listened and obeyed.

Liv spun back around, a dancer in every movement, and gracefully placed herself back in the seat at the table with Lara. She looked invigorated, like the interaction with the large crowd had fed something in her.

Fleck jumped into Lara's lap, pulling her attention away from the woman across from her. He snuggled against her chest and pawed at her knees. His fur was soft and long, and Lara was suddenly aware of how very heavy he was getting. He could still curl up in a ball on her lap, but she remembered that first week where she had hidden him under her cloak and few people had even noticed him. Things were changing. When he got to full size there was no way that they could travel without these types of scenes. The thought concerned her, but she could only focus on the current problems right now, and that black out was the most serious she had experienced.

She steeled herself and asked the question she had come to Laran to ask. "Liv, I need to speak with Soren. These episodes have something to do with the connection I have to Fleck, and Soren's experience with Exu might be our key to finding answers."

Liv looked just a bit shook. "Your connection is causing you to pass out? Oh dear. Soren and Exu would definitely have the answers I expect, but they are out in the Canyon. To be honest, none of us really understood what was happening when they left, but Soren was adamant that he had to get them space, and then they left so quickly. But we all understood that the connection they had with each other was more important than what he was doing for us here."

"The Canyon." Lara said slowly. "Last night Dale said the only way I would get to the Canyon was by being a terraweaver myself." Lara said the last bit warily. How would they feel about a waterweaver trying for a stone? She was again reminded that she didn't know of anyone who had more than one stone. Was it even possible?

Liv said simply. "Yes. You will need to pass the trials." And then, warming Lara's heart at how quickly she had made a connection, Liv continued. "We better get you ready. Two stops. First, I think you should see Confidence Canyon for yourself."

Confidence Canyon

Liv had taken Lara outside the front gate of Laran, which Lara learned was the only way in or out of the city. They had begun a long hot walk around the outer walls. When they reached the far side of the circular wall, Lara was taken aback by the sheer vastness of the open space. She had never really seen a view so far. Nothing was breaking up her vision and it was disconcerting after living her whole life at the base of mountains. And in Azural they had been surrounded by cliffs. She found herself turning to look back at the city, just to alleviate her feeling of unease.

Lara had grown up with the mountains surrounding her, and she felt the openness unsafe and exposing. She suddenly missed the walls around Laran.

"Soren is in the Canyon, the only way to find him will be to go there yourself. It isn't an easy trip. It's far and would be dangerous for anyone who isn't a terraweaver." Liv said as they walked along.

Fleck jumped up onto Lara's shoulders to listen into the conversation. He awkwardly flung his front paws over her left shoulder and his back paws to the right, his tummy curled around the back of her neck. His new position worked better than perching up on her shoulder since he was getting heavier. His tail wrapped around her neck for added stability. "Would there be a terraweaver who could come with us instead? I don't want to assume I can get the stone, and you can see from my earlier episode that I need to understand this Pelanor connection better."

"To be honest, the trip will take weeks just to get there. I don't know of any terraweaver that would be able to just up and leave their life for over a month."

"Wow," Lara really hadn't realized how far away Soren was. "So, it would take longer to get there, than it took me to travel to Laran from Calambria." Lara felt a bit defeated, but Fleck just purred in her ears and the light rumble eased her tension. "I guess we aren't really on a tight timeline. But how does it make a difference if I am a terraweaver?"

Liv reached out her long arm, an artist in how she moved, and pointed ahead. "Look, you can see your first glance of what this canyon truly is."

Lara looked over ahead to the right, following Liv's long finger. There she saw her first glimpse of a cliff ahead. It reminded her a lot of the mountains back home, but these were moving downward instead of reaching toward the skies. As they walked, their angle brought into clearer view the deep canyon. Lara realized that the vastness of this open space played tricks with her mind, things were much further than she realized. In the far distance she began to take in the far banks of cliffs reaching out in the distance, cut into the ground in a strange, uneven curve.

Lara walked in silence for a while, caught up by the sight in front of them. But the walk continued. After awhile Lara broke the silence. "You know, one of the things I am hoping to find out is about my daughter. When she left Calambria she discussed coming to Orange. I wonder if she is still here. She wasn't sure where she wanted to land, just that she wanted to go out into the world."

"Laran is a large place. Most folks go regularly to the evening Festivals. What's her name?"

"Brie."

Liv stopped short and turned to her. "I know her! Of course you would be her mom. I thought you looked familiar in a way, the first time I saw you."

Lara's eyes popped. She couldn't believe she was so lucky. "She's here?" She started to turn back toward Laran, suddenly not interested one iota in the large canyon or the prospect of her meeting with Soren.

Liv didn't follow. "I'm sorry Lara, she was here. But she's gone."

Lara turned back toward Liv, she felt the elation leave her and pull her down. Squaring her shoulders she continued the walk. "Tell me everything you know!" Lara said, then realized how harshly it had come out and added, "please."

"Brie joined us at the drum circle a few years back. She loved the circle. I remember she was there every night. She jumped in quickly with everything. She danced at first, but then she started even learning and taking turns at the drums. She was here for at least a year. But then she suddenly spent most of drum circles sitting and meditating. In the end she told us she didn't think this was where she belonged. She was going to head to Purple. She said that Morchast might have the answers she was looking for."

"Morchast." Lara whispered it. She had walked right past the entrance to Morchast on her way to Azural. It had been up in the mountain heights, but it was so close to home. "I wonder why she didn't stop by to see us at home?"

Liv's eyes darted over without turning her head. "It might have been because of the young man that traveled with her?"

Lara's heart ached. Yes, that would be it. Young love.

Lara walked quietly for a bit, at first heartbroken, and a bit jealous, that her daughter had been so close, and that Liv had spent so much precious time with her. But as she walked, she warmed to the knowledge that Brie was okay. She had made it to Laran, had learned what she could here, and had moved on. "Could you tell me more details? I miss her so."

They walked for another hour, the canyon stretching out in the distance ahead of them. As they moved, Lara listened to stories of Brie's dancing skills. Lara remembered Brie's energy as a youth, and her love of music, dancing and singing in Jada's living room. Wild spins and squeals. Liv told another side of that. A more controlled, yet still exuberant young woman, pouring her energy into the movement and thrilling at the music. Lara could picture her beautiful daughter wearing loose clothing similar to Liv and what a sight she must have been, her long curly tresses spinning with her in the circle every night.

The time passed much more quickly with her mind filled, and before she knew it, they were following the hard packed path up to a stone wall about chest height.

"Well, here we are. No one is ever really prepared for this sight. It will take your breath away."

Lara walked up to the wall and leaned her elbows on it. Her first look was downward, and she immediately regretted it. Her stomach dropping at the sheer depth of the canyon below. Bringing her eye-line higher, she focused on the far-off distance, and found that it was still a bit harrowing, the sheer vastness of this canyon was something she never could have even comprehended without experiencing it herself. The edges of the canyon curved inward and outward from the surface, but all of the edges were sheer drops, all as high as the top of Grist Mountain. It would be impossible for her to travel down there.

"How?" She stammered out finally. "Liv, how do you get down there? How can Soren even survive down there?" She looked across the basin and saw not a single tree. It was all dust, gravel, and rock.

"Like I said. You will have to be a terraweaver to even make it down. I have seen a few terraweavers travel down the sides, making a little rock shelf to travel down on. I have seen others travel down through a cave that they dug to get down there. But it is not stable, and you have to be able to protect yourself from the ceiling collapsing on you. Again, you need stonecasting abilities."

"And that isn't even considering what happens when you get to the bottom." Lara again found her voice a whisper. The vast space felt like it needed her reverence. "Down on the bottom, you'd need protection from the heat in the daytime. I guess a terraweaver can create a shelter of some sort?"

Liv spun and again lightly stamped her foot, pulling stone from the ground to the left and with a curve of her arms, the glistening orange magic curled the stone wall into an overhang, casting her and Lara into the shade. Immediately Lara felt cooler, reminded of just how hot the sun was here. "I only know of one that has ever stayed down there. And that is Soren." Liv shook her head.

"You're right. I will not be able to do this without the power to control the rocks." Lara walked over to the overhang Liv had just conjured up. Pushing her hand against it she felt the strength of it, and it helped build up her resolve. She turned her back on the scary beauty behind her. "Let's go. I have some work to do."

Gym Time

Once back inside the walls they headed to the basin and found Delly's booth. Lara wanted to return Fleck before she continued with her afternoon. He brought a lot of stares, and she wasn't comfortable with the attention.

Lara was drawn immediately to the bright orange designs on the table. She picked up a larger dinner platter that looked to have been made by Ida Mae but was covered with intricate spirals in different shades of rocks and pebbles. "You made these? They are gorgeous!" Lara exclaimed when she saw Delly's work. "I love it! Not only are they gorgeous, but they are useful." Lara beamed at her friend.

Delly's cheeks had turned beet red at the praise, but she was obviously sure of herself. "Thanks, I had missed making them. I am glad to be back to it."

Liv came up behind Lara and greeted Delly, "Oh, sweetie! It has been too long. How is your mother?" Lara was taken aback at the saccharine tone of voice first, and then the question. She hadn't even realized until that moment that she hadn't yet thought of Delly's mother. She felt a moment of despair at being a bad friend, until she saw Delly's face.

Delly had schooled her features in a way Lara had never seen before. It was so obvious, because Delly was so plainly herself in every moment, that the control she was having to project read plainly on her face. At least to Lara. "Hello, Liv," Delly's voice was even, controlled. "You remember that my mother is traveling. I haven't seen her since my return from Azural." She gave Lara a flick of the eyes that Lara quickly read as a controlled eye roll. "But when she returns, I am sure she will be joining you in the Basin. You know that." Delly grinned a wide smile that did not touch her eyes.

Ida Mae came up behind Delly and with a gentle pat on her shoulder, she greeted Liv with much more practiced kindness. Lara recognized the voice as a customer service voice. The octave was just a bit higher than when she was speaking with the family. "Liv, so great to see you. I'd love for you to see the mugs I was just working on. The form of them was inspired by your dance last week. I think you will see a glimmer of your magic in the artistry."

Ida Mae led Liv over to the far side of the long table, and Lara saw Delly's shoulders relax. "What was that?" Lara asked quietly.

"Liv and my mother have a long history. We can talk about it another time." Delly gave another flick of her eyes to Liv and when she saw she was engrossed in the lovely orange mugs Ida Mae had credited her with, she quietly continued, "Liv is such a diva." Here she gave the full eye roll. "And so is my mother."

The view of Liv suddenly was blocked by a group of women rushing up to the table. Lara quickly turned to better see why they were in such a hurry. Fleck was sitting on the table preening himself. The dust from their walk was almost gone, and his color was again a bright white. As he sat there licking his paw and then using his damp paws as a cat might to clean the tufts of fur on his ears, the group of women cooed. "Awe, Exu was never so very small, was he?" "I can't believe I am this close to a Pelanor; I was so scared to get close to Exu!"

Lara and Delly moved around to the back side of the table. Lara to protect Fleck, and Delly to go in for the sale. After comfortable conversation and Fleck getting a happy helping of attention, the three women left with a platter each.

"Fleck, you are a great salesman!" Delly exclaimed.

Liv returned from the far side of the table with her own wrapped up package, which Lara assumed contained the mug that Liv herself had inspired. "Well, Lara. I need to be getting on with some other plans for my day. Why don't we head over to the gym?"

Delly smiled a genuine smile. "Oh, Lara, that is a great idea! That is the best place for you to be spending your afternoons. But..." she looked pointedly between Fleck and her artwork. "Maybe Fleck could stay here and help me sell stuff?"

"That was totally what I was hoping too," Lara laughed. *What do you think Fleck?* She sent quietly so that she might get an answer without upsetting Delly. His answer was simply to jump into Delly's arms. "Okay, I think that answers that." Lara turned to Liv, "Let's see what this gym is."

Liv led her to an open section of the basin covered with a high fabric ceiling, the dark orange canvas snapping as the wind caught under it. The hot, open air drifted through, but the sun didn't beat down, and Lara instantly felt the relief of the shade.

The shaded area was full of training equipment. There were lots of people, all ages, stretching in groups or lifting rocks to strengthen muscles. It was an interesting space full of people with a common goal. Everyone here was doing the trials. Lara recognized a few of them from last night.

Liv left her here with a plan to meet up later when the terraweavers started their usual shows in the early evening.

Lara started by heading over to the group stretching on thick pads laid out in the front right corner. As she slowly brought herself down to sit on the mat, each movement felt difficult.

She had always been in motion, running after children, carrying laundry baskets. At home they had all worked together to care for the fencing and keeping watch for wolves. She had traveled to the blue realm and walked all the way here to Laran. But last night had been more than her body had ever been through. Her muscles had tightened up and her body fought her as she tried a simple reach to touch her toes.

She sat on the ground with her head resting on her bent knees, studying the soft, thick blanket below her, and realized it had been hand-woven. As she considered the work it must have taken to create such a large piece, she startled herself by realizing she was avoiding the problem at hand. One more time, she slowly laid her legs softly in front of her, knees bent, and she realized that the simple act of sitting with her legs straight out hurt. Lara knew she had to push past this pain. She took her calming training and relaxed her mind, slowly reaching toward her toes. When her hands reached about her knee the backs of her legs burned too much to continue, she let out a pained groan of exasperation.

"Keep at it." A kind voice said behind her. Turning slowly to not twinge any muscles, Lara saw a young skinny kid, his voice had cracked, the usual way a young man's did at his age. "I've seen a lot of people give up after one day. It's impressive you are back today." He saw her quizzical look. "Oh, I saw you yesterday. You looked so confused when the course first came out. And from the way you were dressed it was super obvious you weren't from around here." He nodded toward her pants. "Much better choices today. You are already on the right path."

"Thanks, I just got into town last night. I was a bit blindsided by the course. It is such an undertaking. How long have you been at it?"

"Oh, I used to do it when I was little," Lara laughed to herself, because she thought he was still fairly young, probably around 12. "But this is the first year I got serious. I have been training every day and run it once a week. And I am getting pretty good. I got to the stairs last time!"

Lara didn't know what that meant, but figured she would learn soon enough. "My name is Lara."

"Oh, I'm Skip." He said pointing a thumb to his chest proudly. "Nice to meet you. Well, I best get back to training. But I'll see you out on the course, huh?"

"Yes." Lara smiled as she watched Skip run over toward the weight training area. She was always happy to befriend youths. They had so much energy and such an optimistic outlook on things.

As Lara finished stretching as much as she felt capable of, she considered the group of people around her. She realized that although the heat seemed to bother her more than those around her, she was confused by another related difference. They all seemed to be slightly dehydrated, which made sense with the limited water supply, but she was still getting accustomed to actually being aware of it in those around her. The odd thing was that she wasn't drinking more water than those around her, but she wasn't dehydrated. She remembered years of living with limited water, and was really shocked by the idea that maybe somehow being a waterweaver kept her from dehydration?

She moved over to the weights. She was a bit nervous about the new items. New spaces were always difficult for her, until she had been through the motions a few times. Without Liv she felt suddenly even more intimidated and wondered if she might just ignore the weights for today. But then Skip jumped up. He bounded over toward her. "Want me to show you around?" Lara breathed a sigh of relief.

"Oh, thank you. I was a bit intimidated. How would you recommend I begin as a complete beginner?"

The pride of being asked for his expertise showed clearly on his face. "Right this way. These are the best to start with. They only weigh a few pounds, and since they have the handles on them, you can strengthen your hands along with your body and also not worry about them falling on your toes as much."

Skip led her to a row of medium sized rocks that had handles like her teapot. Lara laughed at the comparison as she bent over at the hips to grab two of them.

"Oh no!" Skip interrupted her. "You don't want to do it like that. Here, watch me."

Skip stood directly over one of the stones and reached down between his legs bending both knees and keeping his back upright, then grabbed the handle with both arms. He lifted the stone just until his legs were almost straight. "You should probably just stop here for now. You can do that like ten times. Then take a break. It seems like it isn't much, but you will feel it tomorrow. And I promise you will be able to do more if you keep at it."

"Why thank you, Skip." Lara smiled at him and tried to mimic his lift of the ball. She immediately felt it in her legs as she bent down, but she pushed through and grabbed the handle. Lifting, she straightened her legs and noticed her arms and the pull at her shoulders and neck.

"Good job" Skip encouraged. He counted off as she got through her ten. Halfway through she thought she might have quit if Skip wasn't there counting off. By the last one, she was feeling it in her whole body. She was thankful when he reached ten.

She set it down and suddenly her whole body felt lighter. She laughed, and realized she felt amazing. Even though she felt pain everywhere. How strange. "So, do you think I should do more? I am pretty sore."

Skip looked very serious for a second. She felt like she could see the wheels turning in his head. "I think you better wait. Especially if you are doing the course tonight. But tomorrow you can do it again."

"Skippy, Skippy, don't be drippy." Shouted a larger boy, who Lara recognized from the night before. This was Terraweaver Dale's son. He stood on the end of the weights section. He was standing over a bar with heavy rocks on either side. His muscles bulged and he looked a bit angry.

Next to her she saw Skip's shoulders sink. He shrunk in on himself. "Very funny, Dean." Skip's voice squeaking again as he raised his voice to respond. The confidence he had just a moment earlier as he had helped Lara deflated.

Lara felt a surge of motherly protection. She felt her shoulders go back and almost piped up, but then Skip turned toward Lara and said under his breath, "He's an idiot, not worth the effort." His words were strong, but he sounded defeated. He was looking at the dust below kicking up small clouds of it. Lara would have liked to see Skip stand up for himself, but she knew it wasn't her battle.

She thought it best to ignore it and focus on what had obviously made him feel good. "Well, Skip. I really appreciate your help. I am a bit overwhelmed by all of this, but I have to reach the plateau. It is urgent that I stonegraft with an orange stone." He looked at her with eyes that looked close to tears, and she decided right then and there that she cared about this young man already. She whispered conspiratorially, "You see, I have to go meet Soren and Exu, because I have a Pelanor who wants to meet them."

"You do not!" But his eyes were already holding the spark of excitement that Lara loved to see when people knew about Fleck.

"Yup, want to meet him?"

Drum Circle

When Lara had returned to the market booth with Skip, they had found Kit there playing with Fleck. Delly said the young terraweaver had been searching for him after she had learned from her aunt she was here. Fleck loved her as much as she loved him.

Delly, Skip, and Kit were racing around the short stone wall of the market booth chasing Fleck. Lara could feel the sheer joy that it brought him. It reminded her of the days with her own kids running after each other playing a version of tag, catch and turn, where no one really knew who was doing the chasing, or catching. They all just had fun running and either reaching out with arms or turning quickly to avoid the kid next to them. Tiny Sally squealing as Anna came in and scooped her up before Petey could tag her and then Brie tagging Petey and the animated argument ensuing of who had been 'it' in the first place. Small memories always brought a strange mix of happiness at the time she had enjoyed, and remorse that it was over.

But she was reminded, watching this bunch, that there would always be a fun group of young folks living life to the fullest in the moment. She wanted to watch for these moments and enjoy along with them.

Fleck was leading a wild chase getting faster and faster, the three behind him slowly getting further behind. Lara felt his surge of confidence that he had won the game, when Delly, who had been slowly falling further behind and was almost lapped in the small enclosure, turned suddenly and let Fleck race right into her arms, they all squealed in laughter. Kit still racing behind Fleck continued at full speed until she wrapped Delly and Flecks long tail in a tight hug.

Lara fanned herself with her hand and took a step backward under the fabric Delly had hung over her table. She was amazed at the difference between the chilly evening walking to the Kindred House last night and this midday heat. Even a simple spot of shade felt like welcome relief from the blazing sun.

The people of Laran didn't seem to notice it nearly as much as Lara did. She had lived most of her life with the sun shielded behind thick clouds and the cold wind whipping between the mountains of the Wastes. Even breathing felt a bit like a burden, she felt the heat in her throat.

The sun was starting to set, and Lara was more than glad to see the shades of oranges in the sky. Delly carried Fleck over to Lara, "Liv said for you to meet her at the drum circle, right?"

"Yes. Is it about time?" Lara asked.

Skip came up behind her. "Oh, any minute now we should be hearing it."

Kit peeked around from behind Delly, where she had been floofing Flecks tail. She had it wrapped over her head like a handkerchief. "I'll join you! I am supposed to be there." Then she stood a bit straighter, "All terraweavers are expected to join in the drum circle." She stood tall for a simple moment, and then jumped forward, tickling Fleck under his chin. "Is Fleck coming too?"

"Yes." Lara said, and as Kit pulled Fleck along to the entrance, Lara turned to the older two youth. "Skip, want to join us?"

Skip shook his head quickly back and forth and looked down at his toes. He took a deep breath and sighed slowly as he kicked the dust up beneath him. Lara immediately knew that something was bothering him and met eyes with Delly. A small shrug from her, told Lara she wasn't sure what was up either, but they both waited for him to speak first. They all watched until the small dust cloud had settled.

Skip looked up and his light brown eyes showed extra bright under the sheen of unshed tears. Lara's heart ached for him. "Um, I only run the course on Mondays." His voice was so low, that Lara felt like she had to almost squint to hear it, but when it registered, she gave a quick surprised look to Delly.

"What?" Delly gave him a friendly push, "But you are so serious about your training. I don't think anyone is at the gym preparing as much as you are. You should be attempting every night you can!"

He looked up at her with so much sadness that even Delly understood to be quiet. She took a step backward in her confusion and looked up at Lara, shoulders raised and shaking her head, not knowing what to say.

Lara kept her voice low, "Why do you only go on Mondays Skip?"

His shoulders slumped, and he kicked the ground again as he said, "That's the only day that Dean doesn't run it."

Delly's eyes shot open. "What! Is that jerk keeping you from running! He has no right."

Skip just looked at the ground. "It's just not worth it. I have tried to run on the same days as them, but since he runs it with his friends, I never get any peace. They are always pushing me out of the way. It isn't worth it."

"They run as a group?" Lara asked.

Delly chimed in, "Oh, a lot of people run together."

"Oh, that sounds kind of nice. Like a team?" Lara put her hand on Skip's shoulder gingerly. "Any chance you'd run with me sometimes? I need as much help as I can get, and you were so helpful with the weights."

Skip turned his head up and looked at her, his eyes a bit hopeful.

Delly jumped in, "I haven't run the course in years, but I will join you for a bit, if it will help. I hate that they made you feel like you couldn't run it."

"Really?" Skip looked back and forth between them, his shoulders straightening as he stood there. "I would feel a lot better if I had you two with me."

Delly laughed, "I think it will be fun. Let's start tomorrow though. I am supposed to close down the market tonight."

After a final quick goodbye to her old and new friend, Lara walked to the entrance of the enclosure.

"So, which way?" Lara turned to ask Kit, who was currently tickling the fur on the tips of Flecks ears. "Isn't that fur the softest he has! I love to do that too." She bent down, even though her knees screamed at her and lightly pet the fluff on Flecks other ear careful not to push on the actual ear as it stuck up into the air. Fleck's ear twitched as it tickled him, and he growled out the most adorable purr and Kit beamed up at Lara.

They were right at each other's eye level, and Lara got a chance to focus a bit on the young girl. Her eyes were large and deep brown. She had scars similar to Delly's, and Lara had an epiphany that they came from the course. Any of the people who were scrabbling on the flying rocks would end up with scrapes and cuts. There was definitely something much more physical about these terraweavers than the waterweavers.

"So, your aunt Liv told me that you stonegrafted with her?"

"Oh yes," Kit jumped up, excited to talk about it. Lara stood a bit more slowly, placing her hands on her knees to push upward while Kit continued. "That was a whole year ago. And now I am a full terraweaver just like the rest of them!" She sounded so proud that Lara's heart warmed.

There was a sudden wild beating of drums, a cacophony that had no rhythm or song. It sounded like chaos. Loud and non-stop, the frenzied sound reached over the whole of Laran, and Lara saw most everyone around her pause with a smile on their face. However, Kit's face looked stricken.

"Oh dear! We have got to run. I was supposed to be there before it started!" And she tore off. Fleck perked up and spun, following right on her heels. Lara started after also, but she was not nearly as quick as the two. The long day before, along with her workout this afternoon, were wearing on her physically. She realized she would have no problem finding them, the sound of the drums called out to anyone wanting to join them, and the excitement was radiating from Fleck, even from the distance. She slowed her pace and let herself walk at a leisurely stroll through the crowded market paths.

After about two minutes the chaotic non-beat of the drums crescendoed to a height and then suddenly stopped. There were about two seconds of silence where even the conversations around her stopped, then she heard a deep voice call out "Tamba!" And the beat began.

A steady beat, slow and deep, began and Lara felt it reverberated deep within her; she found her steps matching it as she walked toward the sound. Again, the voice called out, "Bally!" And another beat was added. This one was syncopated, quick for three beats and then a pause and a hard longer fourth. Bap-bap-bap...bum...

Lara reached the crowd watching the drum circle, and she could feel the people around her moving to the beat. A young man wearing torn up orange shorts tied up with a woven belt and no top at all, swayed near her to the slow steady Tamba hythm, swaying and stepping back and forth. While a woman years older than Lara shuffled her shoulders to the second quicker Bally drum, her clothes had strips of layers and layers of thin material, in shades of oranges from almost yellow to brown.

A third call from the voice, "Ho!" And suddenly Lara was immersed in the same multitude of drums sounding at once as earlier, but this time it was with a steady and layered beat that she felt deep in her soul. The drummers followed the Tamba beat and fit whatever they were called to drum into that steady flow.

Everyone around her broke out into dancing. The dance was a blend of chaotic and flowing. No one did the same moves, but everyone moved together in the same way the drumbeats blended so well. It was organized chaos and Lara loved the freedom of it. She danced around too, letting the beats tell her body how to move.

After a while she was tired and moved forward, closer to the circle of drummers. There was a group of people sitting on the ground around them enjoying the sounds while closing their eyes, instead of moving, and Lara sat at the back of that group.

There was so much to take in. Behind her the dancers moved, she could feel their motion, and she was amazed at how comfortable she had been dancing with them. She had always been a bit shy about dancing back home. She realized that there was no expectation here, everyone was focused on their inner enjoyment, and it was beautiful and freeing.

She laughed as she caught a glimpse of Fleck's tail flicking to the beat as Kit spun with him in her arms. Her circle skirt enveloping him in its material.

She moved her gaze to the center of the circle. Ten drummers sat around different styles of drums. A few were sitting on stone pedestals, and some sat on woven blankets. The size and shape of the drummers were as diverse as the size and shape of the drums. Large strong arms on all of them were the only similarities. These folks drummed every night, and it showed from their muscles to the quality of the sound.

She moved her gaze to the group sitting around her and was reminded of her afternoon Calm classes back in Azural. She closed her eyes and found she was able to center herself quickly, the beat of the drums helping her along. Back in the gardens by the Great Stone House, Lara had learned to close out the sounds around her, here she didn't have to do that. The sounds around her were strengthening the beat of her own heart and blood through her veins. She was instantly able to focus on her inner peace. She used this time, as her classes with Waterweaver Han and let the thoughts come and go.

> *there is a thrill to these beats - Brie must have loved this, where is she now, still in Morchast - and Pete in yellow, I am sure he is still there, but how is he - it is nice to know that this time there is no stress about the folks back home surviving, they have water, and a way to begin trading for supplies, I can enjoy myself - my tailbone hurts sitting on this dusty hard packed sand, or is it just rock - next time I should bring a blanket too - bap, bap, bap…bum - there are so many different beats - pata, pata, pata, pata, pata, -*

Eventually, the thoughts slowed and the only thing in her mind was the beats of the drums and silence, and she welcomed it. Deep breaths and calm consumed her.

She was so focused that it took her a minute to even realize the drums had stopped, she sat quietly still, enjoying her peace a moment longer until it was interrupted by the loud voices around her. As they broke through her meditative quiet, she heard "water," "blue," "weaver." Immediately she opened her eyes and saw that the silence was not a normal thing. Everyone was staring directly at her. And it was obvious why.

The blue magic was emanating from her body like a tight second layer of skin. Her connection to peace, a strong blue emotion had triggered her magic stone and even as she was not mentally initiating the magic, it had answered. Humming around her waiting to be called on.

Everyone here now knew that she was a waterweaver, and the looks on their faces were filled with amazement and a bit of disbelief. The silence hung for a moment longer until Kit squealed and ran over to her throwing her arms around her and breaking off the tension that Lara had suddenly felt being the under everyone's focus. Fleck arrived with Kit and rubbed at her left shoulder, mirroring the wave of emotional comfort he sent her.

"I can't believe it! I have never seen anything so beautiful! What can you show me? Let's both go over to the plaza; I want to see some waterweaving!"

Lara stood awkwardly as Kit was already pulling her towards the trial stage area. She looked up to see that everyone around her was smiling wide smiles. She didn't see anyone here upset with her, angry that she was from Azural, or any dismissive looks. Every face she saw looked excited.

Behind her she heard the deep voice call out "Tamba," and the deep slow base beat began behind her, but most of the folks who had been dancing, turned to follow Kit's lead to the center of the basin.

Waterweaving

Lara was pulled along by the strong tiny hands of the young terraweaver. "You have got to join in with the shows! We do shows every night before the trials in Pebble Plaza," the little girl's curls bounced up and down as she spun to look over her shoulder at Lara who, even with her longer legs, was behind the young girl practically running. Kit continued to ramble, "but we all just call it the Plaza, but I like the sound of Pebble Plaza."

Lara's blue magic had dropped immediately at the interruption and her feelings of anxiousness, and the trepidation of performing her magic for all of these people loomed in her thoughts.

Back home she had tried not to use the magic in front of people out of fear of them seeing her differently. A similar feeling was taking her over now. However, here it was strangely on a larger scale but bothered her a bit less. The idea of strangers seeing her as a waterweaver with strong magics felt less of a burden than her close friends seeing her as one.

The drumbeats sounded behind her, but the crowd surrounded her blocking her view of them. It seemed to her that all of the dancers from the circle had come along. She recognized dancers and mediators alike in the faces, all watching with the eager excitement of seeing something new.

The elusive waterweavers had hidden behind that waterwall over these past decades, and now Lara was in their midst. These folks had seen so many wondrous things that Lara could not begin to imagine. Color magics that she hadn't even begun to learn about, but she brought them blue.

In the moment she was a bit overwhelmed with what she might show them, then she realized they would be happy with even that bubble she had made for Liv earlier, and she needed to focus a bit more on tapping into her emotions if she wanted to show them anything at all.

She shook her shoulders out, easing the tenseness from her earlier workouts, and started going over the tenets of Blue, those emotions that controlled the water magic through her blue stone. Calm was not going to happen right now; this was too thrilling of an atmosphere. Responsibility was a stretch. She didn't have much of a connection with this community yet. Order might work, but in the moment, she felt the chaos of the crowd more than the controlled order of it, even though she knew that they followed clear expectations, for she hadn't yet seen a single accident in the bustling crowds. Intelligence might work but focusing on that seemed a bit stiff.

That left her with honesty, and it felt like a good fit. Here she could work through two large issues. On the large scale, what Azural had done to the world at large and her part in opening it up. On the small scale, what she was doing here. She appreciated how the magic helped her sort through these things and supported her in opening up about things she used to keep tightly under wraps.

As she began to focus on her honesty in the moment, she saw the blue light grow from her shoulder. She closed her eyes and felt for water nearby. The basin was dusty and dry, but the people were well cared for here. Travelers brought the water they needed to stay hydrated. Most every person had a water flask at their side.

Lara looked at Kit. "May I?" She asked motioning toward the young girl's flask.

Kit's eyes lit up as she jumped to Lara's side. She held out the flask to Lara, but instead of reaching for it, Lara pulled at the water inside.

With an explosion of droplets, the corked cap was pushed out from the water Lara pulled, falling and dangling from the cord. The water sprayed in a patterned splash that Lara created mimicking her crocheted doilies back home. The points of a star in a lace-like pattern reached out in a tiny star at first, but as Lara's magic continued to pull, she sent the water into the air, above the crowd. The light of the setting sun caught the droplets, and Lara could hear the calls of excitement from the people watching.

She watched the droplets in the air herself slowly shifting the shape of the star by adding little details. When she tired a bit of the lacework, she pulled it quickly into a tight ball of water. The crowd murmured in a satisfying way. They were definitely enjoying the show.

It was kind of stunning that it was such a small amount of water.

She had never performed for people before, but their attention wasn't on her right now, it was on the water. It was only a small amount of water, but the fluidity of it and the ability to make it into any shape she wanted allowed her to play. She pulled the water into a sheer thin layer flat above the audience around her. It shimmered, and made the sky look a little out of focus. Lara imagined throwing a pebble in the surface of a pond and created rings of a wave, circling out and creating an even pattern until it hit the water's edge.

She loved the calm feel of this imagery, and the repetitive waves as they rose and fell, and reached across the sky. Lara was tempted to try adding another set of waves, but realized she would not be able to make it look right when they met, she didn't think she had those skills.

Instead, she pulled the water tight into another ball. She chanced a look at the crowd in this moment and saw it had grown. She felt her heart rate increase and closed her eyes, listening to the drums above the sound of those watching her.

The steady beat soothed her and she started bouncing her water-ball to the steady Tamba beat of the drum. Bouncing it right above the heads and then back up into the sky. The sun was setting and Lara realized it was close to time for the trials to begin, she saw the other terraweavers watching in the crowd and realized that they weren't doing their usual performing. Everyone was watching her. Pushing her anxiousness into the water she created a finale that she hoped would satisfy.

She spun the water-ball around the exterior of the crowds, slowly at first, giving everyone a chance to watch it, and even a few jumped to try to touch it, those successful coming down with a spray of water droplets. She slowly built up the speed of the ball and as she did, allowed a tail to pull off the back so it began to look like an orbiting comet. She had it go faster and faster, pulling the circle it made into tighter and tighter revolutions until it reached the center and snapped to an instant stop, the tail funneling into it as it followed the pattern.

Here Lara gave the show one final explosive shower of water that pushed upward and outward into a fountain of tiny droplets that reached out over the crowd. She allowed it to rain down on the people, and the faces of the onlookers turned upward to feel the cool spray of water mist fall over them.

Shouts and applause filled the air, and Lara felt a mixture of happiness and also embarrassment at the praise. But mostly, she felt the joy of having fun and creating beauty.

Practice

Lara tightened her muscles preparing for the leap. Timing the jump would be key, and her head hurt from concentrating, or maybe it was from her last fall where she had bumped her head on the hard ground. She coiled down and narrowed her eyes and as the boulder moved closer to her — she jumped. This time she made it, just barely, falling forward and clinging to the far edge. It was only about two feet wide, and her fingers dug into the far ledge finding finger holds in the rough orange rock.

Scrabbling her feet up onto the boulders flat top, she stood in a crouch to keep the motion of the boulder from pulling her off like it had last time. Keeping her eyes closed and her hands on the edge, she took some deep breaths to calm her racing heart, which felt as if it was shaking her rib cage. Once she felt her pounding heartbeat lessen, she opened her eyes to look at her next jump.

The next rock was actually larger, but it had a rounded top. How was she going to do this one? She just sat watching it for awhile, feeling the rhythm of the motion of her current seat. It moved in a triangle shape about 10 feet above the sand below. She knew that the sand was not as soft as it appeared from her last eight failed attempts to reach this current boulder. Although it gave way a bit more than the dirt of her homeland, and was softer than the boulder she perched on, it was solid and painful to hit.

Plus, if she fell again, she would have to go through the last four jumps again, and she didn't think she had the emotional fortitude to try it again. Failure had a strange effect on her: she found that it could either spur her on to just keep going when she thought she was done, or shut her down completely, even when she thought she should go on. It was a strange dichotomy.

"Focus Lara," she said aloud to snap herself back to the task at hand. Shaking her head, she looked up from the sand below and studied the next boulder. It was probably about twelve feet across, so plenty of room to land, but the rounded top was intimidating, especially since the last four had all been flat and she had gotten into a comfortable expectation of scrabbling and holding onto the far corner. This one had no corners.

As it came back toward her, she studied it a bit more closely, it had pock marks in it. Deep jagged holes about the size of two fists every three feet or so. Interesting, so those could be used to secure a hold somehow.

She watched the boulder drift away in its triangular back and forth path and set her plan. She would jump as it was coming up on her left and focus on finding four holes to put both feet and hands into. She knew it was going to hurt, every jump so far had hurt, but she had made the last boulder. And so far, she hadn't seen many other people get this far today.

As the round boulder came up on her right, she prepped herself, again tightening her leg muscles and shaking her head, loosening her shoulders and hyping herself up. It would be returning in a few seconds from its far turn.

And as the boulder came close, she took a deep breath and even though her brain told her "Jump!" Her body did not listen, and she watched the boulder travel back along to her left.

She let out a frustrated scream and reset. Looking behind her she saw another few folks trying the boulders she had already completed. A young man of about twenty fell, and as she watched him hit the ground she cringed, remembering how it felt.

Ahead of her, she saw the young man Dean and two of his friends. Lara had been watching them as soon as she noticed them arriving. The line had already formed, and they just walked themselves to the front of the line. An older man had been up front and the three had physically pushed him backwards. Lara had hated the cocky stance they took waiting for the gong to start the trials, but when the course raised up out of the ground and the three started up the sky path, it was obvious they knew what they were doing. They were at the end of the path before any of the people behind them had made it to the third steppingstone. Lara had watched them for a few minutes, but when she had reached the beginning herself, she had pushed them out of her mind.

As she sat here, admittedly wasting time, she thought about how upset Skip had been. There was no reason to pick on someone just because you could make it further in the trials. Lara had no patience for bullies. She watched them jump from boulder to boulder above her. They had definitely slowed down now. This section was not so simple for them as the beginning path.

Lara realized she was just wasting time. She would never make this next jump if she didn't even try it.

As the boulder came across on her right, in a split second she decided not to wait for it to come back around and just jumped. Her distance was a bit short, and she hit the side of the boulder. Her hands finding the holes quickly and even securing holds. She had built up quite a bit of finger strength from all of her years building fences and carrying buckets of water in the Wastes. But her original plan of finding holds with both hands and feet was confirmed as the right plan, when her feet flailed below her off the rounded side of the rock.

Try as she might, she couldn't pull her legs up high enough to reach the hole she saw next to her hips. Her fingers began to ache as she felt them slip in their grips. Then as she was attempting to tighten her core and bring her left foot to reach a hole a bit lower than her knee, even though it was below the curve of the boulder she was taken by surprise as the boulder reached its path end and switched direction. The change in motion of the boulder took it right out of her grasp and her body continued in the direction it had originally been going, then quickly fell to the ground.

It hurt. But her anger in the failed attempt covered some of those painful feelings. She lay there for a few moments. She knew she needed to get up, but she was not ready. It was already getting dark, and she had spent a very busy day. Taking a deep breath, she sat up.

Lara took a moment to take stock of how she felt. The pants that Delly had given her were tattered at the knees and she had a scrape along the right hip that went through her pants and also scraped her skin. She stood and began dusting herself off, wincing as her hands, scraped and bloody from the rock got dust in a cut.

She looked up above her and realized with a shock that she was two rocks farther than she had ever gotten before. She grinned. Every muscle in her body hurt, her hands and arms were likely scarred for life, and she was probably going to have to patch these pants up tonight. But she looked up at the round boulder she had just fallen from and laughed.

She was getting better at this.

She looked beyond the failed round boulder to the multitude of rocks hanging in the sky going off into the distance ahead of her. She knew that to stonegraft orange she had to make it to the end. It was much further than she had imagined the first time she looked at this magical obstacle course, but she had gotten two big steps closer today.

That felt really good.

Delly's Family

Delly's family looked different sitting around the table than Lara's own family, Delly's brothers in their twenties and thirties, the grandparents, and Delly all at the large table. Even with the differences, Lara was reminded of her own happy times at the dinner table back home surrounded by family. People sat shoulder to shoulder at the table, talking over each other. Everyone obviously cared about each other, but there was also the honest, but fun, playful ribbing that came from a lighthearted sibling dynamic.

Delly's oldest brother Frank was the loudest of the bunch. His volume turned especially high because he was in conversation with Gary, Ida Mae's husband and the grandfather of this bunch. "I told that son of a lollygaggin' snipper that he best not mess with my schedule, I had to be at the Forge in ten minutes!"

A younger sibling, Lara still hadn't caught his name, sat next to Lara rolling his eyes. He responded to no one in particular. "Well, if he had been willing to carry half the equipment I had, I might have been able to pick up my pace." There was no anger in the response, and it gave Lara the impression these two went through this regularly.

Ida Mae sat on Lara's right, quietly eating her meal of roasted squash. She seemed to soak in the energy from the youth around her. She moved slowly, but her eyes were full of life, and they darted around keeping tabs on all of her beloved grandchildren.

When the meal was almost finished Ida Mae looked up at Delly across the table from her. Lara noted the gears turning in the old woman's mind. When she spoke in her normal voice, Lara was sure it would be sucked up in the crowded rumble. "So, Delly, I heard from a reliable source," Lara was amazed to hear silence. All of the grandchildren had immediately silenced to allow Ida Mae her words, "Janice, that's little Skippy's grandmother," she said as an aside to Lara, "that you were planning on returning to the trials."

The whole table turned as one to stare at Delly. Lara felt the weight of their stares and imagined that Delly felt it times ten. But Delly simply flicked her hands at her five brothers and her grandparents, "It's not like I am trying to stonegraft. Skip told me and Lara that Dean was intimidating him from even attempting the trials. He was only going on Mondays when Dean and his buddies took their rest day." She looked up, ignoring the rest of the table and met clear, sincere eyes with Ida Mae. "I'm doing it for him. I still have no plans to become a terraweaver."

Lara felt the tension seep out of Ida Mae next to her. Confusion filled Lara's thoughts. She thought she knew Delly fairly well, but there was more going on here.

"That Skip is a good kid, and he definitely is working hard for it. I am proud of you for standing up for him." Ida Mae said and then took another bite of her corn. The table seemed to accept that it was all over, and the hubbub began anew. Lara's thoughts swam in every direction wanting to figure out why Ida Mae and the family was so upset about Delly attempting the trials.

When dinner was over, Lara stood to begin helping clear the table, but Ida Mae stopped her. "Let the yunguns do that, I think you should join me." Lara turned back to the table and realized that the family had already efficiently cleared the whole thing, one sibling had grabbed all of the plates, another the glassware, they had their roles, and all pitched in. It was amazing.

"Lead the way, Ida Mae." Lara giggled at the unintentional rhyming and saw the granny's shoulders shake in humor in front of her as she led Lara down the narrow hall. She left Fleck, as he was having too much fun running circles around the feet of the younger kids in the kitchen.

Lara hadn't been toward the back of the house yet and found it a bit of a maze. The adobe walls were smooth and cool but there was not much extra space in the hallways, leaving as much space in the open rooms as possible. They passed a few workrooms and a few bedrooms and finally got to a door at the end of the hall.

"Welcome to my oasis." Ida Mae grinned ear to ear. When she opened the door, Lara was surprised to see they were heading outside. There was a very tiny courtyard with tiny orange lights hanging along the outer wall. There were only two chairs out here, and that filled the space fairly completely.

"Oh my!" Lara exclaimed. "I can see why you call this an oasis; one on one conversation must be extra special in this home."

"Oh yes, I love sitting with my grandchildren one on one. But tonight, it is your turn." The older woman lowered herself into one of the garden chairs and pulled a blanket over her lap. The night was indeed cooler out here.

Lara sat next to Ida Mae and they both just enjoyed the silence for a while. Lara studied the space as she sat and realized there was something different about the lights. From her vantage point they let off a sparkling orange cast, unlike any she had seen before. It wasn't fire. She stood to get a better look.

The lights were little individual containers that were works of art themselves, likely made by one of Delly's brothers at the forge. But as she got closer, she saw that inside was magic. The swirling orange sands and the sparkling magic that kept moving in an infinity spiral. Lara knew the magic to make these had been precise and powerful. Tiny magic moving was a skill that she was still trying to grasp with her Waterweaving. Lara was sucked into it for a moment, and then broke away and turned to Ida Mae, "How did you get these?"

"Have a seat. But why don't you bring one of those and set it here on the table. We have a lot to talk about."

Lara took the handle of the metal cage and marveled as the magic moved contained in the open space inside. She could have reached in and touched the magic. Setting the magical lantern on the small table between the chairs, she sat down, ready to listen.

"What has Delly told you about her mother?"

Lara thought back to Delly and her conversations at school in Azural. "She said that they traveled a lot, that she had been to most of the color realms with her mother, traveling often with the Brown

Traders." She racked her brain. "To be honest, I don't remember much else."

Ida Mae nodded and seemed to collect her thoughts. "I think I should start back before her mother was even born. When Carlie first came back with that magic stone our whole world here in Laran turned upside down. We had been just a small village, and as the terra magic began to congeal around us and more stones arrived and more terraweavers stonegrafted, our village turned into this hubbub. I was young at the time too, so easily pulled into the excitement that was buzzing around. The growth boomed. The terraweavers built walls and buildings, they created the trials right away. Carlie had said that all of the finders had agreed to protect the stones and set trials to make sure that the deserving earned the right to stonegraft."

Her voice trailed off and Lara saw that Ida Mae was reflecting inwardly about the memories. "I used to love watching the trials. I even joined in a few times, but when my friend fell and broke her arm, I decided that it just wasn't for me. But people came from far and wide, and the trials grew. There were more terraweavers, and the evening festivals began. I made a good living with my art, and benefited from the constant stream of visitors, but sometimes I sit at my booth and remember when The Plaza was simply a flower field by the town square."

As Ida Mae paused, Lara looked up from the swirling dust in the lantern. "I completely understand what you mean. Our town square began crumbling before I was born, but by the time I left for Azural, it would have been unrecognizable if someone had left and come back."

Ida Mae nodded sagely, "The whole world has broken. And the real problem is that so many don't see what is wrong with it now. They lack perspective, seeing things only through the lens of what they know."

"That was the biggest problem I had in Azural. Even convincing them that The Wastes existed, and that people outside of their borders were in need of the water they were holding was impossible."

A click of the doorway opening pulled both of their attention out of the memories. Ida Mae's husband peeked around the door, just his fingers, forehead, and eyes showing, his grey hair in thin chaotic swoops flopping to the side as his head tipped. "I hate to interrupt, but someone wanted to join you." He looked down pointedly and both Lara and Ida

Mae laughed as they saw Fleck mimic the old man peeking around the door, paws holding onto the edge. The white fluff covered claws dug into the wood to help him hold the precarious position.

"Come on in Fleck." Ida Mae invited, and he immediately bounded forward and curled up on Lara's lap. "Thanks honey. Kitchen all cleaned up?" She asked, then at his nod, "Don't wait on us. We might be a bit yet."

His eyes were light from aging, but Lara saw the love there. She thought of where she and James might be in 20 years, and hoped it was something like this. "Fireside stories are always a bit spicier when you aren't there." He giggled, as the door shut behind him.

"Oh, pish-posh. That's not true. I usually tell the spicy ones." She resettled and drew in a deep chest full of air. "Let's jump forward in our story." Lara nodded, she really wanted to hear about Delly's mother. "Old Gary and I only had one child. Hard to imagine with all of this lot running around, but when we were parents, it was pretty quiet in the house. Although Tanya was so full of energy, she could fill the place herself sometimes. She was always a powerhouse — excitable, energetic, moving nonstop until she slept." Ida Mae's eyes held so much love, and Lara understood the emotion to her core.

"When she turned 14, she became obsessed with the trials. It was unhealthy in our opinion, and Gary sat down with her each morning." Ida Mae laughed a cryptic laugh. "She always did listen to him more than me." Shaking her head she continued. "Each morning, he would try to center her in her emotions and make sure it didn't consume her. But that was all she knew. Full force or full stop. She stonegrafted the next year."

Ida Mae looked at Lara. "I can see that Delly never told you. I'm not surprised."

Lara figured that her shock showed. Her emotions were always clear on her face, unless she was intentionally aware and putting an effort in schooling them. "I had no idea." Lara let out quietly, still puzzling out why Delly wouldn't have said anything.

"We don't really talk about Tanya. She broke too many hearts in this home, but I thought you deserved to understand a bit of the history. And also, I need you to understand why Delly doing the trials is such a big deal in this house."

Lara looked into the older woman's light eyes and nodded. "I love Delly dearly. She was there for me when I needed a friend in that backwards thinking Azural."

"Yes, she told us all about you. And Iris, Van, all of her adventures. We love a good story time after dinner. They are probably all in the living room now cozied up on the couches. This family is not what I saw for myself." The older woman's eyes took a far-off look again. "Tanya was an only child, and when she stonegrafted she became obsessed with the evening shows. Every night she was down there blasting her magic. She loved the thrill of the power over all things Terra: rock, dust, pebbles, she could even pull metals and crystals up from the depths.

"She also, more than anything, seemed to love the adoration she received from the crowds. There were fewer weavers back then, and less folks coming and going; we were still in the younger years of Laran. She fell in love with a young man, Jasper. He had been our neighbor for years. He was strong, and handsome, and artistic. He never once attempted the trials. I think sometimes, that was one of the things she liked best about him."

She looked up at Lara, who was very interested. "Oh, my. I am letting myself get off track. To sum up. In their young years they had the brood you see in this home, boy after boy." Ida Mae barked out a laugh. "At the time, I was a happy grandmother, excited to play with them all each night when mom went off to the Plaza for her shows. But when Delly was born, something changed. It was almost as if Tanya woke up. The routine of her life caught up to her. One morning, when Delly was three, she looked at all of us gathered around the table and said she was leaving."

"Delly had said her mother took her to all of the color realms aside from Azural and Morchast. So, she took the kids along?"

"Only Delly, Harry, and Benny. That's the two youngest of the brothers."

"And she left the rest with you?"

"Jasper was still alive then. He loved the family and raised the boys to love art and hard work. When he died, we all were heartbroken." She sighed. "But on with the story. Tanya traveled the realms. She was desperate for excitement. She was driven for the thrills she had felt when she had first begun terraweaving. At first each realm gave her that, but there was something broken in her. The younguns, were like a weight to her. One day, when Delly was 8, she brought them back and dropped them at the door. She didn't even stay the night. She gave me a hug and was gone."

"None of us have heard from her since." Lara let her sit quietly, waiting for her to be ready. How heartbreaking it all must be. Lara wondered as she sat watching the bright orange sand shift in the lantern what her own grandchildren might look like. What she might be to them one day. Would she be there for them the way Ida Mae was for this family? She hoped so.

"The morning after Tanya left, Delly went down to the basin and watched the carnival set up. She stayed out of the house as much as possible, only ever coming back to sleep. I think she was hoping to find her mother there." A tear slid down the woman's cheek. "It was within a week that Delly began the trials. She was fierce and angry. She threw herself into them with abandon, scraping knees and falling constantly, but always getting back up and back in line. She spent 3 years of her life obsessing. When most kids around here were playing and painting, she was pushing herself to meet some standard that many adults never achieve."

Lara pictured little Delly, with her curls and freckles, wiry and thin as a youth, the scars she was familiar with on her arms as fresh wounds, and the fire in her eyes, that she had occasionally caught a glimpse of. Her heart broke a bit for her young friend.

"One evening when it should have been time for the trials to begin, the door opened, and Delly walked in. She was twelve and had just reached my shoulder. She walked up to me and just sagged into my arms. I led her straight out here and in this quiet space we just sat and cried together."

They sat in silence for a few minutes. Lara pictured her young friend sitting in the same chair she was now, broken by the world, and hurt by the mother, who was supposed to protect her. Lara wiped a tear that escaped her eye and wandered down her cheek. She rubbed it between her fingers. And Ida Mae also dabbed her eyes.

"It took a few years of family dinners for her to really open up, but you know her now. She has done a fantastic job of healing. She really is a happy young woman. But she has demons." Ida Mae looked up and met eyes with Lara. The woman's gaze was penetrating, and Lara found herself breaking the eye contact quickly. She wasn't comfortable thinking these things, and it felt too raw. "I think we all do. It's important to remember that about the people around you."

Lara nodded in agreement. "We all have our own stories."

"Well, Delly's demons pushed her to Azural and returned her home. And now she is attempting the trials here again." Ida Mae sighed. "But. She is older. She is wiser. And she is not her mother."

Lara thought about the word wiser. She often thought of wisdom as something that came with age. She was wise because she was almost 50. But Delly had wisdom too, and she was just at the end of her teenage years. Perhaps wisdom really came from experience, from seeing the world for what it was, accepting it, and figuring out how to take it on. Or not to take it on at all.

She felt a confirmation from Fleck and was reminded that often her thoughts were not just her own. She had a constant companion. *You are getting wiser every day too, my little friend.*

Lara turned in her seat, repositioning her furry friend with his bottom and tail sat next to her on the seat, so that she could look her new friend in the eye. "I am so sorry for all that you and your family have been through." Lara said, feeling the emptiness of the words and wishing there was more.

Ida Mae reached out her hand and placed it on Lara's left forearm as it rested on the arm of the chair. Her hands showed age, but were strong from her artwork, and the sinew stood out. The knuckles looked large and gnarly in her hand, and Lara found herself comparing her own hand to that of the older woman. Before, where she had seen her hands to be wrinkled and the skin beginning to roughen, now they looked so young in comparison. While Lara still felt old, she knew there was so much more life ahead of her.

"I am telling you this because I know Delly. She is ready, but there will be times that her emotions hit her. I think it will help for you to know what is going on behind her happy smile, you know, when her eyes don't match."

New Rhythm

The days were moving by so quickly. Lara and Fleck had gotten into a routine that helped the days fly by. Each morning, they had breakfast with Delly's family. They were welcoming and reminded Lara a lot of her own family when the kids were all teenagers. So often she heard people say that boys were rowdier than girls, but having raised three daughters and a son, she found this to be untrue. Youth had energy, no matter the gender, and she enjoyed being around it.

Although, she loved being reminded of the chaos of her happy days as a full-time mother, she also was beginning to appreciate her slower paced alone times. So, after breakfast she walked with Fleck through the streets of Laran. Visiting shops, seeing the sights and noticing all the differences that the orange stone had manifested in this Realm comparing it often to Azural. The regimen of blue was gone, the rigid structure and expectation of the civilians was gone. Here everyone moved to the beat of their own drum and seemed to focus on the excitement of the moment and worked together.

Then it was time to meet Skip and Delly at the gym space in the basin. She pushed herself every day, but the pain of the growing muscles kept her from pushing too far.

The afternoon was spent connecting with people on a more personal level. She had coffee with Delly, or met with some terraweavers, or chatted with the artisans in the tents in the basin. Everyone was so full of energy here. The pace of the days moved at a speed that reminded Lara of her days when her kids were young: fast, and frenetic, and fun.

She could tell that the hard work at the gym was helping her. She wasn't as winded as she leapt the first steppingstones and was faster at it too. The larger stones were getting easier also, her muscles more able to control her jumps and hold on as they moved beneath her.

She was growing in more ways than she had thought she needed to. The thing that was most interesting to her was that she was getting so much more comfortable doing the Waterweaving shows for the crowds. It was actually the part of the day she most looked forward to. As she was pushing through the pain of lifting the weights with Skip, she was imagining different motions the water might take, ways that she might inspire and awe the crowd.

The novelty of having a waterweaver had lulled with the larger crowds now, but every day new travelers came into Laran, and they all were excited to see their first glimpse of the elusive water magic.

Orange Tenets?

Lara knew the only way to get answers to the Fleck headaches, and maybe about his history, was to keep at her push to get through the obstacle course. At night she was having fitful dreams, but she wasn't sure if they were hers or Flecks.

The large Pelanor Exu stood over them, wings outstretched, the teeth sharp and glinting in the sun — a tall wall of stone, smooth to the touch and repeated futile attempts to climb it. In the nightmares she scrabbled to reach the top of the wall, but the smooth surface of the stone gave her no place to hold. When in the dreams she decided to give up and just use her Waterweaving, the blue stone at her shoulder would glow for an instant and then go dark. Her nightmares spun into a mix of attempting to jump, fearsome teeth, falling to the ground, and seeing her blue stone go black.

The next morning the images haunted her as she ate breakfast with Delly's family. She was pretty sure that the stone needed her to be honest to work, and she couldn't get past the feeling that it was cheating to use her Waterweaving powers to reach the top, when no one else on the course could do that. She also was unsure if there was even enough water around here to push herself up in the air. When she had flown above Azural, it had been over the river, using the water below to keep her aloft.

She sat over her plate pushing her mind to think of some new idea to scale this wall, and realized the whole family was all looking at her. She shook her head to clear it, "Sorry, what?"

Delly's brother, the taller one with the swooping haircut, said, "We were just wondering what you were so intensely thinking about that you didn't even notice that Fleck ate all of the carrots off of your plate."

Looking down, Lara laughed. "I am pretty sure I will never get to taste carrots again in my life. But a growing dragon needs his favorite food." Then her face straightened. "I think I am letting the trials consume me too much. I have been having nightmares about them."

Delly looked up, concern all over her face. "Nightmares? Maybe you should take a few days off."

"You might be right." Lara looked at her plate again, and over at Fleck who was still nibbling his last carrot with the tiniest sharp-teethed bites. She could feel his enjoyment and choice to make the last bite of carrot last. "Sometimes I am tempted to just use my waterweaving to blast up to the top. But I feel that would be cheating."

Delly laughed, and said "Lara, we keep telling you. There are no rules, you just have to get to the top. No one has used waterweaving before, but there is no reason not to." Delly's brothers all nodded their agreement. Lara knew Delly was genuine in the statement, but deep in her gut Lara felt differently. She was learning that the stone cared about emotions in a different way than rules or expectations of the realms. Isn't that what her experience in Azural had shown her?

Her thoughts were interrupted when Delly continued, "Maybe it's time for you to take a bit of time today to learn the history of our terraweavers and think about the tenets here. We might not have them plastered all over like Azural, but they are still an integral part of the trials and who our terraweavers are."

Lara sat back and realized in all of her rush to get to the top she had focused on her fitness only. She hadn't even once considered that there might be more. Well, she was definitely feeling physically up to the task now, she just had to figure out the strategy. It was time for her to visit the library.

And suddenly, she felt lighter than she had in ages. She was so excited. She couldn't believe she hadn't been to the library yet. She loved a good book, and she hadn't even stopped inside. Well, she had two hours before her lunch visit with Liv and Kit.

Library

Lara was kind of surprised she hadn't set foot inside the library yet. She loved books, and the library in Azural had been one of her favorite spots, after the gardens. She knew exactly where it was located, because it was one of her favorite buildings in Laran. It sat on the far North edge of the rounded city walls on the furthest side from the entrance.

None of the buildings in Laran were tall, and the library stayed true to this, but it gave a feeling of grandness by adding depth and dimension to the front facade. There were slender beams along each side of the doorway and the outer edges of the walls that were carved stone to look like book edges, you could see the page details and the front and back covers of the books. It piqued the interest. Lara wondered if the sculptor had a particular book in mind as they created the pillars, because they looked so very lifelike. As she walked up to the entry, she slid her hand along the stone page edges and could feel the texture of it. Looking up from here, the door looked the same height as any other, but from further back the slim book ends gave the appearance of height.

Lara entered and found another interesting difference about this building. It was the first time she had heard silence since entering Laran. She hadn't even realized how much noise had been surrounding her until she felt the physical difference of the lack of sound. The silence felt like a weight lifted off her mind and she noticed immediately a tension leaving her.

She knew what the best approach was to find what she really needed in any library, so she headed directly to the librarian sitting at a large desk set up in the center of the room. She looked to Lara to be close to Anna's age, so that would be in her late twenties. Unlike most of the folks Lara had met so far in Laran, this young woman's hair was a deep, dark mahogany brown, and her skin was light with very few freckles. Lara got the impression she didn't spend much time out in the blazing sun.

"Good morning," Lara said, immediately regretting the loudness of her voice breaking the silence.

The young woman seated before her obviously had lots of practice speaking in the hushed tones expected in a space like this. "Welcome, what can I do for you?" Her voice came out in a pseudo-whisper that poured out like honey, slow and steady.

Lara was good at mimicking though, and her next question, she was very glad to hear, came out sounding much closer to the young woman's. "I am hoping to find some books on the history of Orange stonegrafting. And if you have any information on the tenets of Orange, that would be amazing. In Azural, all of the tenets of Blue were posted everywhere, it was very obvious. Laran seems much less concerned about the rigidity of rules and expectations. But I am feeling like if I understand a bit more about the orange stone, and its emotions," Lara cut off her last word, a bit embarrassed because it hit her that she was running on and getting markedly louder with each word she said. Taking a breath, she lowered her voice again and added, "I will have a better chance in the trials, if I know more about the history and the tenets. Sorry, I got loud there."

"Please, no need to apologize, we have a lot of exuberant folks here in Laran. Follow me." She stood and Lara noted that the young woman walked with a cane. The steady beat of it rang out through the stacks of books, reminding Lara of the tamba beat.

Lara followed quietly behind, looking at the huge resource filled stacks of books. The library here in Laran was easily four times the size of that at The Great Stone House. Seeing all of the paper, she was glad she had left Fleck with Delly at the Market. She didn't want to risk any of this amazing collection with his lack of elemental control.

The librarian stopped in a darker corner of the stacks and turned on a tiny lamp that flooded the space with a warm light. There was a small open wooden desk. "Why don't you wait here, I will bring you a few books to look through. We don't allow books to leave the building, but you are welcome to keep a few pulled from the shelves here at this desk. I will assign it to you for the next week, and we can see if you want it longer."

"Oh" Lara said, startled by this news. She had expected to take the books she found back to the house. Instead, she had a seat in the chair and found it was very comfortable; the perfect height to sit in front of a large book to read. The desk was not large, but definitely big enough to hold a stack or two of books and maybe keep a notebook and some pencils. She decided that she would look into finding some paper to take a few notes since she couldn't take the books with her.

Almost immediately, Lara heard the sound of the young librarian's cane beating the tamba beat, and she turned to see her deftly carrying four books in her other arm. Lara was impressed.

"Thank you, this is amazing." Lara stood thinking she could help transfer the stack to the desk but quickly realized her mistake. There was no need for help, the librarian maneuvered her second hand with the cane in it and still simply placed the pile of heavy books onto the desk. The young woman's core must have been iron. Lara laughed at herself, realizing her hours at the gym had her thinking of muscle strength in every scenario.

"I have a few more in mind but wanted to get you something to look at right away. When I think of more, I will just bring them over. Feel free to come and go as you please, the books will remain at the desk unless another patron needs them."

Lara sat back down and traced her hand along the engraved title of the first book. A large orange tome with the simple title LARAN. "Oh, thank you. This is going to be a big help. My name's Lara, may I ask yours?"

The little librarian smiled a quiet smile, the curve of her lips so slight that if Lara hadn't been really paying attention, she might have missed it. "Oh, I know who you are. My name is actually Lenore, but everyone calls me Libby. You know, because I am always at the library. It used to annoy me, but now I love it. I'm happy to meet you, but I will give you some space to get reading."

"Thank you, Libby." Lara answered, a bit distracted as she was already opening the first book.

Trouble with Dean

That evening Lara was distracted as she did her usual water show. Opening new books felt so intimidating. It was as if the information was too much to take in. She had looked at tables of contents in all of the books Libby had stacked up for her, and she had read for hours. All of the information felt disjointed and none of it felt like it made any sense.

There was a book on the planning of the layout of the city. Apparently, Carlie had worked with a few of the earlier terraweavers to pull the walls around the city and create the Basin. Lara had poured over the text with keen interest after seeing Soren's name mentioned, but the only information she got was that he had been in charge of the Western section.

There was a book on the magic stones, which had seemed to be a lucky find, until Lara realized all that it had in it was basic information. She already knew more than the author of that book seemed to. She kept reading in case it had helpful information.

"The stones seem to be powered by emotions. When our terraweavers show excitement, the power seems to flow through them. And all of the people who have stonegrafted orange are our most extroverted and social."

Lara had closed the book with a huff, feeling like it was useless. But now, as she stood in the center of these watchful eyes, she thought she might understand what the book was saying in a deeper way. Sometimes the most basic way of saying something was the best way to get it across.

A young voice broke her out of her thoughts. "Where did the magic go?" And Lara snapped out of it. The little girl was staring at her, and then Lara realized that all of the people around her were looking confused.

Embarrassed, Lara mumbled, "Sorry." The weight of the eyes on her made it a bit difficult to focus, but she turned inward and pulled the blue magic through her and around her. She focused on the most obvious weight on her shoulders right now. Her responsibility to Fleck.

The young Wish Dragon was important to her, and not just because he was connected to her. She had seen in him a wisdom that came from years of living. He was kind to all of the people he came across, inquisitive about the world around him, patient with those who wanted to interact with him. She owed it to him to help him find this other dragon. A mentor for him in a world so lacking in his own kind. The responsibility she felt for him, fed her magic, and the show went on.

Blue sparks of magic mixed with the droplets of water in the sky and Lara watched as enthralled and happy, as the crowd around her. When she created the thin bubble in the air, she noticed that the light from the setting sun caught the water and turned it a shade of orange.

She pulled the water into a tight ball and finished the same way she always did. The ball spun above them; the tail of water pulled out behind. When it reached the center this time, she realized she was bored and switched it up. Rather than sprinkling the water over the crowd, she pulled the large ball straight down into the ground. The magic sparkles following it down.

The young girl in the front ran over to splash in the puddle before it seeped into the ground to disappear forever, the blue magic settling into the surface. Lara watched waiting for the ground to dry, but it never happened. Instead, the water in the center of the puddle seemed to be pushing up, and suddenly, a tiny geyser shot out of the center of the water.

Around her the crowd audibly gasped and then clapped, still thinking it was part of the show. Lara stared, unsure what to think of this. Her mind reeled, she hadn't done that, had she? Had she pulled this water from underground somehow, without even realizing it? Was the water answering her without her even concentrating on it? She thought about her hydration compared to the others around her. Was she unintentionally pulling water from around her? This worried her a bit, especially when water was such a rare resource around here.

Lara watched as the girl and the others who joined her splashing around in the sandy murky water. Another came and drank from the spout of clear water before it landed into the muddy puddle. Others lined up to drink from the new fountain. Lara was worried but also thrilled that she might be able to help if she could just figure it all out.

She needed to talk to another weaver. Pushing her way through the crowd as it seemed to tighten around the bubbling spring, Lara found where the terraweavers were performing. Dale and Gage were throwing rocks back and forth between them. Large rocks bounced off of sparkling orange magic right before it hit one of them and was sent back to the other. Lara watched with new eyes. Rather than watching the rocks, or the weavers, she focused on the magic sparks. And sure enough, as it settled in the ground, Lara thought of how overly orange the whole realm had become. What a mess this world was.

She looked at Liv as she danced, and the stream of dust that she spun around her looked terrific. Light from the setting sun hit the dust cloud that was like art as it spun in exaggerated mimicry of her own body's motions. Lara again focused instead on the tiny pricks of magic that slowly settled into the basin below them.

Lara saw Skip standing to the side watching Liv and walked over to him.

She jumped right in where her thoughts were taking her, "I think we have really messed this world up." He looked up at her, obviously not knowing what she was talking about. The young man had been a great friend and support to her, but he was barely a teenager and had never been outside of Laran. She shook her head. "Never mind, I have a lot on my mind."

"I know! Me too." Skip turned to her excitedly, "I have been getting so much better now that I am doing this more than once a week. I can't say how glad I am to have you and Delly with me." His eyes kept darting past Lara over her shoulder, so she turned to see what he was looking at.

There, Dean stood with a few friends. All of the older teenagers were big and strong. They seemed to take up more space than necessary, and

Lara realized that the people around them gave them extra room. There was a wariness in the eyes of many of the local Laranians, as they gave the group a wide birth. Ugh, Lara hated bullies.

Just then, Liv finished her show with a flourish, the dust flying into the air and then compressing into a tight small boulder that she slowly brought down to fall into her hands. Lara was keenly aware of the orange sparkle that continued down past her hands to the ground. Liv handed the ball of earth to an older woman nearby and gave a flourished curtsey to the crowd as they applauded. Lara felt like she could see the terraweaver glow from the attention and then wondered if maybe she actually could. The orange magic hung around her as she basked in the adoration of the crowd. "Thank you all," Liv was saying, but Lara felt the thanks was insincere. This woman was starting to rub Lara the wrong way, but she couldn't quite put a finger on it.

Lara turned her back on the terraweavers, forgetting why she had wanted to talk to them anyway. "The trials are about to start; we should go find Delly."

They walked along with the crowd at a steady pace to the line. Delly was standing near the front of the line, but when she saw them, she moved back to them. "Hey there. Did you learn anything at the library?"

"I don't know. I am beginning to even wonder what it is I am looking for. There is so much information. Maybe I need to figure out what my question is first."

Skip laughed, "Oh, that's easy. How do we get to the end of this course!"

Lara laughed. "True. I think I got distracted by all of the information. I want to know all about this world, about all of the stones, about all of the magic. I want to understand how everything got so bad that my home lost all of our resources. I want to know where the magic comes from, and why the magic works, and how the magic works. And I need to know about the Pelanor. Why are there so few of them? And about these headaches, and our connection."

"Whoa, whoa, whoa" Delly laughed. "Maybe Skip is right, focus on the first question?"

Lara looked right into Delly's eyes and saw the laughter there, and it lightened her. "Yes. How do we get to the top of this course." As she said it the course was beginning. The rumble of the ground beneath her had become familiar, it almost felt comforting. She softened her knees and stayed on her feet. The excitement surged through her, she was beginning to look forward to the risky jumps and even the falls.

As Skip turned to look at the stone steps rising before them, he suddenly was shoved to the ground, his wiry frame crumpling from the force. Lara looked to see Dean's back as he had already moved far ahead of them, or she might have done something, she could feel righteous rage fill her, flaming up. Instead, she stamped some of her fury out on the ground and reached out with Delly to help her friend up.

"That fiend!" Lara spit out. "Why doesn't his father do something about this?" She hadn't intended it as a real question, but Delly answered.

"Dale was the same way. Arrogant jerks all of them, that whole family. Grandma says Gage was like that even before he stonegrafted. He's Dean's grandfather."

Lara saw Gage and Dale standing near the start of the course, intent on Dean's progress. The young man sped up the first section and was already bounding easily across the larger boulders that Lara was struggling with, his friends not far behind.

She heard a shout from Dale, "Focus Son." Lara felt the weight behind the words, and for an instant felt a bit of sympathy for the kid racing ahead of them to the oculus. That was, until she turned to see Skip dusting his pants off.

They had moved to the beginning of the course, and Lara took her anger and put it into her jumps. The movement felt good, and she calmed down. She could think about all of these problems tomorrow. Right now, she would just focus on the next step, the next rock, the next boulder.

Libby

When Lara asked if Delly had been to the library before, she answered with exuberance. "Of course! I grew up here, you know. And I always did love learning a bit more than my brothers. I think it was one of the reasons I wanted to go to Azural. I knew they thought intelligence was important."

They entered the large entry space and Lara's whisper echoed into the empty corners of the stacks of books. "I have a desk all set up this way."

"Okay," Delly giggled, her whisper, somehow much louder than Lara's.

The desk had two new books stacked on it. Lara read the titles and found they were history books. She opened the first book as Delly pulled a chair over from a neighboring desk. Her light brown eyes popped as the scrape of the chair rumbled through the quiet space. She paused and then awkwardly lifted the heavy wooden chair and carried it over to Lara.

They both read silently for a while, not finding anything of great interest. Just as Lara's eyes were starting to water from looking so long at the tiny letters, she heard the sound of Libby's cane hit the floor. As Libby rounded the corner, her eyes grew wide when she saw that Lara wasn't alone.

Delly jumped up, a light in her eyes. "Libby!" She ran to the young woman, and Lara realized they were already acquainted. Of course. They were close in age after all. And although there were a lot of people coming and going through Laran, the locals were sure to be familiar with each other, especially if they were close in age.

Libby's eyes showed they were not as happy to see Delly, however. Lara wondered at it, until she saw Delly follow behind Libby to the table. Delly's eyes held a sadness as she watched the other woman walk ahead of her, her focus on the injured foot.

When they arrived at the desk where Lara still sat, Delly's face showed only genuine joy at seeing Libby. "How have you been Libby? Sorry I haven't come by to see you, I guess I usually just catch up with folks as I bump into them in the basin. But you haven't been by."

Libby looked cautious as she spoke. "I have been busy here. The library is a big job." She motioned to the stacks of books.

"Sure," Delly responded, "but it's nice to get out sometimes too?"

Libby pointed at the books, obviously in need of changing the subject. "I found a few passages I thought would really help you here." Delly took the cue and had a seat next to Lara in the chair she had carried over.

"Won't you sit with us too?" Lara asked.

Libby looked at Lara. It was the first time they had met eyes.

Lara felt a pull there, but also, her curiosity seemed to be pushing a bit. She felt a dizzying whoosh, the library around her blurring, and was suddenly standing high in the course, looking down from the center of the large boulder section, but she wasn't herself, she was Libby. The boulders moved beneath her, and she was comfortable with it, she had done this before. As she was preparing for the next jump, someone hit her from behind. Lara screamed out in Libby's voice as she spun down toward the ground. She felt the fear raw inside her and caught a glimpse of Dean on the boulder above, preparing for the next jump, not even watching as Libby hit the ground, a sharp crack sounding at impact. Lara pushed past the raw imagery and found herself in a more echoing version of reality. Instead of clear human images, she felt pushes of emotion, the honesty of held back anger, the clear intelligence, bright and open, the peace of acceptance of a new reality, the strength from the responsibility for the library. Lara pulled herself back through the haze to herself.

She had never been on the driving side of a soul gaze, and she found herself a bit dizzy from it. "I'm just going to sit here on the table, you can have my chair." Delly was saying, the sound of her voice echoing a bit as Lara shook herself back to the present.

Lara remembered being on the other side of the soul gazes and knew how exhausting it could be, so she forced herself to snap out of her own haze. "I'm so sorry. I didn't know I could do that, or rather, I didn't know it would just happen like that." She was speaking out of deep fear that she had crossed a line. She felt it was inappropriate, and unwarranted, and just plain wrong to have invaded Libby's mind. "It just…happened."

Delly was folding her legs criss-cross as she perched on the corner of the desk, but she looked up at Lara's words. She too had experienced the soul gaze in Azural and knew what it meant. Concern immediately showed on her face. Delly popped down off of the table and took Libby's hands in hers. Libby was seating herself in the chair that a moment before she had denied needing or wanting. The soul gaze winded people, and even though when Lara had been on the receiving end, she had never seen anything that the waterweaver hadn't wanted shared, she knew that it felt disconcerting.

"You okay? It passes quickly." Delly looked over to Lara with a bit of reproach, and Lara hated how she felt. Delly had confirmed her own regret at the situation. But then Delly saw Lara's face, which must have shown her absolute horror, and she reached out and took Lara's hand too.

Delly knelt on the floor, holding a hand of each of them. She talked slowly and much more quietly than her usual chipper tone. "Libby, you just experienced a soul gaze. It is one of the waterweavers abilities. Both Lara and I had to deal with them multiple times and they really just exhaust you for a moment. We all bounced back quickly. Just take a few breaths, and you will be back to yourself in no time." Delly was looking intently at Libby waiting to see if she was alright, but she gave a quick flick of her eyes to Lara.

Lara was amazed at Delly's ability to forgive and care for her so quickly, when she was still struggling with forgiving herself.

"Libby, I am so sorry." Lara slumped back in her chair beside Libby and waited quietly. But Lara had seen into Libby's soul and knew she would recover. She was a fighter, no matter that she kept it quietly to herself.

As Delly had said of their experience from Azural, both Lara and Libby recovered quickly. Lara gathered her thoughts and sat up straighter and turned her shoulders to face Libby, careful not to keep her gaze too long.

"I am so sorry. That was the first time it happened; I will be more careful in the future."

Delly's curiosity took the lead, "So what was it like on the waterweaver side? I always wondered what they were seeing when they looked in us."

"It was like I was in her memories. I felt her emotions, I saw what she saw. It was like a small window into her experience." As she said this, she felt worse again, "Libby, I am so sorry." The words felt empty to her.

Libby shook her head, "I've been through worse." She shrugged her shoulders and after a moment, picked up the book at the top of the pile.

Journal Entry

The three women sat quietly searching the books for the next thirty minutes, until Libby broke the silence. "Listen to this is a passage from Carlie's journal."

Delly had been on the floor, but jumped up from the ground next to Libby, "The Orange Founder? That's awesome. I bet there is some great information in there." She bounded back up onto the tabletop, folding her legs again, and rested her elbows on her knees. To Lara it didn't look comfortable at all, but Delly chose the position.

Libby opened to a page and pulled out a little slip of paper she had used to save the location. Lara saw that Carlie's handwriting was neat, but off beat in its style. The first letter of every sentence was large and in a different font. Libby began reading, and Lara sat back in her chair to listen.

"We had our first official Color Council meeting this morning. All seven of us, new and improved, sat at a table together and discussed what we should do. The magic is different in all of us. I can't speak for everyone else, but mine is seeming to power only the ground. I can move sand and rock. It's been a crazy exciting time. I already figured out how to pull the rock from the ground. I made the table we all sat at.

Most everyone else's powers are fairly obvious, except pink and purple. We are still figuring those out. The rest are based on elements. Water, ground, plants, light, fire.

It's been a bit hectic. Sometimes, the power takes a lot of concentration, but then other times, it just happens. Like at the beginning of our meeting, we were discussing what to call ourselves, and Artie had an idea, and he literally blinded us all for a few minutes. He said he didn't mean to, it just happened.

That type of stuff has been happening to all of us. Magic just popping off every which way."

Lara interrupted here, "This reminds me a lot of what we are going through with Fleck."

Delly nodded her head, "It's so crazy how young they all were. I mean, they were all at least five years younger than we are now." She said to Libby.

Libby nodded slowly, "I have thoughts on that for sure. But let me finish this entry.

We all decided that we needed to have names. We did decide to all be color weavers. That was a great start, but then, at first, we all tried to name each other, and that didn't go well. Blade got super mad when people recommended fireweaver to him. Let's just say he got really hot about it. He ended up choosing flamweaver. He said it sounded cooler.

I struggled a bit for mine. I also didn't want something basic. I wanted something exciting, rockweaver felt boring, earthweaver felt boring, stoneweaver was confusing, because we all had magic stones. Then, I figured it out! Terraweaver. It felt like a warm hug. It was just right.

So, after everyone had named their magic, we moved on to what to do next. Already, there has been a crazy rush from others around us, adults and youth, to find more of these magic stones. Since the magic only works for the one that has connected to it, people are desperate to get their own.

Axel says, and we all agree, that we should protect the magic as best we can. We are going to find the stones and keep them safe. To keep troublemakers and bad guys from getting the magic we are going to keep them in chambers and only allow folks who have passed trials proving themselves worthy to try to connect. I'm supposed to do my best to find all of the orange stones, and I am going to bring them to my hometown up North, Laran.

We decided on rules:

1. Find as many of the magic stones as we can before bad people can.

2.   Keep the stones safely in special chambers. (Everyone agreed that I got to design them!)

3.   Make trials that highlight the ideal magic user for the color stone.

(We did all agree that this should be decided individually. It is very obvious that my magic is not the same as Becca's, for example.)

I already have a great picture in my mind if I can pull it off. Flying stones, and boulders. A racecourse. It sounds so exciting!"

Libby finished the last sentence dripping with irony. The three women sat over the books for a moment in silence.

"They had no idea what they were doing." Lara said. She pictured the beautiful town square from her childhood and remembered the stories from her grandmother of it being even more lush and colorful from her own childhood. She closed her eyes and saw it for what it was now. The water flowed in Calambria, but the other stones were still missing — the land stripped of its beauty and life. All because a few kids had decided that was how it should be.

But she remembered Axel's words to her back in Azural. *You can undo what we have done.* The magic was still there, the stones were still there. The magic could be returned to the corners of the Chroma Realms.

"You brought water back to Calambria, maybe we can do that for everything?" Delly voiced quietly. The broken world weighed heavily on the three of them sitting in this tiny closed off corner of the library.

"But how do we even begin when we can't even get to the orange stones?" Lara said dejectedly.

Libby stood up, her right hip at a strange angle to support her weight on the injured foot. "We study, we research, and we learn." She took her cane in her hand, "I'll keep looking for more books. You two read through what we have here. The lessons we need to learn are here. I know it." And she slowly made her way down the corridor between the shelves of books.

Lara watched her for a minute and then looked at Delly and was a bit surprised by what she saw there. Delly was making doe eyes at the young woman as she walked away. Lara was old enough to recognize that look. Her little Delly was in love. Lara kept the information to herself, but instead said, "that was a powerful speech. What an inspiring young woman."

Delly seemed to shake off whatever she had been thinking and threw herself into the books. They both read for a while before Delly closed the book, she had been reading with a bit more energy than was necessary. The sound echoed loudly, and Lara snapped her head up.

"Why did that soul gaze have to happen?" Delly said, emotion raw on her face. "She has had enough happen to her; she doesn't need some stranger pushing into her mind."

Lara placed a loose paper in the book to hold her place and set it on the table. She looked her friend directly in the face. "I didn't mean to. Just like Carlie said, I am trying to figure all of these magics as I go. I didn't have enough time training with Axel before I left. I don't even know how to make the soul gaze happen; it just did." Lara looked down the stacks that Libby had walked down earlier. "Actually, there was a tug there, a tiniest hint of a pull, if it ever happens again, I am closing my eyes immediately." Lara did not want to experience one of those ever again.

Headaches & Trials

On the evening of her third week in Laran, Lara stood in the line of competitors for the trial. She had learned the names of most of the everyday locals. Many were like her, coming from other places to try, some had grown up in Laran, and tried everyday, while others just occasionally jumped in for the fun of it.

She was wearing the outfit of the regulars, tight fitting top and bottoms that wouldn't get caught up on the edges of stones and also held her chest tight and she had found it helped with her muscle's recovery. Her shoes were like slippers, that were tight to the foot too, but with a sticky sole made out of suede.

She was surrounded by friends, Skip at the front, and Delly behind her. The atmosphere was always humming with excitement. As they waited in line Delly showed her a trick she had learned years ago to boost confidence. How to stand with her feet spread apart, and her hands on her hips, chest thrust forward. Her elbows stuck out and although she was sure she looked strange, she felt strangely powerful. Like she could take on anything.

Today she knew she would make it past the second round of obstacles. The first with the tiny steppingstones was a breeze, and Lara had been learning the motions of the larger moving boulders for the last few weeks. She knew when to jump and where to place her hands. When it was better to wait for the motion to be heading toward her or away. She was confident today. She was going to do well.

As she reached the front of the line, she waited a moment to allow Skip to get to the end of the steppingstones. Lara preferred to run them quickly, a light step on each stone, allowing the speed to take her along the path.

When she reached the larger boulders, she got to work. Jumping from boulder to boulder, waiting for the right moment.

Lara landed on the large boulder easily. She looked behind her at the course she had completed. The boulders slowly zigging and zagging and swirly on their preset courses. Why did it look so very different now? Likely because she had spent the last weeks studying it from the other side.

She stood up and slowly turned to face forward. She wasn't done. This was just the second section. She had heard about a lot of people getting this far and then after a few weeks giving up and heading home. Would she be able to figure it out?

She was finally close enough to get a good look at the next section of obstacles. Ahead in the distance there was a block larger than all of these floating and moving boulders. It was stationary and wide. And it looked a lot like the wall in her nightmares.

She studied the block, which instead of being a jump ahead as the current section was, this was above her. Like a step up into the air, giant steps that led up so high she couldn't see the ends. There must be at least twenty of them. A stairway into the sky, but for a giant.

She knew she couldn't make it to the top of even that first step. There was no way that a single person could jump that high. It was at least nine feet, and the wall of rock was smooth. She studied it for what felt like hours, looking for any fault in the smooth surface. She couldn't find any. This was what had been plaguing her in her dreams. And she realized it had been plaguing Fleck too; he had seen this before she had. His premonition abilities were just one more annoying mystery.

Finally, she sat down and closed her eyes. This wall was just another problem, and she knew that the first step in finding a solution was to clarify the problem. So, how does one jump up a nine-foot wall with no purchase? How did little Kit do it?

Maybe she could bring a tool along with her and dig holes into the rock? She needed to get a closer look. Jumping back up, Lara prepared to jump over to the next stone, trying to bring herself back to what was in front of her. It was large and flat, and wasn't moving, but the one she was on was moving and the gap between these boulders was the biggest she had seen.

With her mind half on her future plans for the large stone steps ahead, she prepared to jump. There was going to be a perfect moment in 3, 2, 1… and just as she started to leap her vision turned a startling, brilliant, sparkling red. Fleck had done it again.

She heard screams from Skip who had been behind her on the path, and then everything was black.

Lara couldn't remember falling, all she knew was the intense pain when she woke up on the ground. As always, her head was splitting, but there was more pain. Her right arm was scraped with a deep cut, Lara could only assume it was from the missed attempt to grab at the large boulder in front of her, now looking almost like the size of an orange in the air. Her right leg must be broken, she slowly began to sit up, but Liv was there holding her down with kindness and sadness in her eyes.

"No, Lara." Liv said. "Sit still. We have the medic on the way."

Lara's head was clearing, and she started again to feel Fleck's emotions meld with hers. He was worried, and he was coming. A moment later, he shot through the knees of the crowd of watching people and nuzzled her neck with his nose. Lara knew he was upset that she was hurt, and that he understood it was his fault, but she also knew that he did not know how to stop the magic or control it. Neither of them did. It was why they were here in Laran, after all. She needed to remember their overall goals here. She needed this stone to get to Soren and Exu.

As she sat up slowly, pushing up with her right arm, because her left was throbbing too much, she got her first glimpse of the leg. The gore of it broke her heart. There was no way she would ever get up to the stones now. This was the kind of injury no one would ever fully come back from. She turned to look at Fleck. His eyes were round and watery, the light grey taking on the burnt orange of the sunset.

What are we going to do now?

Fleck came up close. He placed both front paws on her cheeks and Lara leaned her head down so that he could push his forehead lightly against hers. This was always comforting to her, but right now, she just broke, and began to cry.

Fleck let loose of her and went to look at her leg. She couldn't bring herself to look again, the image of the awkward, unrealistic angle from her knee still blazoned across her mind. She closed her eyes to welcomed blackness, but suddenly everything was bright pink, and she was in darkness again. She escaped into the darkness with happiness.

When she awoke for the second time, she didn't really want to open her eyes at all. Until she realized the only pain she was feeling was the now, well accustomed headache.

Opening her eyes, she sat up stunned, staring, as the crowd around her was, at the fully healed leg. Fleck calmly back on his haunches, studying his work. He turned to her and tipped is head quizzically.

She felt his question.

Yes, much better! What did you do?

These mysteries needed to be solved.

Rules

The next morning at breakfast Lara shared some concerns with Delly and 'the boys' as she had begun to call them. After Fleck's very public show of healing Lara's leg last night everyone in town was buzzing about it.

Frank, the oldest of the boys, and honestly, a full-grown man probably only 15 years younger than Lara, leaned forward, his strong hands laid out flat on the tabletop, "This sounds like it is very dangerous for you Lara. I hadn't realized," here he looked around at the rest of the family, and they all seemed to nod in agreement. "We hadn't realized how serious it was that you get to the Canyon and see Soren."

Lara tried to laugh it off, as if it was no big deal, but the laugh caught in her throat. "Actually, the truth is, I never would have left home again if it hadn't been important."

Around the table the boys all sent out grunts of agreement. They all appreciated family, and Lara was so grateful that she had them to lean on when her own was so far away. Delly, however, was seated right next to her and jumped out of her seat and hugged Lara where she sat. Of course it was completely awkward, with Lara still holding her fork, and pushed in close to the table, but Lara leaned her head on Delly's shoulder and soaked in the intent of the hug.

Delly, after a few breaths, stood and looked around the table. "What can we do?"

All of the boys seemed to look as one to Frank. He was the oldest. Granny Mae was at the market, so they all turned to him. He just raised his shoulders in question himself. "None of us have completed the Trials, and mom never talked about it…" his voice faded off at the end, and Lara was glad Ida Mae had shared, so she understood not to press the issue.

Instead, she said, "Sometimes problems are so very large that they overwhelm you. And in my experience, the best thing to focus on is the next step in front of you. So, let's just look at the next step, and ironically it is a big stone one. I have been worrying over the third phase of the course. Last night, right before I fell, I saw the third phase of the course for the first time with my own eyes - the large stone steps. I just don't understand how anyone, let alone someone Kit's size, could have ever made it."

She looked up at the family, and although they were often a rowdy bunch, talking over each other and going in different directions, right now they all were invested in what she was saying. They all were here for her. And as she looked across the table, and saw Fleck curled up happily in Frank's lap, they were here for her little friend too. Sometimes, if others can't help by bringing you the answers, they can help by listening and telling you if your answers make any sense. Voicing thoughts often helped one clarify them.

"Well, I had a few thoughts. I wondered about bringing some sort of tools?" She let that drift off waiting to see any reaction from the group. Was this against some unwritten rule? Taking stock of their nonplussed reaction, she continued. "I wondered about maybe taking something to dig small hand holds into the rock and climbing."

Frank sat back in his chair, folding his arms over his chest. "Not a terrible idea, but that is a lot of steps, and you would have to dig holes large enough to use for footholds too. Not to mention carrying the tools with you through the first jumps." He looked around the table, then said calmly, "any other ideas?"

"To be honest, I have even considered waterweaving, but I worried that might feel like cheating, and even if it wasn't I don't think there is enough water here for me to accomplish that much." Thinking out loud, she continued, "but maybe I could bring enough water to use to make the holes in the rock? But I just feel like that would go against my blue honesty tenet."

Delly reached out and pushed Lara's shoulder with her fist. "Lara, how many times do I have to tell you. There are no rules. Like literally, we are the opposite of Azural around here. Maybe waterweaving would help?"

"Well, I think going to the library helps. I have got to try to figure out some options."

Delly's face lit up, and said, "I'll go with you, maybe we can figure this out together." Lara laughed warmly knowing Delly had ulterior motives, having to do nothing with books, and a lot to do with a certain librarian.

As one, the boys stood, as if they all understood that the next step had been addressed, and it was time to get to work. The table was clear before Lara could even push her chair back.

Breakthrough

When Lara walked through the library door, she hadn't expected the force of guilt that hit her when she saw Libby. Immediately, she was reminded of her fully healed leg thanks to Fleck and the unfairness of their situations. Why had she been allowed to get back up, when this amazing young woman was dealing with her injury years after it had happened.

"Hey Libby," Delly chirped happily next to Lara. "Do you have some time to join us, while we do our research?"

"I don't want to get in your way." Libby said in her honey whisper.

Lara felt her cheeks tighten in a smile she couldn't hold back. "Libby, you are one hundred percent helpful. Delly and I just fumble along, there is no way you could be in our way."

"I'll head back after I shelf these books here."

"Great!" Delly cringed at the echo of her voice through the stacks, "Sorry." She mouthed with no sound coming out at all.

At the table Lara found a new small book on top of the pile. The title was simply 'Pelanor.' Libby must have heard about Fleck. It looked to be a memoir style journal from a local Laran elder.

There were a few tabs marking passages:

"The great debate of my childhood had been if Pelanor were real or just fairy stories. There had been many who had claimed to see the dragon fly over Laran, but the few who told these tales were laughed at. It wasn't until our own Terraweaver, Soren, returned from a trip in the Canyon with Exuberance, that the answer was clear. Pelanor were real.

But how can these legends of fairy tales, be here in the present? How can we meld the stories with the truth?"

Lara looked up to chat with Delly, but she was ensconced in another book, so she decided to read on. The second marked passage:

"Soren named his dragon Exuberance, but this dragon had obviously been named long before he had met Soren. He was indeed the dragon of memory from our ancestors' stories. He stood tall over the people of Laran, his soft exterior, and flowing fur did not hide his sharp teeth and claws."

A few pages later:

"The dragon shows the ability to use our orange ground magic, but also the magics of the other color realms. Soren has shared little of what the dragon has communicated with him. The council is frustrated by our lack of understanding, but they are too proud to push him on it. The stories from childhood tell us the Pelanor are magical wish dragons who can solve our problems and watch over us. We have seen this from Exu. Stories have emerged about the color magics being used in town, a flash of light to guide a family down a back alley late one night, a fire started in a hearth with no kindling, a rainstorm over just one back yard garden that was wilting. The dragon has magic. Magic that echoes the fairy tales of old."

Lara so wanted to understand what had happened. She wished she could have been present with those who walked up to the basin and saw the large dragon. There was only one more passage marked:

"Many of those traveling to Laran for the fair and festivities pulled back in fear, and there was a shift in the mood in the basin nights when Exu was present. I fear that Soren will choose to leave, it is too much, even for one so social as him."

Lara took a moment to look at the pages that hadn't been tabbed and saw that they were rambling without much helpful focus, and she appreciated Libby's effort in picking out what was useful.

She really needed to get to Soren. She was sure he would have the answers she needed.

Delly looked up with a grin on her face. "Look what I found." She began to read aloud.

"Orange has its own unique characteristics. The realm is energetic and adventurous. The people here are confident, courageous, and spontaneous. They are social and inviting to all other color realms. There is an air of encouragement and support for those around them. They work together in a community of extroverted, artistic folk." Delly smiled, "I like the sounds of that. Much better than what we experienced in Azural huh?"

Lara nodded. "They were so closed off and unwilling to accept those unlike them. I think one of my favorite parts of Laran is seeing all the colors walk into the basin. It is wonderful to see all of the different realms welcomed."

"It's not all pumpkins and poppies here though" Lara jumped as Libby came up behind her. "Orange has as many downsides and difficulties as Blue. Terraweavers are known to be superficial and insincere. They are risk-takers and," here she paused and gave Delly a caring but knowing look, "they can be arrogant and prideful. And finally, what we see around here most often is they are exhibitionists, as the evening basin shows us every night."

Lara was speechless for a minute as she took in what Libby had shared. In a few sentences, Libby had turned Lara's thinking on its head. The problems weren't just in Azural and Calambria, there were problems everywhere.

They all sat quietly for a few minutes lost in their own thoughts, until Delly spoke softly. "Mom struggled a lot with this stuff. She was so wrapped up in the risk-taking and the arrogance, for sure, but she also craved new things. She was so antsy. I think that probably plays into it too." She looked up at the two of them, still speaking more quietly than her usual boisterous self. As if she were telling a secret she had held and was still unsure she wanted out there. "All those years when I was little traveling to different realms, the first thing she would do is announce herself as a Terraweaver and put on her shows. Don't get me wrong, the people were sincere in their excitement at seeing the orange magic, but it wore off, and she needed more. So off we went, back to the Wheel & Spokes. As the three of us with her got older, it started embarrassing us. We saw the need in her for adoration, and we started complaining about leaving friends we made along the way. That was when she brought us back."

Lara reached out and rested her hand on Delly's elbow. What could she say to salve the raw pain on her friend's face? "Oh, Delly. I know it hurts, but you do have a wonderful family here. I am glad you have your brothers and grandparents."

"The thing is," Delly was starting to get a bit louder again, "I was so angry with her when she dropped us off and left. All I wanted was to be here with her. To have my home and have her. But she left. I jumped into the trials with way too much of my energy. It was ridiculous that I even thought I would be able to connect with a stone in that state."

Libby spoke, and her soft tone alone was soothing in its warmth. "Delly. You were so young. I ran a few of those earlier trials with you, and both of us were doing it for the wrong reasons. The energy in the basin can be chaotic and a maddening, driving force for those who cannot harness it."

"I was so hungry for a solution to how I was feeling. And when I realized that I might never be the terraweaver my mom was, I started thinking about what could help me. It was why I went to Azural. Lara and I can attest that Blue is a salve for all of those negatives. I came back from Azural with a lot of skills to even out all of the hectic orange energy we get bombarded with here. We know the world is broken; Lara's hometown is evidence enough of that. All of the realms seem to be so extreme. So hyper focused on such a small piece of their personality."

Lara nodded, "Blue and Orange do balance each other a bit."

Delly shook out her shoulders as if to put her emotions behind her. "I think my favorite orange emotion is confidence. I think if you balance out the calm of blue with the confidence of orange, you might be able to do anything Lara. Even stonegraft orange and solve your problem with Fleck's magic."

Lara looked up at Libby, "Thank you for the Pelanor book. I have so much to figure out when it comes to Fleck. I," she paused, unsure of how to go forward. She knew she should say something, but didn't know the words. They tumbled out anyway, raw, "I, wish Fleck could have been there the night you fell." The soul gaze had given Lara a real perspective on what had happened to Libby, and even with all of that insight, she didn't know how to address this. But she knew that saying nothing would be worse.

Libby looked at her giving the slightest nod. Lara felt a weight off her shoulders that she hadn't realized she was carrying.

Unaware of what was transpiring between the two, Delly continued on their previous line of thought, "The information here is helpful, but what we need is to focus on our big question." She looked up at Libby, "You should come watch us tonight! We have gotten pretty good. I think we will all three get to the stone steps soon.

Libby shook her head. "I don't go to the trials."

"Why not?" Delly asked, but Lara knew. If others felt the way Lara initially had, focused too much on the injury, rather than the person, she would get a lot of attention, that she probably didn't want.

Libby was looking into Delly's eyes and there was a light there, that Lara had always seen. Delly was one of the most genuine souls she had met. There was a light in her that didn't see Libby as the injured librarian. And it was clear that Libby realized it too. "Oh, Delly." Libby laughed lightly and pressed her hand to Delly's leg that was perched in front of her on the desk. "Who knows, maybe I will have to come see you on the course for myself."

"Yes, you will." Delly stated with finality. "Wonderful, we have all sorts of information here, but what we need is how to get to the oculus in the sky."

Libby laughed. She laughed loudly. Delly and Lara looked between her and each other in shock. It seemed that once she had started, she could not hold back. It was the kind of laughter that is infectious, joyful and free. Delly and Lara found themselves laughing as Libby gasped in breaths between her laughs, and just as they all began to slow, Lara gulped in a jagged breath that made her snort and the peels of laughter from all of them continued. Delly gave Lara a look that questioned why they were laughing, and Lara shrugged her shoulders unable to speak a word. Her shoulders shook and it made her laugh harder.

After a good long time, the laughs seemed to turn to giggles, and finally the three women were sighing loud sighs with an occasional titter until they had finally silenced.

Delly was the first to get herself together, "What was that all about?"

Libby looked back and forth between the two of them with a sparkle in her eye. "I know how to get you to the top."

Workout Chat

"Learn anything useful?" Skip asked as he took a rest between his rounds of twenty light lifts. As he started back with the kettle weight, lifting it steadily up and back down, Lara took note of his athletic position. The bent knees and position of the back were something she would never have paid attention to months ago, but now, she was keenly aware of the importance of it.

"I actually did!" Lara was also lifting, so their conversation timed itself between the rounds. They had been training together long enough that their comfort with the conversation lulls felt natural. "I was focused on two main questions. What the Orange tenets are, you know the Blue tenets helped me so much when I was in the stonegrafting chamber. I really focused on what the emotions behind the magic were, and how they were represented and important to me." Her interest in what she was thinking over from her reading made her set the weight down after her count of twenty.

She walked over so she could focus on the conversation a bit more. Skip was still lifting, so she paused as he finished his count. When he set the round weight down, she continued. "And the second thing was learning about the history of past stonegrafters. I didn't really clarify why it was interesting, but maybe we can discuss that. However, I got a ton of answers to what emotions are behind orange." She was feeling the emotions take over as her excitement to share peaked. "Come on, let's get a drink of water, and I will tell you."

They walked over to sit on the edge of the stone wall. After a deep drink of water, Lara jumped in. "In Azural, the Great Stone House had five clear tenets that were their road-map and a basis for the whole society there. Everything was separated into clear classes on each trait. We had classes in Order, which just basically went over the rules, classes in Calm, which taught us to meditate. All of the realm was built around the tenets, and their government was a mirror to that." Feeling her anger rise, she took a breath, "Actually, it was a bit of an extreme of the Rules and Order tenet mostly."

Skip had heard enough of her stories, that he understood, and she knew it was not healthy for her to get stuck on it. "Here, I was expecting to find the same focus on the tenets of Orange. What were the rules and expectations, but there was nothing. I didn't see any signs, there's no classes. Heck, you don't even have to sign up for the trials, let alone take classes. So, the question I needed answered was, what makes the orange stone tick? What is the energy that is being infused into Laran and the people here? The magic is fairly clear, right? The terraweavers can control these rocks and pull them and move them. But the power to do that comes from the emotion they use as they are harnessing the magic. What emotions?"

"And you found your answer?"

"I think so. Well, Libby found the answer. It isn't as cut and dry as Azural, but it is starting to be clear to me. And spending time here really helped me see it as I was reading about it too. Orange is a blend of the raw, stimulating energy of red and the light, happy energy of yellow. Orange energy comes out as excitement and enthusiasm. The people here are welcoming and believe in community and are quite extroverted. There is a level of confidence, courage and a positive outlook at life. Some clear examples are from when folks throw themselves into the trial, they use instinct, courage, and determination. And also, here in Laran, there is a belief in the freedom of choice, that is such a stark contrast to what I was dealing with in Blue."

"So, I feel much more confident in the emotions that are needed to stonegraft, and I see why the trial is the way it is. All of the emotions are heightened and necessary to attempt and complete the trials and make it up to the top. But the really interesting information Libby shared, is from the history of folks actually stonegrafting orange." She leaned forward like she had a secret. "They often have two people stonegraft on the same day!"

Skip looked up. "Really?"

"Yes, it looks like a lot of the times they add a terraweaver to the list it is two, or three even on the same day. Not all of the time, but I think this is a clue." Lara paused because she saw Skip's mind moving quickly, trying to process the information. She gave him a moment, then sped his thinking along. "I think they are using the Orange emotion of community and teamwork to work together to get up the big steps!"

There was a glint in Skip's eyes, "A team…"

Teamwork

Lara and Skip had decided immediately to come up with a plan for how working together might help them.

"I keep thinking about little Kit and how she might have helped Liv." Lara moved a step closer in the line to the start of the course, head bowed and speaking in hushed tones so that only Skip heard. "She couldn't have pushed her up, but maybe Liv stood on her back or shoulders for a boost up?"

"And Liv then reached down and pulled Kit up?" Skip wondered aloud.

They had decided that it was definitely the answer. The stone steps were much too tall to get up without a boost of some kind. But coming up with a plan on the ground was one thing. Lara was certain, that they wouldn't have answers until they were there sitting at the base together, which was easier said than done.

First, they had to get all three of them to the base, and Lara had only made it that far the one time. Skip said he generally was making it to the base about every other attempt lately. Second, they had to be next to each other in line, so that if they all reached the base they would get there together.

So, with Skip in front of her and Delly behind, they shuffled toward the start.

Fleck usually ran around on the ground in the crowds when Lara ran the obstacle, but today, he was right by her side. She was surprised to notice he had grown. The tips of his ears brushed against her thigh. She tried to remember the last time he had been on her shoulders. It had been a week or so. He was getting too big. She had a moment of sadness at how quickly children grow. Then she pictured her four children grown with an image of grown Fleck towering over them. It was a powerful feeling; she had trouble describing.

Fleck pushed against her thought, a reminder to stay in the moment. They were at the front of the line, and she watched as Skip leapt from steppingstone to stone. She waited until he was almost halfway through so that she could move with her favored speed. She lightly tapped a foot on each stone, and laughed at how simple it was. As she pushed off the final steppingstone, she felt a thrill at how far she had come.

The crowd below had become silent, and Lara felt a strange sense that something was happening. She looked behind her to see everyone staring and pointing as Fleck leapt onto the first steppingstone. His fur flowed sleekly against him as he sped along the stones. He looked like the wind he was so quick and before she could think about more than how beautiful he was, he was beside her. His joy and exuberance were contagious, and she heard the crowd below roar in appreciation for her little friend. Delly was just behind Fleck and the four of them stood on the first large stone of the second section of the course.

"You coming along?" She said aloud for Skip and Delly's sake.

He sent her an image of the two of them in the basin of the deep canyon walking toward a large Pelanor in the distance. "Ok, Fleck feels confident in us. Let's get this done."

So much had happened since yesterday's fall that she had almost forgotten the fear, until it hit her suddenly facing the large moving stones again. The start of the second section of the obstacle course was much closer to the ground, so the fall would not be as painful, but it was in the back of her head the whole time she worked across the jumps, especially when she had to wait a long time for the timing to be just right.

Ahead of her she saw Skip working his way, leaping when the timing was right. His body was slim, but his work with the weights gave him a lot of control over his muscles. He was able to tense up and stop or flow with the motion of the new stone. Lara tried her best to mimic the motions he used, but she had been at training for a much smaller time, and her body shouted at her when she pulled up tight too quickly.

When she reached the rounded top of a particularly large boulder, she splayed out her arms and legs and just laid there to catch her breath and center her emotions. The fear was getting stronger as each stone brought her higher into the air, and also closer to where she had fallen. Fleck perched on the base of her back, and she could feel his excitement. *Glad you came along this time, aren't you. See all the fun you've been missing?*

His agreement came through as a wave of sheer joy at the view he saw from up here. She had not spent any time looking outward in her many passes, so her first view of the landscape came through his eyes. His shared views were always a bit like a dream, the edges hazier the further from his focus. She sat up, Fleck jumping off of her before having to say anything. They were so synced. Instead of studying the next boulder in her path, or looking down at the ground, she looked out around them. They were high enough to see past the buildings and walls of Laran.

Her first pull was to look toward home, but Calambria was much too far, and the twilight made the distance blur. She could just make out a darkness of what she believed to be the mountains in the distance. Turning her head to the left she looked toward where Azural was. She could make out the Wheel Road still, wagons and groups walking, but the lighting made it difficult to see past the tangled tall trees in the center of Chroma. She looked directly to her left where she could see the fields of wheat that stood outside Amara. The yellow realm was so close, that would mean that Pete was so close. He had been there for under a year, but so much had happened to her, she wondered what had changed for him in that time. She knew now, how much the world could introduce to you. She still felt like the same Lara, but also so much more.

The Yellow Spoke Road broke from the Wheel Road leading through the fields to a large building that shined yellow against the setting sun, catching the light in an almost magical way. The building was simple to see because the light surrounding it highlighted it in the darkening evening. Pillars that looked to be taller than the walls of Laran held up an open palisade. She could imagine Pete walking up those wide marble steps.

Shaking her head, she turned to look behind her. The view caught her breath. The canyon stood laid out before them. Fleck had already been looking for that way, and now they studied it together. It was a long way, but Lara could just make out a speck in the sky. A flying speck of white, that moved along the edge of the far side of the cavern. Fleck perked up and leaned against Lara, bouncing, he was so excited that Lara had to hold onto him for fear he might slip off the rounded top. *Well, it's a long way, but we know how this works. Let's focus on our next step.* Fleck sent her an image of Kit's stone shining at her knee.

"Yes, but first, just this next boulder." Lara laughed and got ready to jump.

Stone Stairs

It took them four days to actually all make it to the large steps of the third stage. The first time, Lara had fallen again in the same spot, fear taking her over from her memories, but she controlled the fall this time, since she was conscious and only had some bad bruises from it. Delly also fell quite a few times, it had been years since she had taken the course seriously, and she had needed a few days to get back into the swing of things.

Ironically, Skip had made it every time until the first night both Lara and Delly had made it. He was behind them, and when he was close and saw they both had made it he jumped up and down cheering, forgetting that the boulder beneath him was still moving along its designated course. They all laughed about it that evening but were fired up at how much better they were doing.

And so, finally with the setting sun glinting behind them, all four stood at the base of the tall stone staircase. They had a clear plan. They would take turns being the base, the middle and the top. Fleck could scamper up them when they had their human ladder built. That way none of them would get too tired from pulling others up or holding others on their backs. Lara was the first base. She made herself into a table and Delly climbed up to stand on her back, wobbly at first. It took her some time to figure out where to place her feet on Lara's back and then once she was able to still, Skip climbed up. The weight of the two young people was almost too much, but Lara was determined. She held firm, tightening her arms and legs and back. Just when she wasn't sure she could take it, and her arms started shaking and feeling weak, the weight lifted as Skip boosted himself up onto the top of the next step. He immediately reached down and took Delly's hands and the weight on her back was halved.

After Lara felt the weight leave her completely, she stood. Looking up she laughed; there she saw three faces peeking over the ledge. All three grinning. The angle was hilarious to her, and she broke out laughing. Fleck's grin looked much more ferocious from this angle because his rows of tiny sharp teeth were in full view.

"Well, don't just leave me here." She laughed. Delly leaned over as far as she could, and they found that the height allowed her to just brush Lara's fingertips. If Skip and Delly leaned over and Lara jumped just right, they could each grab an arm, and Lara could walk up the side of the wall. It took them a long time to get it right, but they all stood on the next plateau pleased as punch. Until they looked above them and realized they had to do it again. They actually were going to have to do it 9 more times.

The next time was Delly's turn on the bottom and Skip as the middle standing on her back. Lara scrambled up and as she was pulling her knee onto the top of the next level, she felt Fleck's sharp claws clip into the material at her neck. "Can't you just pop up there?" Then she realized her mistake. He sent her an image of her lying at the bottom of the course. His memory of the incident made it obvious he had as much scarring from the experience as she did. He was doing his best not to use any magic.

The three of them worked together and got to the fourth stair and suddenly the course was shutting down around them. They had taken too long, but they had gotten so far.

Delly just stood dusting off her hands as the stairs lowered into the ground. "Next time we will be a lot faster at our human ladder."

Stonegrafting

The final stair didn't look any different looking down, but when you looked up the endless wall of stone above was gone and instead from this angle all Lara could see was the darkening sky.

It was Lara's turn to be the middle, and she scrabbled onto Delly's back, settling her feet, one at Delly's hips and one at her shoulders. She bent her knees in an athletic position but kept her back leaned straight against the wall behind her.

"Ooh, the stone is getting cold. I think we better hurry, we are so close, but it is getting late."

Skip started the climb up their human ladder. They had learned through mistakes that it was best to use specific footholds to get up. Stepping onto Delly's back, he grabbed ahold of Lara's arm holds, which she had akimbo holding on to her hip, like the confidence-boosting stance Delly had taught her in line. "I don't want to get ahead of ourselves, but I think we've got this!" He said, stepping up onto Lara's knees. The trickiest part was always getting from the knees to the shoulders, and they had all been in very embarrassing positions over the last few weeks, but now they were adept enough that Lara knew when to turn her head, and when to push to give him the extra boost. She also knew to settle down to absorb some of the pressure when he first stood on her shoulders.

The final bit was for Skip to jump off of her shoulders to scrabble up onto the top of the next step. Lara repositioned her palms under his feet. As the climber it was his job to count down. "Three," they all tensed up, "two," they all coiled up their energy, "one!" All three of them pushed upwards. Delly just a bit, because the weight of them only allowed her a bit of motion. Lara a bit more, taking the bit of energy Delly sent her way and pushing against Skip's feet as he pushed off against her hands.

"Yes!" He screamed. Lara turned on Delly's back and leapt up to grab his outstretched hands. She hung there for a moment while Delly stood and then tensed up her body to make it simpler for Delly to push her upwards. Once she was high enough, she scrabbled herself over onto the dais. She fought the urge to turn and look at their goal of the oculus right behind her, instead focusing on getting Delly up first. They reached down and caught Delly's arms, pulling her up. Fleck was hanging onto Delly's feet and as they pulled back, all four of them rolled onto the ground at the top of the stairs, cheering in their exhaustion.

"Ha! Take that stupid stairs," Delly laughed through her ragged breath.

Fleck darted off behind her and Lara turned to see as he headed into a doorway of the familiar but new domed structure.

Lara jumped up and grabbed Delly and Skip's hands, pulling them up. "We better hurry!"

And so, with the last rays of the setting sun, blazing the evening sky a deep burnt orange, with Delly skipping along beside her and Skip chasing at Fleck's tail they ran into a room that Lara had seen before. She might as well have been in the oculus room in Azural, aside from the lack of water around the exterior, instead the room was surrounded by a circle of gravel. And the most obvious difference, the stone pedestal in the center of the room, sitting under the oculus, was topped with orange stones.

The three of them were still pumped with endorphins from the crazy success and energy it had taken to get to the top, and for a moment they stood silently around it. Then the energy still pumping through them, they couldn't keep quiet, they all started laughing. Skip let out a "whoop!" And Delly grabbing their hands, they all spun around, Lara feeling like she was six years old again in the meadow with Jada back home.

They all stopped suddenly as sparks started flying off the pile of stones. The orange magic rippling upwards and outwards. Tiny tendrils of power floating out from the pile, surrounding them. They dropped each others' hands and turned in their own little circles, watching the wisps circle around the room. Lara caught Delly's face in a moment and imagined her own mirroring the awe shown there. The tendrils became thicker and more pronounced, almost as if reaching out one might be able to touch and grab ahold of them. A larger one swooped around by her feet and Lara found herself jumping over it.

And then there was a stone flying up into the air above the pedestal, Lara watched with light in her eyes as it reached out and sped toward Delly's thigh. There was a bright blinding light, causing Lara to close her eyes to protect them, and when she opened them, she saw the stone fused in Delly's leg and watched as the orange magic tattooed its way along her leg up, down and around.

Another stone jumped into the air, and she saw it flash toward Skip. Again, the magic spread across his leg, in a similar pattern. Tiny pebbles that continued outward until there were full sized boulders, in the bright orange of the stone.

Delly was already over by the gravel, pulling it up into the air playfully. Skip ran over and joined her. Lara was so happy. She turned back toward the pedestal, and while the magic still swirled around, no stone was jumping for her yet.

Suddenly, the ground beneath them began to move downwards.

"Oh no!" Delly screamed, looking at Lara in alarm. "No, not yet!"

"Not much time left." Lara said. She stared at the stones. She felt the burden of time and her need crush at her, and she saw the embers of magic slowly start dissipating. Her joy when she walked into the room, slowly seeping out of her.

Skip stood tall, and looked twice his age when he yelled out, "No way. Not if I can help it! Come on Delly." And without another word they were out of the room. Lara didn't know what they were planning, but suddenly, she felt the downward motion of the large room halt. They were using their new stone casting to hold the oculus up. Giving her time.

Her heart was overrun by heartfelt joy. She looked at Fleck beside her and marveled at the community they had built here. She had made fast friends, and they had made it this far. Fleck pushed a pounding, thrumming beat into her mind, and she let her body spin to the Tamba beat. As she picked up speed, intentionally letting go of the reservations she had been holding. She might not be young, but she was still able to be exuberant; she might not be as nimble as her young friends, but she was still determined; she had shown herself a good friend, and part of this community; and she had shown herself, that she could be courageous. She stopped her spinning and turned toward the stone with renewed confidence and determination. The stone jumped toward her.

She was overcome with energy as it fused with her leg. Rather than take her time and watch the tattoo spread, she rushed out to her friends as they stood on the edge of the floating island and embraced them. They had almost reached the ground level and Lara squealed with the delight of a child as they all rolled off the island before it was swallowed up into the ground until tomorrow's trial.

Celebrations

As the three of them stood and dusted themselves off, the community was already in motion. Delly's brothers surrounded her in a tight mob, and Skip was in a tight hug with a woman who was obviously his mother. Lara stood off to the side with Fleck, as family and friends surrounded Delly and Skip. After Delly's brothers gave her space, Ida Mae and Libby came forward to speak with Delly.

Lara's heart swelled seeing Libby there. Sometimes bravery wasn't about jumping onto the highest stone, sometimes it was internal. Lara wondered what the stones might say of Libby's courage to come back and face the basin. The trials might show some of the tenets of the stones but looking past Skip to the far side of the basin, Lara saw Dean standing with his father. Just because you made it through the trials didn't automatically get you the stone. The trial system was broken.

Skip and Delly continued to be inundated with hugs and congratulations from the people of Laran. They had lived here their whole lives and her heart blossomed seeing the love their community had for them, but it wasn't for long that she watched before Ida Mae hobbled over and embraced her. "Congratulations to you too. Why aren't you out there with them?"

Lara smiled at the older woman, "Give the kids their moment. I'm not really part of this community."

Ida Mae pushed Lara in the shoulder. It was so solid that Lara stumbled to the side. "That's nonsense and you know it. Community is made through the relationships you build with those around you. I would say, you have become an integral part of ours."

Lara's eyes teared up a bit. Ida Mae was right. Almost all of these people had been strangers to her a few months ago, and now she knew most of them by name, and many of them she called friends. "Thank you, my friend. It always helps to hear wisdom that we know in our hearts out loud from a friend." They both watched as the final burnt rays of sunshine disappeared from the sky. As the sun set, Lara ventured to ask Ida Mae, "Are you worried about Delly?"

Ida smiled, and it had an interesting effect of making her look both older, as her wrinkles creased, while also making her look younger as her eyes lit up. "I think Delly has something that Tanya was always searching for, so I think she will be alright."

Lara was a bit surprised. What had changed Ida's mind? She ventured, "What's that Ida Mae?"

"Tanya was always searching for stability and balance. The terraweavers are all about stone, ground, earth. That should give stability and a strong base. But what Tanya never understood, and Delly did long before she stonegrafted, is that you have to look outside yourself for those things too. Delly has her brothers, she has her friends, she has mentors like you," Ida reached out and squeezed Lara's elbow, and Lara was again reminded of the strength of this woman. "But more than anything, she knows when to turn to those supporting her for help, and she doesn't feel less when she does. She learned from her mother's mistakes."

Lara was about to respond when Ida stepped behind her and pushed her to the center of the celebratory mob. The people of Laran welcomed all, and she was one of them now. It was dark, but no one was walking home. Lara had never seen what happened when there was success at the trials, but she noticed the coordination of those around them.

More torches were brought and lit, the drummers arrived with smiles and shouts and before she could even catch her breath, she heard "Tamba!" Followed quickly by "Bally!" and "Ho!" And the frenetic experience surrounded her. The power of the beat filled her, and she found herself in one moment swirling around with little Kit and then hugging Delly, then laughing with Liv and then, just jumping with joy with Skip. She was filled with exuberance as the music swelled, she saw the crowd step back, leaving the three of them in the center. She realized what this was. It was a rite of passage into the terraweaver group. All three of them glowed orange from the emotions running through them.

Lara focused on her newfound power, following a similar path as with her water magic. She closed her eyes and felt for the emotions of orange. The excitement and community of this moment had her orange power at the ready. The stone in her thigh felt warm and ready, reaching through her calf toward the solid ground. There was a firmness to the power that was very different from her waterweaving. She reached toward the ground that the orange stone called to and raised it below her feet. Feeling herself move upward, she opened her eyes and saw she stood on a circle of stone about three feet higher than before. She tested the control she had and moved back down and spun around pulling tiny gravel pieces around her into the air. She played, testing different sizes and weights of rock. This wasn't about putting on a show, this was about the sheer amazement of learning a new ability.

Fleck moved through the group having as much fun as the rest of them. He pounced on pebbles that Lara had sent in a shower around them as they fell to the ground. He jumped in the air to bump rocks back toward Delly as she tested her distance. He spun in the tiny dust cyclone that Skip created. And the crowd loved every second of it.

Lara stepped aside and Fleck joined her, sitting next to her feet. He was just the height that he could look directly at her orange stone as he sat there. From her angle looking down at him, his eyes reflected the orange of the stone, and with the orange dust layer covering him, he looked almost as if he were some orange dragon rather than a Pelanor.

He lifted his paw and placed it on her stone, and she felt the magic spike just a smidge at his touch. She crouched down so that her knee was still where he could see it. "Well, this answers one question, and gives us hundreds more doesn't it?" Lara hugged her knees so that the blue stone in her upper arm laid next to the orange.

Fleck touched both reverently and Lara felt a jolt, the power seemed to hum inside her body between the two stones. "Maybe..." She looked at Fleck the question thought rather than out loud, Maybe *we should see what happens when we use them together?*

Lara wasn't prepared to do this in front of anyone, she had no idea what she was doing, or what it might look like. Instead, she headed to the far corner of the basin where she had done her Waterweaving shows. Sure enough, there on the ground was the small gushing geyser, still pushing water up into the air at about a two-foot height. *Let's see what we can do here.*

She thought of the blue and orange emotions and realized that the idea of feeling two emotions at once was too much for her mind to take in. She was too jazzed up from the strong orange emotions surrounding the whole basin. Instead, she decided to just try to create something with all of the orange energy inside her. She started by trying to pull a stone wall up around the water. It wasn't pretty. Lara laughed at the jagged shapes, nothing like the round fountain back home. But as she sat there staring at the failure of a wall, the interior started to fill with the water shooting up in the center. "Well, Fleck? It isn't perfect, but it is a memorial to our first day as a Terraweaver. We have a long way to go."

"I think it looks great. I wouldn't change a thing." Lara spun to see Dale and Dean walking up behind her. Dale continued, "I guess we got the answer. One weaver can earn multiple stones." Lara was a little concerned by his excitement at the idea.

"Looks like it." She responded, hoping she sounded lighthearted. She had a sudden fear of what this might mean. How many others might try for it. What kind of power might be unleashed? Fleck felt her anxieties and pushed back at her thinking. It was a gentle reminder to slow down in her worst-case thinking.

"I think the fountain wall should stay as it is to memorialize your success here today. But if you don't mind, I can add a floor and reservoir below to keep the water from getting muddy?"

"Oh, that's a great idea." Lara nodded happily. She turned to see Dean standing quietly beside her. She realized she had not talked with this young man once since she arrived in Laran. "Hello Dean." She said, and noting that her voice sounded a bit flat, she forced a smile to balance out coldness.

"Terraweaver Lara." He said politely. "Or Waterweaver Lara?" He sounded confused. "I'm sorry, what should I call you?"

Lara turned to face the young man. She had to look up because he was at least a foot taller than she was. "I prefer just plain Lara."

"But you worked so hard to stonegraft. You deserve the title." He sounded dejected, and Lara almost felt sorry for him.

The night flashed with the magic orange light as Dale used his terraweaving to shape the fountain reservoir, and Lara felt a weight on the young man beside her. "Dean, why do you want to be a terraweaver?"

He looked surprised by the question "Umm." After a few moments, he finally admitted, "I don't know? I am supposed to?"

"I think if you really want to be successful, the first thing you should do is really think about that answer. The magic looks into your heart to know you, to know your goals, your purpose. How can it know you if you don't even know yourself? Destiny without purpose is hollow, especially when you must push others down to reach it." Lara had said her fill, and the fountain was in good hands with Dale. She walked back over to the celebrations, and joined in.

No one went to bed that night. The whole town was out til dawn, and the next day the streets were quiet. There had not been a stonegrafting in two years, and the people of Laran knew how to celebrate.

Water & Rock

Lara woke earlier than most, but the sun was already past the midway point. She sat out back in Ida Mae's quiet courtyard, with Fleck curled at her feet. He was still groggy but awake enough for her to talk to.

I slept well last night, looks like you might have needed a bit more though.

He let out a tiny growl as he stretched and started to stand. As he shook out his fur, Lara was amazed at how much he had grown. Not only was he larger, but he was beginning to look older too. His fur was less scruffy along his back, although he still had that magnificent fluff at his ears, ruff on his chest, his tail and his feet. Also, his eyebrows were becoming more pronounced. They pushed up out of his head a bit, which made him look just a touch more serious. Lara thought back to how her children had looked as babies and had a fleeting sadness at how quickly time passed. Until she pictured them grown and how proud she was of them.

Fleck sat back on his haunches and started preening his fluffy ears. Licking his paws and pulling the large soft skin down through his paws. As soon as he let go, the ear popped back up again.

Lara looked at the lantern that sat on the table beside her. Although the daylight illuminated the tiny patio, the orange sparkle of the magic continued to outshine the natural light.

"I wonder," Lara said quietly, and Fleck knew her intent at once, perking up and coming close.

Lara turned inward and thought of two simple emotions that she could meld together. For her terraweaving, she chose the orange emotion, exuberance, for the waterweaving, she chose the blue emotion of peace. She closed her eyes and let the thoughts and emotions fill her. She wanted to leave her friend Ida Mae with a gift, and it was a great chance to try creating something with the two at once.

Lara was at peace out here in this home filled with boisterous family, she was beyond excited about having completed the orange trials and her success at stonegrafting orange. The two emotions mixed in an interesting way. She found herself very happy. It was so wonderful to be excited and thrilled by something but also at peace with it. She felt Fleck encourage her to open her eyes and take a look.

Upon opening her eyes, she was mesmerized by the mix of the blue and orange around her. This wasn't powerful magic, but the thin flow from each stone waited for her to create.

She looked at the wall behind her that closed off the courtyard from the street behind. The stone was marked with designs that the original terraweavers must have added as they built them, or Lara thought, possibly Tanya had decorated them over the years. Lara found a space that was fairly plain and pulled the stone to create a tiny reservoir, then she reached deep into the earth, there was no water, so she added more emotion than just peace, she felt she owed this family for the support they had given her, she owed Delly more than she could put into words for the trust she had in her which helped her believe in herself.

Lara pulled with the responsibility she felt and reached out deep into the ground. There she found what she was looking for, and pulled the water, to the opening she created through the center of the wall.

The tiny splash of a thin trail of water hitting the base confirmed her success. The sound added to the peace of the space, and Lara knew that the water, being such an important resource here would be useful to the family she cared so much about.

We've made so many new friends here, but we have to go.

Fleck understood her unspoken feelings of sadness and jumped up into her arms. Again, he sent her images of them walking in the canyon. This time, she saw the great white Pelanor more clearly. It looked just like the book's images, and she caught her breath. She felt the urgency from Fleck and agreed. She looked around the quiet courtyard, and then went inside to pack.

187

Goodbyes

Lara realized that she was terrible at goodbyes. She hated them. When she had left Azural it had been sudden and without a chance to wrap things up with all of the people she had connected with. She regretted that, and didn't want to have the same thing happen here. So, although she was ready to just take Fleck and walk out into the desert, she waited until she could spend a few minutes with all of the people she had grown close to.

She spent the afternoon packing up her stuff into her and Fleck's packs. When she looked down at Fleck with his pack on, she was shook for a moment at how small it looked. Fleck was probably twice the size he had been when they had arrived here. He was growing so quickly now.

"Well, I guess, you will be able to carry more stuff then." Lara said. "And I think, Sally and Fiero might need to make you a new pack, this one might not even fit you soon." She said as they headed out to the basin. Drum circle was about to begin, and she knew that everyone would be there.

She didn't start at the circle but instead wandered further back where the drumbeat was a quieter reminder of the passing of time. She spoke with Ida Mae at her booth, where Ida gave her a set of clay bowls that Lara had been eyeing to bring Anna. Then she moved over toward the gym area and said quick goodbyes to some of the folks she had worked out with over these last few months.

When she arrived at the center of the basin it was time for the terraweavers to do their shows. Lara sat in the crowd quietly watching Skip and Delly join in. Their faces showed the pride and joy they felt, and it made her so happy to see them. As Delly started sending rocks back and forth with Kit, Skip saw Lara and walked over.

"You aren't going to join in?" He stood beside her looking back as Kit spun and pushed the tiny boulders back into an arch with her glowing orange magic. "I know a lot of us want to see if you might be able to waterweave and terraweave at the same time, none of us have seen someone use two abilities."

Lara thought about it, she had been successful back in the courtyard, but after seeing Dale's look yesterday, she was not thrilled with the idea of a lot of people realizing it was possible. She knew it wasn't her place to tell others that they couldn't do what she herself had done. But she didn't have to be the one who encouraged it.

She also thought she might just be done with these shows. She reflected on her journey these last few weeks. Initially, she had been so embarrassed by the attention, and then had enjoyed it, and now, she thought maybe she just wasn't interested in the accolades, or maybe she just didn't need the outside verification. She was confident enough in herself, that she didn't need a crowd to tell her that what she was doing was great.

Plus, she had a larger purpose for stonecasting orange. She needed to move on. Lara reached out and placed her arm quietly on his shoulder, waiting for his full attention. It took a moment, but when he looked at her askance, he quickly realized something was going on. "What is it?"

"I don't have the time." She said simply. Her voice cracked with the emotion she felt. "In some ways I wish I could just stay here with you all and just keep doing what we have done for the last few months, but I..." she broke off unable to finish.

"You can't. Those headaches are no joke. And the whole reason you left your own family and home was to meet with Soren and Exu." He said it in a way that gave her the determination to accept that this was the right thing. She hadn't realized how much hearing someone else say what she knew would help cement it in her head. Her resolve was bolstered, and it was a good thing, because she saw Delly walking over with a quizzical look.

Skip gave her a quick hug and said, "I know I am going to see you again." he placed his hand on her shoulders firmly, his youthful, wiry body at odds with the solid person she felt before her, "This is a big friendship. The kind that last for life." And he was off.

Delly had heard his last bit, and Lara knew that Delly understood. She didn't say a word. She just fell into Lara's arms, and they stood there hugging quietly. Lara felt a few tears leave her eyes, but she held tight. Fleck jumped up onto Lara's shoulder, pushing them a bit, but he wrapped around the shoulders of both of them so they could hold his increased weight. "Well, at least this time I get to say goodbye." Delly mumbled into her ear.

Lara pulled back and Fleck awkwardly slid between them into Delly's arms. She held him close so that she could get a good squeeze in, but also because he was just too big to hold casually. "I am so beyond glad that we reconnected."

Delly dropped Fleck onto the ground and pushed Lara's shoulder. "Go on. Get those answers. I am making some loose plans for our future that we will go and tell Van all about what you learn on Pelanor, and I will get to show Iris my stonecasting."

Lara laughed, agreeing that it was in her future schedule too.

The rest of the evening was less emotional, having discussions with those she hadn't connected with as strongly about what they knew about the Canyon. "Don't forget you can use your stone casting to create a shaded area during the hottest parts of the day."

"Bring plenty of water. There isn't much in the desert."

"When Exu was in town, he was a bit finicky about new people, best take care when you meet him."

"Soren was always such a friendly guy, but something changed. By the time he left town he was so reserved."

Lara's head swam with warnings new and old, but she knew this trip was not for fun. She had questions that she needed answered. And so did Fleck.

And so, knowing that it was best to travel in this area during the cool nights, Lara and Fleck walked out to the Canyon. Kit had insisted on walking with Fleck to the cliff's edge, and Liv came along with her niece.

Lara had pushed a bit of her water magic into creating a bubble of water pulled from fountain that she had created. It pulled along behind them with little effort from her. Leaning on the wall looking over into the deep cavern, Liv said, "Well, you needed to do it, and you have. You are ready for this."

Lara looked at Liv and thought about the layers of character all people have. She had put Liv into a box earlier when she had said those things to Delly that first few days. She had labeled her selfish and vain. And yet, here she was keeping an eye on her young niece, walking the long trip to the Confidence Canyon's Cliffs edge. That wasn't a selfish act. She realized she barely knew this woman and had no right to judge her so harshly. "I want to thank you for all of your help, Liv."

Liv laughed, it was as musical as her motions, "Oh Lara, we are only as strong as those around us. A strong community makes us stronger."

Lara peered down, the shadows of the evening accentuating the drop. "It might take me a bit to get the hang of terraweaving" Lara said, feeling the pressure of it.

Kit jumped up onto the ledge and walked along the top. Lara's initial reaction was to remind the young girl that it was dangerous up there, but then she remembered that Kit was a more practiced terraweaver than she was.

"You'll be fine Lara!" Kit laughed. "I am sure the magic works the same way, and you're a great waterweaver. You don't need to stress about it. You proved you are worthy of the orange stone, so you can trust in that."

Lara laughed at the sheer confidence in Kit's voice.

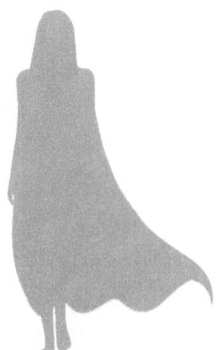

Maya Gouliard

Long Walk

The trip down the side of the cliff had taken a long time. Lara had pulled a boulder from the cliff side and sat with Fleck in the center, lowering it slowly. She was new to stone casting, so she had to focus a lot more on the emotions to get them to work. She also found that the emotions for waterweaving had been ingrained in her, and she felt the responsibility for others at all times, so it was a simple thing to grab onto whenever needed.

Excitement felt more of a fleeting, in the moment, emotion. One that jumped into her heart and then was gone. Harnessing it was a learning experience. Fleck was flitting around her distracting her. At first, she was getting upset with him for pulling her attention away, and then she realized that he was feeding her the energy she needed. He was enthralled with the large bird that flew overhead, then he was scurrying over to study the flower that grew out a crack in the canyon wall, then he was peeking over the edge of the boulder and feeling the wind rush through his fluffy fur. His joy at all the little miracles of the world surrounding them filled her heart and mind also. Finding that energy on her own also; allowing herself to find the exuberance she saw in Fleck was helping her open up to feeling it herself.

Once they reached the bottom of the canyon, Lara was exhausted. They set up camp. Lara pulled a messy rock structure up at an angle to their right. It just reached over their heads to block the suns rays, which were just peeking over the top of the far side of the cavern. And then they curled up on the beautiful woven blanket that Ida Mae had sent with them. And Lara slept.

She hadn't been this tired in a long time, and she slept the whole day away. When she awoke it was because the sun had passed over her structure and the heat of it was enough to wake her.

The following week they fell into a routine. As soon as the sun set, they were off on their walk. There was little need for light on their walks because the bottom of the canyon was a smooth desert, loose sand and dust swirled with the winds, but little else was in the way. As soon as the sun's rays began to lighten the sky in the East, they made camp. Lara's supply of water was plentiful, and she felt no stress about it running out, but the food supply was more of an issue. She made sure they ate enough to have energy for the next night's trek, but she was careful not to eat any more than needed.

On the third night of their second week, the light of the moon was non-existent. Fleck shuffled along behind her, he was getting bored of it all, as she trudged through the shifting sands. She was beginning to feel the monotonous drudgery of the unchanging landscape when suddenly her right step didn't meet the ground. Flailing her arms she reached out in the darkness, but there was nothing to grab hold.

Her right foot finally reached the ground, but it was so much lower that she pitched forward and rolled onto her shoulder, and the steep descent of the ground kept her rolling and bumping along at a horrifying speed. Lara could feel Fleck's fear for her as much as her own, but he stayed at the top as she continued to fall an alarming distance.

When she finally reached the bottom, she felt the thud more than she heard it as her head continued to swim in circles and she coughed up the sand she had breathed in during her fall.

As her head cleared, she started to feel overwhelmed with what she had just experienced, and she found herself laughing and crying at the same time.

"I'm alive." She called out to Fleck, as much to tell herself as him.

Lara slowly stood up and realized that although it had been a scary experience, the tossing and turning had caused nothing more than bumps and bruises, and she was pretty accustomed to those after the Orange Trials.

"The question is, how do I get back up to you?" Her throat was scratchy from the sand and it hurt to talk. The light from the stars gave her little to work with, and she reached out to touch the sandy cliff in front of her. Although the cliff was not too steep, it was soft and the sand immediately shifted as she tried to pull herself up.

After a few attempts and feeling the sand filter between her fingers rather than getting any grip, she sat down and leaned her back and head against the hill. A few deep breaths later, she thought to Fleck to save her the pain, *I think you better just come down here and we can see what we are up against when the sun comes up.*

Fleck was more prepared for the drop, and so he simply slid down. She felt his happiness at the experience, and even laughed aloud when she heard him chitter an exultant sound. Again, she wished she had some light so that she could have seen what he looked like.

Her pack of supplies was still tightened on her back, and they settled in as best they could in the dark of night.

At the first glimmer of light from the rising sun, she was floored by her surroundings. She had really believed the canyon's center to be flat. It had looked flat. Here, she saw that she was wrong. She was not on the bottom of a sandy hill.

In front of her she saw a chasm, deep and dark, the trickle of light not reaching the depths of it. The edges looked similar to the sides of the canyon she passed down to enter, layered orange and browns in a steep decline into the earth. She debated throwing something down to find the bottom, but was too scared to hear how very deep it was.

However deep it was, there was no way she would be able to climb down and back up the other side.

Do you think we could do something similar and create like a rock elevator? Go down this side and the walk over and back up the far edge? She asked Fleck.

He was looking over the edge, down into the dark depths. Neither of them had seen any animals out here in the canyon, but looking down into the dark had Lara imagining the most fearsome things. "Maybe," Lara said out loud, as much to herself as to Fleck, "we wait for enough light to see what it is like down there?"

Fleck sat back on his haunches and sent her agreement. They passed the next hour sitting at the edge of the new cliff, watching the sun rise. The colors were amazing, mostly oranges and yellows, that would blend together and hit against the sands making the ground glisten. Slowly, the light reached further and further into the depths of the newest canyon before them. Lara waited, and waited to see the bottom.

The full sun was visible on the far edge of the cliff now, and the heat was becoming more than Lara could handle, she pulled a rocky overhang above them to protect her a bit. She was getting better at it. This outcropping of rock bent above her in an arch, and she was pleased with how smooth the stone looked. Fleck had no trouble with the heat, he spent the free time, playing in the loose sandy bank behind them.

Lara had been beyond lucky to have decided to stop last night, a few steps further and they would have been down in that chasm.

When the sun finally reached the pinnacle in the sky, directly above the deep gulf, Lara saw what they were up against. Even with the light shining down, there were shadows at the bottom.

Frustration surged through her. The fear she felt when looking into the darkness below her was foreign to her. She had faced the unknown before, but this was too much for her. She sat staring off at nothing in particular. Her mind racing.

They had come too far to turn back. She was so close to finding answers that she and Fleck needed. If they turned back, she would have to climb that stupid sandy incline and then trek back all that way just to have nothing but exhaustion to show for it.

She thought of all she had braved so far. She had traveled to unknown corners of the realm. She had stood up to Shauna in Azural. She had jumped on rocks flying through the sky.

Wait! Fleck! The rocks from the Laran Trials! She stood up and looked at her situation with fresh eyes.

Instead of looking down, she looked across from her. She looked at the cliff on the far side of that scary deep darkness.

Big Magic

Lara pulled a boulder sized ledge of rock out of the side of the canyon cliff's edge, just as had when she was heading down the first cliff at the start of the canyon trip. But this time, she needed it to go across, so she pulled it all the way away free from the side of the cliff. She knew there was a way to leave magic behind, so she envisioned fusing her orange magic into the boulder. As she let her terraweaving go, the boulder shivered in the air, as if trying to hold on to the magic Lara had left for it, but then it crashed downwards. It hit the wall of the cliff as it tumbled down, breaking off rocks and debris. Fleck and Lara just stood, waiting to hear the thud as it hit the bottom.

It took much longer than either of them was comfortable with.

Lara looked up at Fleck and they both silently agreed they needed a better plan. Lara thought about how she had taken her waterweaving and created a thread of magic in the river back home that she had been able to leave behind and keep the magic flowing. What was the problem here?

"I'm not confident enough. I think the fear is getting in the way of the orange magic."

Fleck agreed. He sent images of the darkness below them. He was scared too.

"So," Lara spoke out loud, because she realized it was helping her organize her thoughts. "We need to think through our emotions."

She purposefully turned her back on the chasm below and walked back to where she had rested the night before. The evening was already much cooler, so sitting with her back resting on the sandy surface, she soaked in the last warmth from the evening sun. A whole day wasted.

"The emotions of orange are confidence, excitement, social skills. How does any of that help us here?"

Fleck sat back on his haunches; his tail flicking left to right in a clipped pattern. His frustration showing in the tail as much as his face. His large cat-like eyes were covered with a scrunched-up brow, and his wide mouth, which was almost always smiling, was twisted in thought. Lara laughed a bit at how serious he was. "Well, we needn't fret that much! We will figure it out." She reached out and scruffled his fluffy ears and his face relaxed a bit.

They sat in silence until suddenly, Fleck pounced upright. His body seemed to shiver he was so excited.

"What?" Lara asked.

He bounded back and forth, reminding her of again of a squirrel. If only Stella could see him now, she grinned.

He finally stopped and closed his eyes, concentrating. Lara closed hers too, so that she could focus on what he was trying to share. He shared a memory of him sitting at the booth with Delly.

Lara watched as Delly turned the page of the book she was writing in. It looked like it was a journal.

The memory of Delly was saying, "Fleck listen to this, sometimes I surprise myself with what I write."

The memory of Fleck jumped up onto the table next to Delly's journal and tipped his head to listen. "Bravery isn't always for the people who just do the dangerous things. Bravery is the person who is most scared to do it but does it anyway because they must. The person confronting the fear. That's bravery."

Lara was pulled out of the memory instantly as Fleck let the moment go. He looked at her expectantly.

"But I thought that Bravery was a red tenet?" Lara was surprised when Fleck rolled his big grey eyes at her. His frustration clear. He closed his eyes again, and Lara again concentrated on what he was trying to share. This time it wasn't a memory; it was simply colors. All she could see was orange, until he pulled the colors, separating out the red from the yellow. Lara thought of the map of Chroma and how the red and yellow realms sat on either side of Laran. "Well, I guess we can use that. If bravery is a red tenet, and orange is a blend of red and yellow... ugh, what are you trying to say?"

Now Lara was getting frustrated. Why couldn't he just talk like the dragons in the story books. Then it hit her. "Wait, of course. Courage is an orange tenet that uses bravery. I guess we have to be more courageous when we confront our fears. I would say we have a lot of fear to use here."

Lara decided to pull their magic stone vehicle up from the ground further back from the edge so that if she dropped it at first, she wouldn't have to start all over after it fell into the depths.

When their makeshift transport was hanging about a foot above the ground, Lara jumped up onto it, and Fleck followed.

She turned to look at the far side, at her goal. From this vantage point it didn't look too far. If she and Fleck were just going to walk it straight it would probably only have taken 5 minutes.

She looked at Fleck. "We must do this. We came all this way; past pink and red, into orange, the trials, and the canyon so far. This is not something we can just turn back from." She determinedly looked into the scary black depths and felt the fear inside her, but she also knew that she was going to make it across. That they had to make it across.

She fueled that knowledge into her orange stone and the tremors of power rumbled down her leg into the boulder below her. As the power pooled below her, she pushed it out against the sandy hill she had fallen down last night. As the magic hit it, sand splashed out reminding Lara of a large rock hitting water in a pond. Lara marveled at the sandy pattern for a moment before she realized she needed to concentrate on staying upright as her transport took off in the opposite direction, pushing out over the dark depths.

Lara focused on the need to reach the other side, and as the power kept them aloft, the thrill of her magic turned from courage to excitement. When they reached the halfway point, she looked down at Fleck and saw that she had made a serious mistake. This conveyance she had pulled from the ground was not a hard boulder like the ones in the trials.

They were standing on packed sand, and as they moved across the expanse the sand was slowly blowing away from her feet. Their transportation was slowly disappearing in the wind. Lara freaked out. In an instant, her anxiety took hold of her emotions. She looked ahead and saw their goal. It was just too far! The sand beneath her would run out before they reached safety.

No. She would not let that happen. She was strong, she knew it. She felt the terra magic answer her call quickly, her need connected with the determination she felt bordering on stubbornness. She reached down pulling from the strength at her knee and the magic of the earth answered, surrounding her with sparks and swoops of bright orange. She let it build up, let it feed on itself; seeing the magic just made her more excited and it grew and grew. Then with a force of will, she focused the magic, pulling it upwards toward her hands and pooled it in front of her, then she reached out, sending her orange terraweaving to the far cliffs edge. She imagined grabbing the edge and yanked with all of her might.

In her mind she had imagined bringing an outcropping toward them they could jump to, or a second boulder from the far edge, to make it the last bit of the trip. What happened shocked her.

The whole of the cliff shifted. It leaned toward them, answering her magical call. The power had consumed her, and she was exultant with the understanding that she could do these monumental things. Just as she had called to the water back in Azural and pulled the Waterwall down, she could now call on the earth and literally move mountains.

Just as Lara's feet began to sink into the sand of her poorly planned transport, they reached the edge of the far side that Lara had pulled forward. Lara and Fleck jumped down on the other side and turned to look behind them. Looking again down into the depths, Lara found they didn't seem so scary now that she knew she could call, and the rocks would answer.

Pelanor

On the sixteenth day of their journey, Lara saw a sight that had her stunned. In the distance was a flying white spot. It was not a surprise to see Exu, flying across the sky, indeed it had been the goal of the journey. She was thrilled that it was happening. However, it hit her like dejavu. She had seen this before. She looked at Fleck, who was prancing around in his excitement to be so close. He had seen this exact moment?

Two more days and they were close enough that Lara decided to travel during the day. It was hot, and she started to regret the decision. The sweat slid down her neck and she had to drink a lot more water than when she was walking at night.

Then she saw it. The other vision that Fleck had sent her earlier. There in front of them, a full dragon and an older man standing waiting for them. And it was identical to the image she had seen when they floated on the boulder in the trials. Fleck wasn't just imagining this dragon; he had already seen this exact moment. *Fleck, you see the future?*

As they walked closer the two just waited. Soren put a hand up as they got close enough to see more detail, but they did not call out.

The space around them had been built up into a camp of sorts that bordered on a permanent residence. There was a clothesline with a few sets of clothing that looked like they might have been hanging awhile, because they were covered in dust rather than looking freshly washed. There was a stone structure that looked much nicer and complete than Lara's past rudimentary attempts. The sun was rising toward the center of the sky, and Lara was feeling her lack of sleep schedule. She had hit the dawn equals bedtime wall, but the excitement of seeing the grown Pelanor woke her up. Fleck's emotions were also affecting her. He was so excited; she could feel a jittery mix of nerves. *Breathe, Fleck.* She reminded him.

When they finally walked into the camp, Soren stood from his place on a stone bench under the eaves of the structure. He waved her a welcome and slowly walked toward them.

Exu laid out in the full sun, obviously unbothered by the heat. Lara marveled at him. She looked first for what she could see of Fleck in this enormous animal. He was waiting for them, and watched with large light grey eyes, so like Fleck's in color, but they sat further apart, the bridge of his snout had a ridge that separated the eyes, giving Lara a much stronger image of a hunter than little Fleck had. His ears sat flat against his head, so Lara couldn't judge how they might differ from Fleck's. His teeth were the same as Fleck's, sharp, pointed and fierce, but Lara felt a distinct fear that she had never felt looking at Fleck. Was it the sheer size of these teeth, or was it because this was a stranger to her?

This Pelanor sat on his haunches, which were much wider than Fleck's, muscles that came from age and action filled out his shoulders too. The talons of all four paws tapped on the loose gravel below him, Lara realized he was in a nest of a sort. The gravel in a loose pile circled around him and then stopped. As his talons tapped, more gravel chipped away.

His fur was white as Flecks and flowed in the canyon's wind. He really did look a lot like a grown-up Fleck. The largest difference was his chin where a long beard flowed. He obviously took great care, because it was knot free, and streamed out to the side with the breeze.

Lara tried to picture the stone statue back home at the fountain in their town square. The representation was close but missed the softness of this creature. The flow of the fur made him almost approachable. Almost. Lara stopped and looked down at Fleck.

Fleck hung next to her, and she could feel his trepidation, a mixture of fear of being a disappointment, and how much his world was changing. A chance to belong, bringing into Lara's awareness for the first time how much he had always been an outsider no matter how much he and Lara had bonded.

Lara's heart broke at the sudden realization of just how much this meant to Fleck. She had been much too focused on fixing her problem. In this moment, her headaches felt trifling next to the momentous weight of the two Pelanor meeting.

"Exu has been expecting this little one for a few weeks." Soren's slow voice was gravelly with age, and Lara thought probably the lack of use. "You are welcome."

Lara bent down and hugged Fleck, sending him all of the physical and emotional love she could.

Go on. She thought softly as she gave him one last tight squeeze.

Fleck started forward again, his pace slow, but continuing toward the adult dragon before him.

Soren stopped beside her, but Lara only gave him a quick glance. He was watching the two dragons also. Fleck stepped slowly. When he was about half the distance away from Lara, Exu lowered down and settled in with a show, turning around and then lying in a circle and Lara almost laughed at how similar he looked to Fleck cuddling up onto her pillows. Her first glance of his tail surprised her though, although it was long and fluffy, it was not nearly so long as Flecks. It wrapped around his body just long enough to rest his head on the tip.

Exu also seemed interested in this new creature heading his way. Lara felt every emotion running through Fleck. He was excited, but also nervous. He wanted to impress him. Lara watched as Fleck turned back to look at her, and she sent both an emotional encouragement and a wave of her hands. Fleck walked until he was just below the nostrils of the great dragon. He reached up his nose and nuzzled the adult dragon.

In that instant, Lara's mind broke open. A tempest of visions, sounds, feelings, words, all hit her mind. She put her hands to her ears, but it didn't help. Crumbling to the ground, she covered her head as best she could to close out any extra stimuli, what was in her head was already too much. She couldn't make any sense of any of it, but caught glimpses that were familiar, she saw a family of Pelanor, sitting by a pond, the space around them lush and filled with colorful flowers. The space was serene, but she was only there for a blink of an eye. She felt an overwhelming sadness that burst tears from her eyes without even understanding why. She felt the loneliness of separation, and the rush of elation at reconnecting. The interaction consumed her but broke off completely within moments. Lara found herself wrecked. She pushed up onto her hands and knees and dragged her breath in, trying to calm herself, while also trying to sort out what she had experienced.

She felt a hand on her shoulder and looked up to see Soren crouched down next to her. While the shaggy hair falling over his face was grey, his eyes were a light shade of amber that glinted, and she felt understanding from him. "You're going to need to rest after that. We can talk after you sleep." He helped her up and she stumbled into the stone cabin. There were rooms inside. They weren't fancy, but it looked as though Soren had been expecting her, because he led her past a first room that was obviously his bedroom, to a second small space with a stone bed. He took her pack and laid out the bedroll she had, and she fell asleep instantly, with an echo of dragons crying out that wouldn't quite leave her.

Lara & Fleck's Problem

When Lara awoke it was the first time she could remember since bonding with Fleck that he wasn't instantly reaching out to her. He wasn't in the room, and she saw through the open window space that the sun had set already.

As she moved out of the open doorway arch toward the center room, she ran her hand against the stone wall. It was grooved to give the appearance of wood. Her fingers bumped against the notches between detailed planks that reminded her of her own wooden home. But the feel of it was hard and cool. As she marveled at the intricacies, including the notches in the imagined wood, she heard Soren clear his throat.

Turning she saw him seated in front of a roaring fire, necessary to warm the cool stone structure on these cold desert nights. His seat was also made of stone, but looked like a bench she might have seen in the old church back home before it had shut down. The short stone pew looked just long enough for Soren to lie down if he wanted to. Although it was obviously a hard surface, there were a plethora of woven blankets thrown about and folded up around; some on the floor, and some on the pew itself. Soren gestured to Lara calmly, inviting her to sit down with him.

Seating herself far enough that she could turn sideways with her leg tucked to the side, she faced Soren. She hadn't really gotten a good look at him before, she had been enraptured with Exu, and then her vision had been hazy as they came inside.

He was unlike any of the terraweavers she had already met. His energy was tempered and calm, and he moved with slow, measured, thought out motions. He sat there, sturdy, and she recalled his image from Fleck weeks before. She hadn't been able to see his face, but she remembered the strong solid outline, she felt the everlasting support of the rocks around her, and realized he was part of that. She added supportive to her mental list of orange magic emotions.

He sat there for a while watching the fire, and the flames cast his face in a flickering orange glow. His profile showed a crooked nose that looked to have been broken in more than one place, and craggy skin that suddenly had Lara wondering how old he was.

He sighed after a few quiet minutes and turned to her. His amber eyes penetrated her. "Why did you have to come?" The question might have seemed simple on the surface, but his tone was almost accusatory. She felt pain from his words.

"I…" she spluttered, unsure if it was a real question or just his pain talking.

He reached a hand up, palm toward her in acquiescence. "No, sorry. That wasn't the right question." He paused, and she just sat quietly. Lara had never been one to feel uncomfortable speaking with strangers. She had loved meeting all of the new people on her journeys and had found comfort in similarities even with folks so different from her. But, here with Soren, she felt on edge. She felt like she was walking on a tightrope and that saying the wrong thing might make her fall, and ruin everything.

"You obviously came because of the baby Pelanor." Lara nodded in answer.

"Fleck," she said cautiously, her voice not sounding like herself to her ears, "It's short for Reflection."

Soren closed his eyes, and she saw his face soften just slightly, the corners of his mouth turned up in a tight smile and he let out a slow puff from his nose that Lara wondered might almost be a laugh. "That's a good name."

Lara physically felt herself relax at that single line. She pulled the nearest woven blanket, an orange and black striped one, around her shoulders to stave off the chill from the side not facing the fire. It wasn't scratchy like the other woven blankets she had used in Laran. It was soft, warm and Lara found herself almost petting it as she pulled it over her arm.

After a few more minutes Soren continued, "It has been a very long time since I have spoken with anyone besides Exu, or myself. I am out of practice." He looked at her and his eyes showed the emotion that his words maybe could not. He was pained, and sorry. He was uncomfortable. "Can you maybe just take the lead. Tell me why you are here."

Lara nodded quickly and then began wondering where even to start. As she was about to start Soren interrupted her thinking, "Wait, I don't even know your name."

And so Lara began with her story from the beginning. She told Soren about her family and years in the Wastelands. About her children growing up, and life being new and uncomfortable without them. She told him about the water shortage and her decision to travel to Azural. By the time she was at the part where she met Fleck for the first time, Soren had relaxed and even asked her a few small questions.

"That first night together, wolves had come to the fire, and they had seen Fleck, he was not any bigger than a squirrel back then, and they had bowed to him. Bowed."

"Hold on, I am just trying to picture Exu that small. He was full grown when I met him." He actually laughed and then motioned for her to continue.

"That was the night we first bonded. It was like a sudden inflow of emotions. I had no clue what was happening, I felt his emotions as strongly as my own." Soren nodded but kept silent.

Lara paused here. She was unsure how Soren might feel about how things transpired in Azural. There were a lot of political ramifications to her choices, and although she did not regret what she did, she knew that there would be some who disapproved of her choices. Rather than having to lie, she decided to skip ahead in her story.

"When I returned home from Azural with the water magic, things were so much better. I was able to return blue skies and fill the well. But things with Fleck were getting worse. His magic use is connected to me somehow. Is that how it is for you? I am getting headaches and even passing out now when he uses his magic."

Soren did not seem forthcoming, instead he watched her encouraging her to continue. "So, we felt the need to understand why this was happening. We only knew of three other Pelanor, two young ones in Grevendale and then Exu, so we traveled to meet you, then heard we had to stonegraft orange to even be able to meet you. The headaches have gotten worse while we were in Laran also, but nothing like what happened here when Fleck first met Exu."

Soren nodded thoughtfully, "I think it might be best to tell you my story next."

Soren & Exu

"I was one of the first terraweavers. Carlie and I had been childhood friends and when the finders started returning with the orange stones, our group of friends would just crowd around in awe. At the time, we hadn't set up any trial courses, we hadn't planned anything. Laran back then had been so different: a lot more balanced, and a lot more political. At first, the older generation was trying to hold on to power, even though things were changing so quickly around us all.

When Carlie had first arrived, she had been so excited to share what had happened. She told everyone, that was when the evenings in the basin had begun. Everyone wanted to see what she could do. Everyone wanted to be a part of the story. It was a couple of months after that the stones started appearing. And with it, more of us became terraweavers. I still remember one evening, looking up after a performance and realizing how much had changed. Did you know that the basin used to be grass? Not anymore. Everywhere I looked the orange of our magic was seeping into the ground."

Lara nodded. "Azural is the same. Even the lettuce is blue."

Soren looked pained. "I was young at the time, and thought it was pretty cool. I was so excited about how we were changing the world. We were making things better, more exciting, less stuffy, less about their rules and more about enjoying life." He shook his head slowly back and forth. "Things weren't great before the stones, but I am not so sure that we made it better."

"Anyway, over the years, Laran turned more into what you experienced when you arrived. The desert grew up around us, the stone walls were raised to close off the strong winds. The obstacle course was perfected and we terraweavers got into a comfortable rhythm of life. Performing, enjoying, living. It was all about the excitement and the energy."

It was about ten years ago that Exu arrived. I remember the first time we glimpsed him. He was flying over the city during the trial one evening. He perched on top of the stone chamber high up at the top of the course. I think it was the first time the city had been quiet. Everyone stared. He had studied us and then flown away. But he kept visiting. None of us knew what to think. The stories of the guardian dragons started up again from our childhood. I was enthralled. I remembered the stories of the dragons granting wishes and bringing gifts to those they had encountered. I had loved the stories as a kid and was starting to sort through the fact that they were real, when Exu one evening, rather than flying to the top of the oculus, instead flew down and landed at the bottom of the steppingstones.

"It of course caused a huge stir, most everyone in the basin stepped back with reverence. Most of the terraweavers moved forward, a few on guard, but not me. I was enraptured. He was awesome sitting there. His fur caught the last rays of the setting sun, and his coloring looked a deep burnt orange. His eyes darted through the crowd of us and seemed to be searching for something. I didn't think much of it, I was too excited about just seeing him. I moved closer and when I was within about ten feet of his toes, he suddenly pounced forward and looked me directly in the eyes, his nose not more than a few inches from me. I froze and stared into his eyes, which I had thought were orange, but up close I saw they were a clear light grey that seemed to pull me in like pools of water had when I was a kid, and we still had them in Laran. I remember feeling exhausted just from the look."

Lara broke in here, "I think that might have been what waterweavers call a soul gaze. Weavers look into the eyes, and it is like they are windows to the soul of the other. I have experienced a few, and can tell you, you see the truth of people in them."

Soren nodded. "The look only lasted a moment, and then with a quick nod of his head and a hot puff of his breath he leaned forward and touched his nose to my chest. In that moment I was hit with something similar to what you experienced last night. Exu calls it 'the gleaming'. The Pelanor have a shared history, they worked together with an almost hive mind at times, and they keep an ancestral history that is linked and shared amongst the Pelanor. What you saw was what your mind could make sense of in the massive dump of information that was shared with Fleck."

He paused and looked at her keenly. "What do you remember?"

Lara thought about it and realized that her memories were even more hazy now than when it was happening. "It all blends together. Beauty, fear, timelessness, protectiveness, community and brokenness. I remember flashes of every color, often blending together and then separating; I remember an image of an oasis with pools of water surrounded by large bright flowers of every color, and I remember a stream of blood through a ditch of black dirt." She realized she was blinking back tears and wiped them away with the back of her hand. "What happened to them?"

"That will be Fleck's story to tell you, not mine. I am sure he will when he is ready." Lara blinked back the memories from yesterday and realized she was crying, unable to hold the tears back.

Looking up she realized that Soren was crying also. "Exu doesn't like to speak about it. I understand that. For a long time, we thought he was the last. He's old, Lara. Older than you and me, older than Laran. He was around before we created these color realms. His ancestors were all gone, and he was alone. It wasn't until a few months ago that he saw a vision of the two of you walking towards us that he knew he was no longer the only Pelanor, and now you say there are even two more."

He turned fully toward her and gave her a penetrating look. "Lara, there's so much we don't understand, and never will about the Pelanor. You and I are in a unique position where we share more with them than anyone else will ever know, they might know us better than ourselves. But they are more than us. They are powerful on a scale I fear I cannot put into words. They are mythic. Do you understand?"

Lara considered this. She knew that Fleck was powerful, and that he was a mystery to her. It was a little intimidating to think that it was a mystery she might never solve, and it didn't sit right within her. "Pelanor are the characters in the stories from my childhood. They are the magical dragons that came to fix our problems when those around us couldn't. They are those mythical beings come to life. I am not sure I understand, and I am not sure I will be able to accept that I never will. But I will not push either of them. One thing I know is that I love Fleck as much as my own family, I don't want to hurt him."

Soren nodded, then looked down to study his gnarled hands, rubbing his fingers over his joints as if they pained him. Lara was reminded of just how old he must be. He was the same age as the initial stonegrafted. Same age as Axel. "I've gone on long enough. Let me sum up by telling you the end of our tale. Over time, the connection to Exu began making me more aware of the brokenness of Laran. He exuded a balanced nature and indeed could use all of the magics from each realm. The connection with him was opening my eyes more and more to how broken things were in Chroma. The color realms continue to become more and more homogenized. I love Laran, and I love the energy and welcoming nature of our community, but those who stayed were all so similar. I became aware of the lack of certain balancing thoughts in our own community. Exu began sharing more specifics about what the world had been like before the fall of the Pelanor. He has even taken me to their nesting ground in the jungles near the center of Chroma. He has shown me memories of a world that was happy and balanced and beautiful. We found ourselves angry at those around us for not seeing the problem, not understanding. But how could they? They hadn't seen what we had seen. They didn't know what we knew. We realized there was little we could do, and the world was too far gone for us to change it back. We came out here to live in peace, away from the continuous reminders of how broken things are." He looked up at her. "But I think our peace is over. For you have brought something I was pretty sure both of us had lost." He turned his gaze from her and looked into the fire. "Hope. If there are more Pelanor in the world, we might actually be able to fix things."

Terra

She took two days, and her catch up on sleep had her a bit groggy, but waking up in the light felt much more correct. She stood out on the front steps of Soren's stone home with the sunrise's first rays reaching over the canyon cliffs behind them. She was worried, for the last few days as she rested and reset, she hadn't heard from Fleck once. "I can't feel him at all." Lara said walking up behind Soren the following day. "Where are they?"

"Exu took him to the far side of the canyon. He told me they needed some time."

Lara's heart hurt just a bit. It felt as if part of herself was missing. She wondered at how much she had come to rely on Fleck as an emotional buoy.

Soren looked over at her, and although it seemed that he saw right into her soul, she did not feel sucked in the way she had with the waterweavers. The blue stone abilities must have included the soul-searching look that saw right into your core. Lara had called it a soul gaze, but had never been trained or taught about it, just experienced it from the more experienced weavers.

Instead, Soren seemed to just be using his mature years to gauge her state. He gruffly said, "Well, I think we should use this time we have waiting productively. Let's get you some training." He started walking into the house, and Lara followed.

"Most important part of training as a terraweaver is to stay well fed." His chuckle was like a low rumble of rocks sliding down the side of the canyon.

After breakfast he took Lara out into the open.

"Show me what you can do."

Lara let out a short laugh. "Not much. I literally left to see you as soon as I stonegrafted. But I'll start with what I practiced on the trip here." She focused her thoughts on the concepts she knew of Orange. She picked a memory of when she had taken her kids mushroom hunting and they had found a huge fallen tree. They all had whooped and hollered and jumped up and down, the excitement of that moment was a firm, solid memory full of exuberance. Once she had a firm hold of the emotion, she opened her eyes and saw the trickle of magic reaching out from her leg, she pulled a structure of stone from the ground beside her at a sharp angle creating her shadow hut. She had gotten much better at it, and it curved to block out the sun for the whole of the day. It was strong and stood firm, even though it curved at a strange angle that looked as if it might topple over, but she had the base counter leveled into the ground.

Turning to see what he thought, she saw his shrug. "Definitely did the job of keeping you cool during the day, but you have a long road ahead of you." With barely a glimmer of the orange magic swirling from his body, he pulled from below them, the ground below Lara shook and she wondered if she should move out of his way, but before she could blink the two of them shot up into the air. Below them, the ground started breaking away creating stone steps that led down to the ground. They stood at the top of a pyramid, with steps leading to the base. "Come on." He started down the steps, and Lara followed.

As they hit the last few stairs Lara saw there was an opening into the pyramid structure. Inside, the walls were covered with carved reliefs, set into the bottoms of the stairs. Flowers, vines and animals practically came to life in their realistic images. She ran her hand along the carvings, "and all of this out of stone…" Lara turned to Soren, "It's beautiful. You are an artist."

"There is a lot more we can do with stonecasting than just throwing some rocks around. Here, let me show you something else. But this one is hard, you will have to be patient." He took her out into the open.

Lara watched him slowly build up his energy. The glowing orange was flittering around him in pulsating waves, that were catching the morning sunbeams just coming above the cliffs edge, causing it to look as if it were the orange of the flames in last nights fire. After a few minutes he pushed his hands down toward the ground and much of the magic flowed deep into the earth. Lara wasn't sure what she was expecting, but what happened next amazed her, Soren flipped his hands and pulled up and the orange magic pulled up and out of the ground. The earth rippled and opened to let a bright shining jewel shoot into the air. Lara had only ever seen something so beautiful in drawings of princesses in the children's books.

Reaching out his hand, he dropped his find into Lara's. "There is so much in the ground. Once you are able to feel it, you will be able to find it and encourage the stone around it to give it up."

Soren had Lara continue her work, but with the added concept of trying to use both a large feeling and a more refined memory or feeling to work on detail. She started just by pulling up a simple solid rock wall with a drawing on it. Hers looked like a toddler's attempt at a person, the arms and legs jutting out from an awkwardly shaped oval body. Her memory of Brie handing her picture after picture of the same style person, with the addition of long princess hair and a crown brought her a mix of pain from not finding her, and joy at the time she had enjoyed with those amazing kids.

After a long morning, when the sun was getting too hot to handle, they headed back for a drink of water. Lara's balloon of water still floated by the doorway. It was getting pretty small.

By the fourth day Lara was getting anxious. She hadn't felt anything from Fleck since the incident when the Pelanor had first met.

Exu & Fleck

Everything Fleck had known before meeting Exu had been within his own interactions. He had traveled from his egg and struggled to eat and find water. When he had first seen Lara walking carefully through the pebbles of the riverbed, he had followed her from curiosity at first, and then she had shared her food and water, and shown her kindness. The connection with her had opened his experience, for as soon as they connected, he not only felt her emotions, he understood her motivation, remembered her memories with her, he saw the world broader than he had, and he loved her fully for all of it. During their travels and time at home he had made friends; friends that he and Lara had in common, but also friends that Lara could not ever have. The animals he met on his journeys spoke to him when he was near. Not with words like Lara and her people used, but through body language and sounds that Fleck understood, the twitch of a squirrel's tail, the howl of the wolves at night.

Fleck had gotten a pretty clear understanding of what this world was. He had thought he understood it. He understood that the color realms were all different. He knew that the magical stones were the reason. In Azural, he had found his magic along with Lara, but in a very different way, and although he was unable to explain it to her, he began to understand it for himself. The realms' magic stones were as much a part of him, as the land.

He found himself innately using the magic without even realizing he was doing something special. He remembered vividly the need to be with Lara and the Blue stones in the Oculus, and the feeling of excitement that had pushed him to pop over to her. Why not? It had just made sense in the moment that he needed to see them with his own eyes. They were a part of him. Lara had been surprised by it, but in the moment neither of them worried much about that when the water magic they had come for was right there.

Since then, more often he felt a stirring inside him to use the magic more and more, and at first, he had. It had been so simple. There was no need to plan, or prepare, he just wanted to do something, and he did it. But his love for, and connection with, Lara confused things. When he would fly to the treetops, she would scream out in pain. When he had started a fire in the yard because Sally was cold, Lara had crumbled with her hands on her head, and he also felt an echo of her pain. He learned quickly that when he used any of these abilities, there were consequences for her. So, he had done his best to hold back.

The thoughts raced around in his mind, but he still did not have words. His whole connection was through feelings. He understood and saw the world through emotion and his experience of it. He naturally saw the flow of the connections and the breakage when there was none.

He had thought he understood the world. He had thought he understood himself. He was wrong. The moment Exu touched his nose, the connection took him on a journey of realization. Opening his mind to all that was true about Pelanor and Chroma, now and before. The initial connection had been scary, Lara had screamed out in pain, and then he had felt her cut off from him. He didn't like it, but he also had not liked her pain.

In a heartbeat, his knowledge of all that was, had compounded, adding the whole ancestral experience of the Pelanor.

Exu was the last of the Pelanor from before times. He had survived through the wars, and the fighting. He had survived because he believed that not everyone's job was to get into the fight. He had witnessed the fall of Pelanor, and he had waited, and Fleck was so glad that he had.

Being cut off from Lara might have hurt more, if he hadn't suddenly had so much new information to try to grasp. The world around him floated between the canyon floor where he stood with Exu in the here and now, and then suddenly he would be standing on a mountain top, seeing carnage as Pelanor fought. He saw blood flow down the mountainside, and when he thought he might not be able to handle another moment - he was again in the canyon with Exu.

Then he was by the seaside, watching a family of Pelanor. Generations were there, there was no mom, dad, children, it was all Pelanor present. They gathered around and Fleck came closer to see what they watched in the sand. An egg, and he remembered his own egg, and his own entry into this world. And then Exu was there with him, watching him break out of his own egg under the dark black skies of the Wastes. He experienced the same feelings again, and he felt Exu reach out in his mind and comfort him. Then they were back on the sunny, happy beach and this other egg, broke open and the Pelanor gathered around the hatchling and cleaned her and with the first touch the young girl was part of the collective, sharing in the experience of those around her. Already at birth holding the ancestral knowledge and powers that Fleck was still trying to grasp. Fleck looked out at the memory of the ocean and saw the waves breaking and it helped soothe his leaning toward hurt and anger. He had taken the classes on meditation with Lara, and they both had learned to use the techniques.

Then they were again in the canyon and Exu was scratching a nest into the stone. Fleck attempted his own, his tiny sharp claws breaking into the rocky floor, chipping gravel up. He worked hard, but as he turned to try to get comfortable, he found his first attempted nest too small and hard. But Exu reached out with his tail and pulled Fleck close. Curled up with the older dragon, he felt the kindred knowledge that he was part of something powerful, legendary, important, and sad. But it wasn't just Fleck himself anymore, it was them (us).

The next few days were a whirlwind of learning to grasp all of the information that Fleck had taken into his mind. He was filled with an ocean of experience, but only the ability to take in one teaspoon at a time. At first, he jumped around, a teaspoon here, a sip over there. Here, he was watching Pelanor hunt in the rolling hills, over there he was watching the ground beneath him crack as overhead a war of magic split the skies with lightning and fire. It was all too much, but then it was never enough.

By the end of the second day, Fleck was slowing down. Rather than jump from memory to memory, he began to experience them more fully.

He sat watching the Pelanor family playing in the pond in the jungle. The magic stones surrounded them, and he could see them just sitting there, out in their natural setting. The blue stone glinted in the water, the orange stone, sat warmed in the sun, on the sands by the edge of the water. Every way he looked he saw stones, and he marveled at it. The world looked so healthy and happy, the Pelanor looked so healthy and happy. He was so happy to see this, but then he was hit with a wave of pure sadness. Why? Who?

What had happened? He turned to Exu, hoping for an answer, but Exu turned his back. Fleck felt his pain. He felt his guilt. He felt his anger. He felt his brokenness.

Fleck tried to find the answer himself. He had it all inside him. He just needed to learn how to find the right sip from the ocean. He allowed the waves of experiences to wash over him in deep rolling open waves, finding what felt close. When he felt the emotions similar to what Exu felt, he dove deeper. The waves began to crash in his mind and although he tried to still them, all he could get was chaotic: a flash of pain here as a Pelanor fell heavily to the bloody ground a large gash along his side; two Pelanor diving through the sky, fire blazing past their bloody fangs to the ground below; stones pulled into the air and rained down, but wait.

Fleck went back to the fire blazing Pelanor, the sky was streaked with lightning and fire, and he looked to see who the enemy was, who had broken and defeated the mighty Pelanor? The smoke from the flames got into his eyes, even though he wasn't really there. The rain streaked his vision, blurring everything, even though it wasn't raining in the canyon. He wiped his eyes, he focused, and he saw.

Heartbroken Fleck cried out, his body stiff and pained, his fur felt matted and dirty from the experience, although it was not. Exu pulled Fleck gently into his soft side and together they wept for their ancestors.

Source

Lara was dripping with sweat, and her throat was dry and caked with dust from the winds whipping up across the canyon floor. All she wanted was a shower and a long drink of water. As they walked up to the house, she let out an exasperated sigh.

"What?" Soren asked, his solid steps slow and dependable behind her as he came to stand under the overhang of his home.

"Just look." Lara felt her frustration overflow. She was on edge, missing Fleck and worrying about him. It wasn't really just about the water. "I just want to cool off, but there's only a limited supply of the water. I don't want to use yours up." She huffed, and then quickly felt like a spoiled child. Sitting down harshly on the stone bench. "I'm sorry. I just wish that they would come back already. I'm worried about him."

Soren sat down next to her on the bench. His mouth was pinched to one side, and he looked like he was thinking a little too hard.

"What?" Lara asked. And then realized she still sounded bratty. She took a breath and pulled a sip of water across the doorway from her shrinking bubble of a water supply. As the cool water coated her throat she instantly felt better. She took a deep cooling breath. "Sorry, again. Don't you ever just get fed up with all of this heat and dust? I feel as if I am coated in so much of it that if I stay out in the sun too long, I will just bake myself into a stone statue."

"Lara, I think we need to discuss the stone's magic a bit more. I am pretty sure you are missing something important." He looked at her out of the corner of his eye, and she saw a glimmer of humor there.

"What on earth is so funny?" She quipped. And for the third time she apologized, "I'm sorry. Again. I can't believe what a grump I am. Please, go on."

"I believe you can figure this out on your own, let's just think about things for a minute." Lara whipped her head around and let out an exasperated huff. "I mean it. Tell me what happens when you use your magic."

Lara rolled her eyes so hard that she felt the muscles in her forehead twinge a little. She remembered the family making fun of Sally as she rolled her eyes at something James had said. She missed them. She was tired of this never-ending dryness, she was tired of the heat in the days, and the flip to cold at night, she was tired of feeling so alone. She wanted her own bed. She missed Fleck, she missed Sally and Anna. She missed Pete, and his solid understanding of who he was, she missed Brie and her chaotic energy and ability to question everything she came in contact with.

Lara closed her eyes and remembered all of them. Her family, her friends, her own bed. Opening her eyes, she looked at Soren, tears tracking down her cheeks. "I miss my family."

Soren patted her on her back — a firm, encouraging pat. "It won't be much longer. Exu and Fleck will return, and then you will head back to them. Let us continue to use our time together wisely." He placed his hands in his lap and again sat as though he were a statue. "Now, what happens when you use your magic?"

"I focus on an emotion, for my water magic, it is a little clearer, they had the tenets all laid out: intelligence, calm, responsibility, truth, order. When I channel those emotions, the stone's magic powers up. With blue, the magic pulls and finds water and I can control the water around me." She looked at him sitting next to her. "With orange it is less regimented. It is energy and exuberance, it is joy, and community, it is about the feeling in the moment. I channel the raw feeling and can pull the stone. Not as well as you, though." They both let out a little laugh at that massive understatement.

"Don't forget that I have been doing this for decades." He reminded her. "Tell me about the realms. What have you noticed about the differences in Blue and Orange?"

Lara felt this was obvious but sat and tried to think of what his point was. "Well, they are overly blue and overly orange. The world broke. The whole problem is that all of the stones have been taken and congealed into a homogenous place, where the emotions of the stone take over and everyone gets so wrapped up in just one facet of themselves." She turned toward Soren. "Like in Azural, no one would have just gathered and done waterweaving as a show for a crazy celebratory crowd. Just like no one in Laran would consider the regimented schedule and stifling calendar.

"Meanwhile, in Calambria and the Wastes, we have to live with whatever emotions we had. The color seeped away, along with the magic."

"You went to Azural because you needed to bring the water magic back."

"Yes." She really didn't understand what he was trying to say.

"Did you bring back water?"

"Yes. I pulled it right down the riverbed. And I pulled it right out of the storm clouds that had hung over us for years. What are you trying to say?"

"I think you have almost got it. Tell me what happens when you use your magic. Describe what happens after you feel the emotion."

"The stone activates, I feel the power build, the light and magic emanate from the stone, and I reach out with it." Soren started nodding. "The magic reaches out and responds to me."

"What happens to that magic?" He asked.

Lara sat silently for a moment. She remembered the first time she had seen Fallon use waterweaving in front of her during classes back in Azural. The glittering light of the magic falling to the floor and seeping into the ground around them. Then she remembered the blue flecks of magic soaking into the ground of her own backyard by Sheila's water dish. Then she remembered the tiny geyser that had shot up where she had performed her waterweaving shows in the basin.

Lara's eyes flew to Soren's wide with the shock of it! "The magic seeps into the land. When it is taken away, so are the resources — leaving behind the Wastes; and when too much is brought into one location, it saturates the land with that resource." She put her hand to her head, covering her face, and whispered. "My blue stone isn't just finding and moving the water, it is creating the water."

Her head reeled from this concept until she could control it. She stood up and rather than turning toward her bubble of water, that she had dragged all the way from Laran, she turned inward.

She focused on her steady breathing, the slow in and out of it. The natural process of her body finding its peace and rhythm. She opened her eyes and saw the slim trickle of blue light pulling from the stone, but rather than searching for water, she condensed the magic. Rather than it falling into the ground, she solidified it, she felt the change and right in front of her eyes, the magic became water. She pushed it up into the air and allowed it to fall down in raindrops, showering the heat and stickiness, the dust and sorrow and allowing the water to refresh her.

The water seeped into the ground around her similarly to how the magic sparkle might have. A teaspoon of water into a canyon of stone and dust. "Of course, the world is broken. I've known this all along living in the Wastes, but it isn't the ability to use the water magic back we needed. It was the magic itself. Why couldn't the finders just have left the stones alone?"

"Human nature?" Soren said quietly. "You were a mother; didn't all of your children pick up the shiny things they found? It isn't just about power; it is about the magic of it. We all are drawn to beauty and magic. How we work together is the issue. Can we think of the people around us more than we think of ourselves? I was not so sure. You want to know why we came out here? Because we gave up. It hurt too much to see the realms breaking apart further and further. Exu saw what the world could be. He saw what it used to be, and it hurt him to see it breaking again. We had given up on the ability of humans to fix what was broken."

Lara sat beside him on the bench. He looked up at her. "But you know what? It isn't just having Fleck here that gives me hope for the future of Chroma." He patted her on the shoulder, and she felt a strange mix of pride and burden from the thought.

Time

Lara jumped up from her seat by the fire. Running out the door she kept running out into the dark. She could feel Fleck running too, and when they were close enough, he leapt up into her arms. The impact made her stumble backward, My, *you have grown this past week,* she said to him, but she could still hold him aloft. She felt just a trickle from him, as if he was keeping himself closed off. *Are you alright?* She asked, suddenly worried.

She knelt on the ground and placed him on her lap. His nose was soft as ever, but when he placed his forehead to hers, she couldn't help but wonder at how much longer she would be able to hold him at all. They pushed foreheads together softly, a remembrance of their connection, and it eased her heart. He was still her little Fleck even as he was growing.

Looking up, she watched Exu and Soren greet each other. Their connection was just as cherished and close, and she wondered at how she hadn't thought to ask how Soren was doing cut off from his own dragon. How easy it is to be self-centered. "How long before he is your size?" She laughed looking over at Exu.

Lara was not expecting the chortle that came from the grown Pelanor before her. It was a rumble, but she felt something more, a wave of cheer came at her from the animal, and she found herself happy as well. Soren, also laughing, turned to Lara. "They don't measure time the way we do Lara. You know Exu was full grown when I met him. He was full grown when the first stones were found by Carlie and her friends. He was full grown when the Pelanor fell. Fleck is still a hatchling and will be for a while yet." Soren looked up at Exu. "He says not to rush things.

Hatchlings take years to mature, and Fleck has a lot to learn. But that he has the knowledge he needs now, just needs to learn how to access it and then how to comprehend it."

Lara looked from the full grown Pelanor standing over them down to her young friend. She was so focused on how much bigger he had grown that she forgot to see how small he still was. She wrapped him up in a tight squeezing hug, and he wrapped his tail around her. *I love you, little one. I missed you and I am glad to have you back.* He sent her back a mix of the thrill of his time spent with Exu, a sorrow she couldn't catch the reason for, and his wish, like her, to return to their comfortable little cottage with James.

Fleck slept with her that night on the woven blankets in Soren's stone house. They both tossed and turned a bit to get comfortable but having each other had them both settled in their minds if not their bodies.

The next morning as Soren began cooking breakfast out front over a grill in the yard, Lara realized that the whole purpose of the visit hadn't even been addressed. "I am glad that Fleck has met Exu. And I am glad to have learned from you. But...I don't think we have solved the issue of my headaches. Is Fleck going to just have to block me out forever? I don't think we can continue on like that."

Exu reached down and looked Fleck in the eyes. Lara saw them nod and then Fleck opened his mind to her fully again. There was so much going on, but it was like a choppy sea rather than a storm. She saw moments flitter past that confused her, a colorful world, and then a bleak barren one, that reminded her of home but was not in Calambria. The images floated by until she felt Fleck pull her mind toward his, and they sat in their own back yard. She could see baby Fleck playing with Sheila. As Lara sat there on her favorite bench watching the goat bounce along the fence as memory Fleck ran on the upper wood beam, there was suddenly another visitor. Exu sat with them.

His sturdy voice echoed through the memory. "Fleck is learning to master the ancestral knowledge. It will take time, but he is devoted to solving this problem for you. He loves you very much, and from what I have learned from his shared experiences, you love him too and are worthy of his choice. I do not have the answers you seek, because I only ever joined with a human as a full grown Pelanor. We live in a different age. One we will have to learn through experience. Fleck will protect your mind now that he knows how to close off the connection. Just remember to give him the space he needs when his memories overpower him."

He watched the baby Fleck jump easily over Sheila's back and then scoot under her big belly, only to jump over her again.

"I will fly you home, it is good for him to have a peaceful place. And then I will travel to Grevendale. It is time I took on my role as the Pelanor Elder. The youth there deserve to be included in our shared story, no matter how sad.

I would recommend you try Morchast next. There are many books there. And it is a place of secret knowledge, and unexplained mysteries. No where in our shared history have Pelanor ever connected with humans, except for one time, possibly. Kira, Princess of Morchast." And with that he was gone, and it was just Fleck and her watching the back yard antics of his younger self. He turned to her and his eyes filled with sparkle and tears and he shared that he wanted to include her in more memory from the Pelanor.

She could feel that he was holding back, he was fighting the wave of emotion that made him want to open up to her about everything. *It's okay little one, you can keep anything you need close to you. You don't have to share it all with me. Tell me when the time is right Ducky.* And they were back on the hot stone ground in the canyon, the sizzle of eggs over the fire and she felt only a trickle of Fleck in her mind. He was protecting her, and she loved him for it, but now, how could she help him in return?

She squeezed him tighter and hoped that for now, the physical could make up for the lack of mental contact.

Return Trip

Lara had never felt the fear that she felt as they discussed Exu flying them home. "He flies me everywhere," Soren said matter of fact, "you just have to hold on tight." And then he, for the first time in her experience, broke down laughing. It had started as a chuckle, the low gravelly rumble she had heard from him before, but he didn't stop. It built and built until he looked up, and catching the eye of Exu bleated out a "Pah," and then there was no stopping it. He laughed dragging in breaths when he could, and Lara was concerned he wasn't getting enough air.

Then she saw Exu begin laughing. She was floored. The Pelanor, who had looked so majestic and controlled, turned its fluffy cheeks up and laughed. It was a different noise, slightly hissy, slightly growls, but his eyes were full of humor.

Lara looked at Fleck, who had such a confused look on his face that she began to laugh also. After a good long time of full belly laughing, they all relaxed and let out high sighs as they got better control. What was it about a good laugh that just seemed to set everything to rights in the body?

Lara looked at Soren, "I think there is a story for us?"

"I fell. Every time. We tried for years."

"And you still want him to take me and Fleck?" Lara was so confused. She began to mentally prepare herself for walking home.

"No. We had to come up with another solution. We had a basket made."

"A basket?" Lara was so confused.

"Come with me." And he walked her around to the back of the house. His orange magic flowing before they even turned the corner. Below him he pulled at the ground and raised a hidden storage compartment. It raised up and there before them stood a storage shed, with a very large basket inside.

It looked like a basket she might use to carry her groceries home from market, or her laundry in from the line. But the size was jarring. There was enough room inside to hold seats and a cot. It was a whole tiny home.

"I've spent the night in here while Exu was flying. We used to travel a lot, before we came out here."

Lara looked up at the handle of the basket. It had leather wrapped around it where she could see Exu's claws had scratched it. "So, he holds the basket as he flies?" Lara felt stupid just saying it. But the idea was still taking hold in her mind. "And we will just sit in here?"

Soren took her closer to the basket. "Look, room enough for all three of us, and Exu is plenty strong. Just look at those arms."

Lara turned to look at Exu who was preening in the yard. He was large, but the slim body belied the strength she saw in his arm and leg haunches. She knew that Exu was powerful in his strength and his magical ability. She was letting her fear take over. Fleck pushed against her leg. His fluffy ears tickling her knee.

With patience, he opened up to her. The flow of his mind was again overpowering, the rise and fall of an ocean of experience, but he was working to control it. He pulled her into a single memory. It was early in the morning, and he was curled up on his pillow in front of the fire at home. The memory version of Lara was sitting on the floor next to him, petting him and singing. James was washing dishes at the sink. As he turned and smiled at the two of them, there was a warm glow of satisfaction and comfort that came from the present-day Fleck- a yearning to be home. Then she felt a push of encouragement.

And she snapped back to reality, with Fleck closing off the connection to a slim almost non-existent line. She knelt down onto one knee, and pulled him into a tight hug, to help tighten the connection. "You are right, of course. We have been gone too long."

Standing she clapped her hands in determination, cementing her decision,"Alrighty, let's get moving." And there was no going back in her mind. Her stomach was telling a different story, and she could feel her heartbeat hammering in her chest, but the decision was made, and she would stick to it.

Take off had been the worst of it. Lara had packed up her few belongings. She had more than she had left with, a few blankets from Laran, a set of bowls she had from Ida Mae for Anna, her magic stone carvings she had made for her loved ones when practicing with Soren. She tossed them into the basket and last threw her blue cloak over the edge. Soren had told her to leave it out, she would need to use it. The only way into the basket was to climb over the edge, and Lara was again happy for the Laran workout wear. She easily leapt over the edge landing on one of the seats.

Fleck had curled up in the center at first, but when Exu had flown above them preparing to grab the handle, Fleck was enraptured. He watched the air shift around Exu, he watched his hands as they grabbed the leather-bound arch above them, he turned his head to see what Exu's tail was doing, enthralled by the slow motion from side to side. Lara laughed to see Fleck mimicking the tail motion here in the basket, until suddenly, they were taking flight, and she could do nothing but try to catch her breath.

Fleck rushed over to the edge and perched with his tiny paws up so that he could see everything, and Lara reached out to hold him, her fear running away with her and seeing him fall, but as she looked at his paws and saw the sharp claws grip the edge, she was reminded of his heritage, the claws just tiny versions of those Exu used to carry them. Fleck was going to be flying like this one day.

She looked out and was taken away. The full canyon was visible to them from here. It had taken her a week to walk from Laran and here she could see the whole trek. In the distance off to the East she saw the pavillion of yellow. Large pillars that stood open to the air, wheat fields all around. She thought of Pete, and how quickly she might be able to get to him traveling this way. But she didn't know how a quick visit from his so changed mother, now a waterweaver and terraweaver arriving with two Pelanor might look like. She was unfamiliar with Amara, did not know how they might react. Although she missed him, she knew the sudden arrival would bring attention, and that was one thing she knew he preferred to avoid.

Pulling her gaze to the West she saw in the distance the sun was setting. They had decided to travel at night, to avoid too many eyes seeing them. Most in Chroma did not know about the Pelanor, and Exu had preferred to keep the stories to a minimum. But that was all going to change now that there were three more of them.

They flew over Laran just as the sun was setting, and Lara saw the obstacle course settling into the earth for another night. Although the crowds were far below, she waved, picturing all of her friends there to see her.

As they started further South they traveled directly through the center of Chroma. To the West in the dark, the red lava flows of Piron brightened the red realm, giving it an eerie, dangerous caste.

Settling into the basket Lara remembered a question she had meant to ask Soren. "On our trip to Laran, we ran into three soldiers from Piron. They freaked out when they saw Fleck. I mean, they were really scared. Do you know what that was about?"

Soren answered, his words careful, as if he was telling only part of the story. "Blade was the original flamewaver. At first, we used to do a lot together. All the original seven and a few of us who stonegrafted early. But emotions started to get in our way. We all noticed problems. You met Axel, he had been madly in love with Becca, and when they had a falling out, he shut himself away. After he closed himself off, it gave permission to everyone to lean into emotions. And also, I think the way these magic stones work, we all harness such specific emotions, it trains us to be hyper focused on only a few aspects of ourselves. Blue, Red, Yellow. They are just a bit more stubborn than the other colors. You know Orange really is a nice balance between Red and Yellow."

"Fleck and I had kind of discussed that. Hey, I thought Pelanor could talk. But the only time Exu talked to me was in Fleck's memory?"

"Oh, he can talk. Can't you Exu?" Soren laughed.

Above her, Lara heard a grinding, rumble. The sound shook her eardrums, and she felt like her skull was bouncing against her brain. The words from the dragon hurt her, even her bones seemed to vibrate. "We can speak your language, but it isn't pleasant. It is better for everyone if we think it."

Lara ran her hands from her forehead through her hair along the back of her head to settle the remnants of the vibration left from the grating sound.

"Exu visited Piron a few times when he was searching for someone to connect with. It didn't go well. He got angry, they got aggressive." Soren shrugged his shoulders as if that was enough to explain things. "We haven't been back."

Lara tried to imagine what an angry Pelanor might look like surrounded by the fires and soldiers of Piron. It wasn't very pretty, instead she looked at Fleck, and thought of home.

As they continued their flight, the jungle below them pulled Lara's attention. She had never really considered the center of the Wheel Road. It was too dark to see anything more than occasional shadows across the treetops.

She remembered the story Axel had told her about him and his friends trekking through this wilderness and first coming across the stones. There was something important out there, but it was too dark to try to see more clearly. Instead, she laid down on the bench to rest.

She awoke to Fleck bouncing on her, clearly excited. Groggily, she laid there, looking up at Exu's body, floating. There were no wings, her mind still wrapping around this. His motion was a soft wave, rising and falling with the tail swishing occasionally left or right as he banked with the wind. After a few moments she shook her head and reached up to wipe her eyes, preparing for more travel, but as she looked up over the edge, she was shocked to see they were already approaching the mountain range around her home. The sun was rising in the east and she could see the purple mountains of Morchast in the distance.

Fleck was on the other side of the basket looking West. Lara perched next to him and she saw her first glimpse of Vaalean. From the ground the pink realm had looked simply like a flower field full of pink flowers, but from here, she saw all it was. A pink cloudy mist surrounded it, giving it a cover from those approaching below, but from up here, Lara could see the castle and grounds. It looked right out of a fairy tale. The morning sun's rays caught the pink ribbon valances and beautifully manicured gardens surrounding. She saw a few ladies walking in what she could only describe as ball gowns in all shades of pink.

She felt as if she was seeing her story books come to life. What court intrigue might be happening down there? But before she could study it any further, the mist enveloped it and she couldn't see anymore.

So, she turned her attention to home. The mountains still brooded darkly; the trees more broken than those in the jungle behind them. She even noticed a smell of decay that she had not realized was there before. Her home was dying. But the Hope River was flowing, and the skies were blue. Lara watched the houses in the distance grow from dots to tiny boxes to the individual homes of those she loved. Exu was too large to land in the town square, so Lara had him take them to the far side of the river near the new dock they had built.

Bridge

Lara could already see the townsfolk crowding up on the far side of the river. The plank bridge across the river only allowed one to cross at a time, but no one was stepping foot on it. Lara looked up above her at the dragon and understood why.

The basket hit the ground with a jolt and then bobbled as the base settled flat on the dirt below. Lara jumped out at the same time as Exu flew further back and curled himself up into a ball. He seemed to realize that the crowd was nervous about him and also must have been tired from the flight. Lara could hear his light snore already as she turned toward the bridge.

Most of the townsfolk were nervous, but she saw Sally and Fiero pushing through their friends to reach the wood and before Lara could call out, Sally was racing across the thin plank board, holding her skirts up so they didn't drag in the water. Sally enveloped Lara in a tight hug. She could barely reach her arms around Lara as she was wearing her cloak and pack, so she pulled her arms lower and squeezed at Lara's waist.

"Mom, it was such a long time." She looked up to study Lara's face. In that moment Lara realized how very much she must have changed. Not only was her body and face slimmer from exercises, but her skin was tanned and freckled. She stepped back from Sally to look her up and down. She looked thin, but happy. Food was still hard to come by out here, but at least the water had improved things.

Anna called out and Lara looked up to see James and Anna weaving through her friends across the river. But rather than wait for them, Lara reached her hands up and said, "Wait there."

Sally started to walk back to the plank, but Lara reached out and grabbed her hand pulling her back. "And you, wait here."

Throwing off her cloak, she stood in her Laran training clothing. The orange brighter in the dull surroundings. She was so glad to be home, the excitement of those around her and the community she had here, powered her orange stone at once. Pulling into the loose black dirt she reached down further than she had needed to in the canyon, but it was still there. Below them, the hard rock answered her call, and she pulled an arch in front of the town. Stone by stone, she pushed the energy into the magic and built an arching bridge across the river. It took her longer than it would have taken Soren, but he just sat by quietly and watched.

When the bridge was completed, Anna tipped her head in question and when Lara nodded in response, Anna ran across it. It held strong and James followed at a more leisurely pace, allowing the daughters their time with her before he came and held her. His solid presence reminding her that she was home. Fleck jumped up into Fiero's arms and Lara could hear the "oof" from him as he took the larger baby dragon into his grasp. Sally was scratching his nose, and the purr emanating from him told Lara he was as happy as she was, even though she could not feel his emotions like before.

In the shuffle of hugs and greetings in the center of the bridge, Lara was turned with her back to the townsfolk. They all seemed to understand she needed time with her family. "I have so much to tell you! So very much happened."

She realized they were all looking at her with an almost humorous glint in their eyes. James gave a slow smile, "We had some excitement here too, Lara." She saw him look past her and she turned to see what they all were looking at. At the base of the bridge was Brie.

Instantly, it was obvious to Lara why she had taken longer to arrive at the bridge than the rest of town. Her waddling steps, slower and more deliberate. Her lovely daughter was carrying her first grandchild. The swell in her chest felt close to bursting, and the only thing to keep it in was to run and hold her daughter close.

The hug brought Brie's belly, and the baby inside, between them, and Lara could feel the child stir. "Oh sweetie. I searched for you in Laran. And you have been here this whole time? I never should have left, what time with you I missed!"

"Oh Mom," Brie's voice sounded warmer than when she had left as a youth, yet still held that ironic humor, that Lara had known would keep her daughter safe in the world. "We all have our own paths. And I think you've made it just in time." Behind Brie a tall young man that Lara did not know stood quietly. His dark skin and orange clothes looked as out of place here in Calambria as Lara did now. Lara felt the urge to ask every question under the sun but couldn't even think of which one to ask first. Behind her, her family came, and they all surrounded her.

Lara spun in a happy circle, seeing the faces of her family again. She saw Fleck in Fiero's arms, and knew that their journeys weren't over, but she also knew that there was no place in all of the seven color realms as wonderful as home.

Exit

The man stood with his dragon, and they watched as the village surrounded their new friends. *They have a long journey ahead of them,* he thought to the dragon.

And the dragon thought back, Yes. But now we have seen the journey, and we have seen the possible ending. It will be difficult, but it will be worth it.

Worth it for whom? Us? They are the ones who must travel the hard path.

The legend's vision swam before him. All that was, would be, and had been. It was a terrible cacophony, layered with a beautiful symphony. He looked forward to the day the young one could embrace all of it together, for that would be the key to the future of Pelanor, and with it, the future of Chroma.

The End

Character List

In Calambria

Main Characters
- **Lara**: Waterweaver — Empty Nest Mother to Anna, Pete, Brie, and Sally — Married to James — Connected to Fleck
- **Fleck**- Reflection: Baby Pelanor — connected to Lara
- **James**: Husband to Lara — Town Recorder
- **Anna**: Lara's oldest daughter — Runs the Inn
- **Pete**: Lara's son — left for Yellow Realm
- **Brie**: Lara's middle daughter — left for orange realm years ago
- **Sally**: Lara's youngest daughter — married to Fiero — leather worker
- **Fiero**: Sally's husband — leather worker

Supporting Characters
- Sheila: the Goat
- Jada: Best friend to Lara since Childhood
- Jane: Farmer Oswald's daughter — best friends with Anna
- Dillon Oswald: Runs the only farm in Calambria — father to Jane and Jeff — Childhood friends of Lara and Jada
- Suzette: Seamstress
- Stan: worker at Inn
- Diane Kelton: Mayor of Calambria

Mentioned Characters
- Jeff: Jane's brother
- Granny Oswald: Dillon Oswald's mother — Jane and Jeff's grandmother
- Ben: Jack of all trades — bff with Griff
- Griff: Jack of all trades — bff with Ben
- Granny Winslow: used to own fabric Store
- Granny Sanders: Neighbor to Lara that used to let her pick flowers
- Mr. Smiles: candy shop owner

On road

- Three red soldiers

In Laran

Main Characters
- **Delly**: Lara's friend from Azural
- **Ida Mae**: Delly's grandmother
- **Libby** (Lenore): Librarian in Laran
- **Skip**: young training friend to Lara
- **Soren**: Terraweaver — connected to Pelanor Exu
- **Exu** (Exuberance): Pelanor — connected to Soren

Supporting Characters
- Liv: Terraweaver — aunt to Kit
- Kit: Very young Terraweaver — niece to Liv
- Dale: Terraweaver — son of Gage — father to Dean
- Gage: Terraweaver — father of Dale — Grandfather of Dean
- Dean: older teen attempting to stonegraft
- Gary: Delly's grandfather
- Frank: Delly's oldest brother
- Harry: Delly's brother
- Benny: Delly's brother
- Sammy: Delly's brother
- Waiter at Grinding Stone

Mentioned Characters
- Terraweaver Carlie: Original Orange Terraweaver
- Axel: Original Blue Waterweaver — Lara's mentor in Azural
- Becca: Original Pink Weaver — Axel's ex
- Blade: Original Red Flameweaver
- Jasper mentioned: Delly's father
- Tanya mentioned: Delly's mother — Terraweaver
- Janice: (mentioned) Skips grandmother
- Waterweaver Han: Calm teacher in Azural
- Waterweaver Shauna: Blue Headmistress and Order teacher in Azural

About the Author

Maya Gouliard is a late-blooming fantasy author who discovered her writing voice after raising her children. Her debut novel "Waterweaver" draws deeply from her own life experiences, transforming personal challenges into magical realms where color holds power and motherhood strengthens the adventures. When not crafting fantasy worlds filled with baby dragons and everyday magic, Maya hosts her podcast, "I've Always Got Time to Talk," where she highlights how an inquisitive mind paves the path to wisdom. Her intimate understanding of family bonds and resilience infuses her writing with authentic emotion that resonates with readers of all ages. Maya's journey from mother to storyteller embodies the same transformative spirit that defines her characters.

https://calmillusion.square.site
https://linktr.ee/mayagouliard
https://substack.com/mayagouliard

Also by Maya Gouliard

Waterweaver

Book One of the Chroma Series

Waterweaver is a captivating blend of epic and cozy fantasy. A tale set in Chroma, a magical realm where colored stones hold power over the elements. Lara, a mother from the Wastes, embarks on a life-changing journey to the Blue Realm of Azural in search of a water stone to save her drought-stricken village. Along the way, her adventures highlight how quiet virtues, and inner strengths can change the world. Strong family values meet intergenerational found family friendships, including one with an adorable baby dragon, helping her discover the strength within herself. This book weaves themes of resilience, family, life-long learning, political dogmatism and narrow-mindedness, empty-nest motherhood, and the quest for survival in a broken world.

Our Journey into

Unschooling

A Look Back from the Finish

Line: A Practical for Prospective

Unschoolers

A candid and intimate memoir chronicling one mother's transformative journey through educational alternatives. From traditional public schooling to homeschooling and ultimately unschooling, this deeply personal narrative offers an honest exploration of modern parenting and educational choices. Part personal story, part guide, the book provides invaluable insights for parents questioning conventional education and seeking alternative learning paths for their children. Through personal experiences and reflective storytelling, the author illuminates the philosophy and practical realities of unschooling, offering hope, inspiration, and practical wisdom for families considering alternative educational approaches.